What Were The Chances?

Albert Stanley Jackson

www.yourolduncleal.com

DEDICATION

I dedicate this book to my Papa David. Through your patience and understanding, I have learned it is more than blood which defines family. I thank you for giving me the strength and encouragement needed to believe in myself.

ACKNOWLEDGMENTS

I would like to thank my editor Devon Atwood
for all her help and advice.

Introduction

Responsibilities

𝕸ost freshmen girls worry about adjusting to their new life as a high school student and making friends. At fourteen, I find myself responsible for the welfare of my younger brother and sister, as our mother is often away for days, weeks, and months at a time. Without knowing when she will return, I am tasked with the responsibility of caring for my two innocent and vulnerable siblings. Watching as they sleep, I fear what the future holds in store for our family. Sadness fills my heart as I tuck them in and tenderly kiss their tiny foreheads, and whisper softly, "Sweet dreams."

On rare occasions, our mother stays overnight, her presence disrupting our lives once again. This evening will be one of those times.

The loud, echoing thud of the back door closing behind her announces my mother's arrival, and I watch as she struggles to keep her balance. Moving slowly and clumsily through the kitchen, she stumbles into our room, collapsing onto the bed next to mine with a muffled thump. The intense combination of alcohol and stale cigarette smoke emanating from her pores and clothing causes the air in our room to grow unbearably acrid. The periodic squeaking of old springs as she tosses and turns, along with her loud snoring, leaves me sleepless. Unable to rest, in a fit of desperation, I clutch my robe and old quilt in my arms and exit, leaving the room we share in search of fresh air.

I wrap myself in the quilt from my bed as I settle into the green metal lawn chair beneath the crabapple tree. The gentle rustle of leaves in the breeze comforts me as the whippoorwill's nocturnal song and the fragrant scent of honeysuckle wrap me in peaceful slumber. I sleep, waking sporadically from wishful dreams, depicting a home filled with love and laughter.

As dawn breaks, a blanket of light blue covers the sky, slowly pushing away the darkness. The sun's warm rays break through the morning clouds, creating a beautiful shimmer on the dew-covered lawn. Taking in a deep breath of the crisp morning air, I watch as blue jays take their inaugural flights, landing on leafless branches for temporary respites. The world slowly wakes, signaling it is time for me to start the day as well.

Slipping into the house, I close the screen door gently as a low grumbling sound echoes from the next room. I watch my mother struggle to find a comfortable position as her breaths become short and labored. Tangled in a mess of bedding, she can no longer move. Once secure in her self-made cocoon, she continues her slumber. If I'm lucky, I'll have my younger brother out of the house before my mom rises. No ten-year-old boy should have to witness his mother in this condition.

Leif gingerly passes through the room mother, and I share. His gaze settles on the lump hidden beneath the twisted and threadbare bedspread. Not wanting to disturb or waken our mother, he tiptoes into the kitchen, so as not to make noise. He places his spelling book and writing pad on the dining room table. He then carefully pulls a chair from beneath the kitchen table, mouthing a quiet, "Good morning, sis." I kiss the top of his head; upset he is so aware of our drunken mother's situation that he has learned to tiptoe around her. I had planned a hearty breakfast for Leif, but now must change my strategy. The inviting smell of bacon frying might wake our mother. Not wanting to risk a confrontation with her in front of my little brother, I silently set out his morning meal of cornflakes, toast, and orange juice.

With his belly full, my little brother slowly closes the creaky screen door, leaving the humble shack we call home. From the kitchen window, I watch as he runs to the end of the driveway, the sound of large gravel crunching under his feet. After washing the dishes, I look out one last time to check on Leif. Standing patiently across the road, his small fingers clutched tightly around his books, he scans the horizon for the school bus. I savor this moment, knowing I won't have another chance to relax today.

The morning after scenario when our mother comes home drunk never changes. She will soon struggle free from her self-induced mummification, her body aching from a much-deserved hangover.

After nursing her first cup of coffee, she will again attempt to explain her many reasons for coming home reeking of cigarettes, booze, and regret. Her stories grow old, and I tire of hearing them. The consequences of this stupor will have a profound effect on our family, leaving a lasting imprint on our lives. This forced homecoming will set in motion a whirlwind of events altering the course of our family's lives forever.

Chapter 1

With Nowhere Else to Go, Mom Comes Home

𝕿hree hours after my little brother boards the school bus, my mother emerges from our shared bedroom. As she steps into the kitchen, the intensely pungent odors which offended my senses last night follow closely behind her. Disheveled and unkempt, she demands something to eat and a cup of coffee. I warm a Danish in the microwave but do not speak. After I place the warmed plate in front of her, she seems to enjoy the soft, flaky texture of the day-old cheese Danish. The dryness of the pastry causes her to take small, yet annoyingly loud sips of coffee. Later, I expect to be inundated with a variety of explanations for why she returned home so late last night. After consuming her pastry, she stands, dusting off the crumbs which have fallen onto her lap, and goes back to the bedroom.

Collecting the dirty dishes, I am thankful she has chosen not to converse, preventing an argument this early in the morning.

After a twenty-minute shower, my mother reappears in the kitchen, the scent of chamomile following her as she walks past. A fluffy white turban conceals her still-damp hair as her beloved, tattered, and worn Chanelle bathrobe drapes lazily over her youthful frame. Reclaiming her seat at the old, worn-out 1950s dinette set, she lights a cigarette as her hands shake. I watch as trundles of smoke lazily escape her lips, creating a veil around her weary face. Exhaling a plume of smoke, she demands another cup of coffee.

"Oh, it's not fresh. I need to brew another pot," I explain.

"Just nuke it and stop being so difficult." Her tone is curt and dismissive.

She sits cradling her warm cup of coffee, the silence between us palpable. Taking one last drag from her cigarette, she crushes the butt out in an ashtray nearby. Exhaling the remaining smoke, she motions for me to sit. Our conversation will be predictably cliché, like a poorly written movie—one I have seen countless times. She will attempt to use this conversation to rationalize her poor decisions without considering the harm they cause our family.

"It didn't work out again," she calmly states. "We will have to move to another town, one where we can make a fresh start and people won't look down on us."

Unable to control the anger bubbling inside, I rise to my feet, pushing the chair back. The sound of metal legs scraping across the tiled floor emphasizes my anger. I cannot hold my tongue any longer. "Mom, people look down on us because of the choices you make and how you choose to live your life. No one knows I exist. It's always the same with you. You screwed up, and now we all are going to pay, am I right?"

"No, you little smart ass," she angrily replies. "There is far more to it this time. Sure, I took money from him. The morning shift at the café pays squat. Do you know how hard it is to find a man who will accept me as I am, much less with the baggage of three ungrateful children? You need to sit down and let me explain why this time it is worse."

"Worse?" I shout, "how much worse could it possibly be, mother?" Weak-kneed, I decide to sit, fearing what she is going to say next.

Unapologetically, she continues, "I not only took a little money from him, but I also damaged his house and car. He accused me of stealing money from him, and I, of course, denied it, until he told me he was pretending to be asleep and saw me take money from his wallet. I got mad and started yelling and throwing things at him. After the argument, he ordered me to get my things and leave. In my drunken state, I started turning over furniture, breaking anything glass or fragile and then," she pauses, "then I did the stupidest thing. On my way out to my car, I scratched the side of his precious Mustang with my nailfile. Sylvia Rose, I may need you to cry and make the cops feel bad for us."

Despite knowing punishment will follow, I must speak my mind and make our mother aware of the emotional toll her actions are having on our family. There is a calming sense of liberation as I complete my tirade. "I can't and won't run to the cops all teary-eyed, telling them how much we love and need you. I no longer have the stomach to utter those words. No mom, I will not lie for you anymore."

My mother's hand connects with my cheek, leaving a searing heat in its wake. I accept the ramifications of my words with steadiness and strength of conviction. Our conversation ends as an awkward stillness hangs in the air long after she exits the room.

This will be the last conversation we have as I go about my daily routine of caring for Paige and cleaning the house. Later that afternoon, Leif comes home and quietly plays outside while I decide what to make for dinner.

Once dinner is complete and dishes have been washed, our mother isolates herself from the family and a ghostly stillness descends upon our home. After tucking Paige in and reading her a story, Leif settles down to complete his homework. A lead pencil scratching on notebook paper is all I hear as a thick and unnerving quiet envelops our home. In the eerie silence, I recognize this to be the calm before the metaphorical storm. Having completed my nightly chores, the evening air beckons, and I take a seat on the front stoop. My iced tea grows warm in my hand as I contemplate our latest crisis. Leaning against the screen door, I close my eyes while the soothing sound of a lone owl's hoot calms me. I must think of a way to keep my family together. As I breathe in the refreshing country air, the starlit sky provides me with the clarity necessary to devise a plan to rectify my mother's recent misdeeds. To accomplish this goal, I will be forced to shed my shy and normally reserved shell. To safeguard my siblings and myself from our mother's manipulative attempts to use us to gain pity, I must step up and become the adult in this situation.

Two hours pass, and I slip unnoticed into our room. Lying in bed, and staring into the thick darkness of night, a wave of anxiety courses through me as I grow increasingly restless.

Morning comes too soon, and I drag my sleep-deprived body out of bed. Exhausted, I enter the kitchen to prepare breakfast for my family. The inviting aroma of bacon frying and freshly brewed coffee wakes my mother from her self-imposed hibernation. My eyes remain fixed on the eggs cooking in the cast-iron skillet as I refuse to look up upon hearing her feet lazily shuffle across the kitchen floor.

"Still mad I see." Her comment uncalled for, I offer no response.

Undeterred, she pours herself a cup of coffee. With that, she exits the kitchen, an undeserved sense of smugness following closely behind her.

After bidding farewell to Leif, as he dashes from the house to catch the school bus, I heave a deep sigh and prepare for the challenging day which lies ahead. Within moments, noises from outside our kitchen window catch my attention. A police cruiser pulls into our driveway. A sense of dread washes over me, and I can't help but think, *here we go again.*

Nervously, I reevaluate the plan I had concocted the night before.

My heart races, and my hands tremble while my stomach churns with anxiety. However, my mother seems unfazed by the situation unfolding before us. With an almost conceited confidence, she exits our shared room in her most

7

provocative attire, using every weapon in her femme fatale arsenal. The screen door leading outside from our kitchen slaps against the frame, reverberating in my ears. Turning towards the sound, I see my mother looking at me through the dirt-covered mesh, and with her overconfident grin, she silently mouths the words, "I got this."

A chill runs down my spine as a second police car pulls in closely behind the first. The simultaneous arrival of two officers signifies a grave situation. Paralyzed with fear, I am certain the worst is yet to come. In past such situations, my mother has charmed her way out of encounters with law enforcement. However, today her pitiful excuses, cries for forgiveness, and provocative appearance will prove futile. She has never had to face two cops. I am certain she is regretting her self-assured boast now.

It is time to carry out the plan I had devised the previous night. I frantically search through my mother's disorganized closet, desperately seeking her most sophisticated dress. Among the chaotic mess, I find a maroon polyester blend gown. Slipping into the dress, it feels as though it was tailormade for me. Slowly, I run my hands over the soft fabric, admiring the peekaboo slit and plunging neckline which flatter my recently developed soft curves. Suddenly, a feeling of empowerment washes over me, replacing nervousness with a renewed sense of hope.

In front of my mother's vanity mirror, a soft light illuminates my plain features. I apply makeup with a light hand, preferring subtle elegance to flashy glamor. Unsure of how to style my strawberry blonde hair carelessly resting on my shoulders, I decide to put it up in an elegant bun. Slipping into a pair of slightly oversized pumps, I walk toward the full-length mirror, awestruck by the woman now staring back at me.

As scuffling sounds emanate from the gravel outside, I am forced to confront the chaotic events unfolding. It is time to present myself with poise, class, and confidence, hoping to offset my mother's scantily clad and provocative appearance. With guilt weighing heavily on my heart, I mentally prepare for the deceitful mission ahead. Taking a deep breath, I remind myself, *you're doing this to keep the family together.*

Through an open kitchen window, I hear my mother's voice, soft and trembling, as she pleads with the officer for leniency. Her words fall on deaf ears as he remains resolute in his duty. Robotically reciting the Miranda Rights, the officer's actions fill me with sickening dread as he reaches for the handcuffs on his duty belt. Hearing the metallic click, I know it is now or never.

I swiftly round the corner and, without giving the officer a chance to respond, I call out, "Stop!" My unexpected appearance catches the cop off guard, freezing him momentarily.

Shaking off the initial shock, he speaks loudly, "This is a police matter ma'am, and does not concern you. Please keep your distance."

Unfazed by his abrupt words, I draw closer and, though filled with trepidation, say, "Officer, my name is Sylvia Rose, and this does concern me. This woman is my mother. Is there anything I can do to help?"

My unexpected and sultry appearance catches the cop off guard.

For a moment, he stands eerily still, as if frozen by Medusa's stare.

The sheer look of amazement taking over my mother's face as she bears witness to my transformation is priceless. With a devilish grin, I silently mouth the cutting words she said to me earlier. "I got this."

As he turns back towards my mother, the dutiful cop places her in the back seat of his cruiser. The two-way radio crackles in the background as he asks mom if she understands her rights, which he had just read to her.

My earnest attempts to convince the first cop to listen to my pleas go unheard, and he remains unresponsive. Frustration mounting, I direct my attention to the second cop, who has been watching the events unfold while silently leaning against his cruiser.

With a steady, determined tone, I ask, "Officer, may I have a word?"

Standing a few feet away from me, I can see him carefully study my expression while considering his response. "Look, I overheard you telling Roger you are this woman's daughter. Do you have any idea why we are here?"

Taking cues from the dialogue of adult actors I have studied on television, I say with great shame, "Officer, I understand my mother may have damaged someone's home and vandalized a car. We have had a long discussion about the situation. Can you tell me what charges you will hold my mother on?"

The cop paints a vivid picture, leaving nothing out of his description. He details the terrible sequence of events which leads to them coming to our property today. His recounting of the incident is almost verbatim what my mothers was yesterday. The officer scans my face for a reaction. He finds none. I worked through my anger last night. Moving the focus of our conversation forward, in a calm voice, I reply, "She told me everything, officer, and as you can see, seems quite remorseful. I am certain if given the chance, she would like to apologize to whomever she has wronged."

As I hear the officer who placed my mother in the back seat of his cruiser start his engine, it is obvious all my planning was for nothing. They are going to arrest and book her, and there is nothing I can do or say to change their minds.

Tipping his hat, the second officer, who has shown more compassion than the first, hands me a card with his name and number on it. "Look," he says in an almost fatherly voice, "we have to take your mom in. She will have to spend the night in jail until the judge from Tupelo can preside over her arraignment. On the back of that card is the man's name and number who is pressing the charges. I suggest you give him a call. He is a reasonable man who only wants your mother to be held accountable for her actions. You have to understand, your mother never let on she had kids. If made aware of this new development, there is a chance Mr. Marlow may consider taking a different course of action. There is precious little time to convince him to drop the charges against your mom, so you better get a wiggle on."

I turn the card over, and in sloppily written blue ink are the words, *Chance Marlow 555-8142.*

Turning the card back over, I see this officer's name is Snoopy Brooks. As I look up and try to hold in a giggle, the officer offers an explanation,

"Nickname," he says shyly.

"Thank you, Officer Brooks. I will give Mr. Marlow a call right now. I appreciate your advice." Elated there may be a possibility of resolving this issue without jail time for mom, I fight the urge to hug the kind officer. "Thank you again," I say, shaking his hand through the rolled-down window of his cruiser.

I watch a trail of dust follow behind the two black and white cars as they speed down the driveway. With a deep breath, I re-enter our house to hear Paige stirring in her crib.

Chapter 2

The Revelation

After tending to Paige's needs, I catch up on chores as I rehearse what I am going to say to Mr. Marlow. With all that is happening, tonight's supper will have to be quick and simple. Frozen dinners for Leif and me and strained peas and carrots for Paige.

Once I put the last of the laundry away, I will make the call, which will decide our mother's fate.

The time has come. I can't stall any longer, so I sit down in the rocking chair by Mother's bed, hands shaking and heart pounding, feeling as if it is attempting to flee my chest. I hope to establish a dialog with someone I have never met, a person who has every right to be angry with my mother and, by proxy, me.

Swallowing my fear, I reach for the telephone and dial the number on the back of the card the considerate officer handed me earlier. A wave of nausea comes over me as I hear ringing on the other end of the line.

After a few tense moments, Mr. Marlow answers the phone. "Hello?"

I hear my voice tremble, cracking slightly as I respond. "Mr. Marlow, though we do not know each other, I would like to talk to you about Connie Turner. The police showed up at our home and arrested her, saying she assaulted you and damaged some of your things. She is in their custody as we speak."

He interrupts. "Let me get this straight. You called to tell me Connie is in jail? Why in the world would you do that? Who the hell are you to be interrupting me at work and what's more, who gave you my number?"

I take a deep breath before answering his questions and decide blunt honesty is the approach most appropriate. He seems like a man who does not tolerate casual or friendly banter. "Mr. Marlow, it was the police officer who gave me your number, stating you were a reasonable man. He suggested I contact you. My name is Sylvia Rose Turner and the reason for my call is to ask you to reconsider the charges you have filed against my mother."

I hear a rather odd thud followed by silence and what sounds like fumbling around. Unless I am mistaken, my guess is Mr. Marlow dropped the phone. "Your—your mother?"

"Yes sir, my mother."

"Connie has a child? You're telling me Constance Jo Turner is a mother? That's absurd. She can't have a child. She lived with me for over a month. Never once has she mentioned having a family."

I take this opportunity to speak up. "Well, that's my mom.
Sometimes I honestly think she forgets."

"Can we get to the reason for this call? I am at work and am a busy man. Time for me is a factor now, as we are in the middle of laying rebar before pouring a concrete slab."

Not knowing how to respond to his abrupt question, a long, uncomfortable silence follows. Finally able to gather my thoughts, I continue. "Mr. Marlow, if you would be so kind as to allow me to explain why I am calling, I would very much appreciate it."

"What's to explain?" he asks. "Your mother damaged my property and assaulted me. I called the cops and, well, now you call to tell me she is in jail. Sounds pretty cut and dry to me. So, Sylvia Rose, is it? What is it you wish to say to me? What in the world would motivate you to call a

13

complete stranger and put yourself in the middle of something you know nothing about?" His tone is hostile and unforgiving.

I realize to get him to understand the entire situation, we will have to meet in person. Perhaps then he will realize why Lief and Paige need Mom back home.

I continue by asking Mr. Marlow if he can come to my house where we can continue this conversation in person. I explain my mother has two other children younger than I and believe it is important he meet the entire family these charges will affect. His response is not what I expected. "Ms. Turner, my time is valuable, and I cannot just take off here anytime I want. I do not see the need or have the desire to meet with you at this time. I cannot see what good it would do, anyway."

"I promise, Mr. Marlow, to truly understand our family, you will need to come visit our home. Please, it's important, and I would appreciate the chance to apologize for my mother in person."

His tone softens. "I cannot and will not accept an apology from you for things your mother did, I hope you can understand that, however, I will consider going down to the town hall tomorrow and talk with your mother and the officers. As I was unaware Connie had children, perhaps we can come up with an amicable solution. The resolution to this issue lies with your mother, not you. I understand why you called; you seem like a very responsible young lady. Your mother is lucky to have you on her side."

Releasing a breath I had not realized I had been holding, and filled with gratitude, I thank him for his understanding.

As our call ends, I hold the phone receiver against my chest and, with a glimmer of hope, I gently place the receiver back on the cradle, thinking to myself, *if nothing else, tomorrow should prove to be interesting.*

Chapter 3

The Other Phone Call

$\mathfrak{T}$he familiar sound of the screen door slamming lets me know Leif is home. From my room, I shout, "Hi, how was your day?"

"It was ok," he yells back. "Scottie Macklemore got detention again because he pushed Susie Washington down."

"Doesn't sound like a good day for them. Now, you go get out of your school clothes and play outside for a bit while I get dinner together." I tussle his hair as he runs to his room and think to myself, *how could a mother allow herself to miss these precious moments with her children?*

As I pull out the fried chicken dinners from the freezer, the phone rings. *Great*, I think, *just what I need. Another distraction.* I set the oven to preheat and finally make my way to the phone. Reluctantly, I answer, "Hello?"

"I only get this one call, so listen close." It's my mother, and she is speaking in a whisper. "I need you to come down here and shed your heartbreaking tears. You need to tell these cops I have to come home because you need me there."

Knowing Mr. Marlow will be there tomorrow, I feel vindicated and able to speak to her in a way I normally never would. "Oh my goodness, you honestly expect me to do that? Seriously? There is no way I can or would ever do that. I could never say that phrase with a straight face. Mom, I don't need you here, and we are doing just fine. Maybe it will be good for you to sit there and think about what you have done to our family."

"This is not a request, young lady. It's an order. Get your ass down here, shed some tears, and get me out of here now!" Her voice is now raised in anger.

"Not going to happen. Too busy here. Making dinner right now and just do not have time to walk five miles one way to get you out of jail. They tell me you won't be able to leave until a judge has his say so. May as well sit tight, Mom. Well, gotta go. So much to do. Good night." I hang up the phone feeling independent and powerful. Without fear of immediate repercussion, I was given the opportunity to say things I have wanted to say for several years. With a slight spring in my step, I place our frozen dinners in the oven.

The rest of our evening is low key. I feed Paige and we all watch Little House on the Prairie, a family favorite. Afterwards, I put Paige to bed and ask Leif if his homework is done. He acknowledges it is, and I let him stay up for another thirty minutes. Once Leif is in bed and sound asleep, I go outside to relax in the crisp night air to think. I do not know what tomorrow will bring, but whatever happens, I sense Mr. Chance Marlow may be more forgiving than he wishes to admit. I feel a significant change is about to come, and this evening, I sleep better than I have in years.

Waking refreshed, I face the day with great optimism. With Leif off to school and Paige changed and cleaned up, I have a few minutes to myself. Sitting at the dinette table, I allow myself to daydream, visualizing a new home for us in a new town. Yet another "fresh start." I see a future where Leif and Paige go to school together and Mom is home to have breakfast with us every morning. A pipe dream, perhaps, but I will never give up on the hope we can be a complete family.

The loud ring of the telephone wakes me from my dreamlike state. Intuition tells me it must be bad news.

"Ms. Turner?" I hear.

"Yes, this is she."

I recognize the voice immediately; he need not reintroduce himself but does. "Ms. Turner, this is Chance Marlow. After a long conversation with your mother, there are updates regarding the charges filed against her. I have taken off work this afternoon to meet with the police and your mom. Once I get her home to you, she can share as much or as little of our conversation with you as she wishes. I am calling to let you know we are leaving the station once her release papers are signed; we should be there in about an hour"

A click and dial tone assault my ear. He hangs up without so much as a goodbye. *How very rude*, I think as I hang up the phone. Luckily, today I have enough chores to keep me busy until they arrive. True to his word, an hour later I hear the roar of a car's engine. As they pull into the driveway, Mom casts down her eyes and head in shame. I guess he scolded her all the way home. Good, I think to myself. Someone needs to tell her the things I can't. I watch as Mr. Marlow exits his truck and walks to the passenger side, holding the door open for my mother. With all that has occurred in the past few days, the man exudes class by showing mom courtesy and respect she does not deserve. I cannot help but think, *what a class act.*

It took the entire hour to make certain the living room was spotless for their visit. All my work was for naught as I watch Mr. Marlow slowly guide my mother to the old green metal lawn chairs beneath the apple tree. As they sit opposite from one another, my mother shouts for me to bring two glasses of iced tea out to them. Confused regarding their decision to converse outdoors, I heed my mother's request. With tray in hand, I deliver the beverages my mother ordered. Mr. Marlow thanks me for the tea, and mom says nothing. I have never seen my mother in such a docile state, and, oddly, it frightens me.

Chapter 4

The Only Thing Certain is Change

𝕴 listen as Mom and Mr. Marlow's words drift through the kitchen window, their voices barely loud enough to hear. The air is thick with tension as their tight whispers emphasize the palpable unease. Straining to hear, my mother's fretful words ring in my ear as she rebuts the man's resolute tone. They seem unable to come to an agreement regarding our family's fate. Though I know it to be best for the family, the daunting prospect of starting over yet again fills me with dread.

As I pretend to wash dishes, I can hear Mr. Marlow's measured tone as he speaks to my mother. Mom's stance is defensive, and her expression is stern as she shows remarkable self- control by not interrupting. The sweltering sun changes position in the sky, causing them to move towards the side of the house in search of a cooler, more shaded area. Their heated voices drifting in from the outdoors wake Paige. Tearing myself away from the ongoing saga, I tend to my baby sister's needs. After feeding Paige, I am disappointed to learn they have settled matters in my absence. Moving away from the back screen door, I watch as Mr. Marlow stands, ending their conversation on what appears to be a positive note. Mom goes for a hug, but the polite man extends his arm, offering a stiff handshake instead, leaving mother with an uncomfortable smile on her face. Once they say their goodbyes and Mr. Marlow drives away, mom sits quietly, sighing heavily with her eyes fixed on the ground. The wind whispers between the trees, creating a tranquil atmosphere as Mom appears to reflect on the life-changing events of the day.

Connie Turner does not self-reflect, at least, the one I thought I knew never has. Noticing this causes a sense of uneasiness to overtake me. Understanding she needs time to think, I allow her the privacy she needs. Behind schedule, I set to work on my chores.

With all housework complete, I flop down on the couch in front of the television, enjoying a much-needed rest after an exhausting day. I inhale deeply and enjoy the lemony scent of furniture polish filling the room. Fifteen minutes later, the screen door slams carelessly against the backdoor frame and heavy footfalls grow close, warning me Mom draws near. Snatching the remote from the arm of the sofa, she turns off the television.

"Hey, I am watching that!" I angrily snap.

I immediately regret my childish outburst once I notice tears in her eyes and an odd mixture of shame and sorrow on her face. She speaks in a solemn voice. "Sylvia Rose, we need to talk. I mean, seriously talk." Joining me on the sofa, she continues, "I've been sitting outside thinking about all that has happened. I cannot change the past. It's behind us. Chance is offering us an opportunity—one I truly don't deserve. Because of what has occurred, the local gossips will have a field day. Therefore, Chance and I agree, a fresh start in a different town is what our family needs, and he promises to help us financially during the process. The next few months are going to be difficult for all of us, especially you. I need to let you know in advance how very sorry I am for what is about to happen. Sylvia Rose, I need you now more than ever."

Uncharacteristically, my mom reaches for my hand, and, using a motherly tone I have not heard before, continues, "With help from Chance, our lives are going to change, and this time, I intend to do things differently. I know it may be too late to be the mother you need, but I still have a chance with your brother and sister. I promise things will be better for our family, and I will do everything I can to make the best of this generous opportunity we are being given. I know I screwed up again. All I can ask is that you forgive me and help our family this one last time." Mom's words relay conviction and show great determination. In her voice, for the first time, I hear a glimmer of hope and believe she truly will try to be the mother Leif and Paige need.

With a move now eminent, it falls to me to prepare for all that will need to be done. I will have to post chores for all family members, and become a strict taskmaster, not only for Leif but mom as well. I cannot do this alone and will need her to be an example for my little brother. This move will be the most difficult for him.

Chapter 5

Mom's History, in Her Words

The past several days have been an emotional rollercoaster and a whirlwind of activity. With so much to accomplish, I pass out assignments for each family member, including Mom. To my surprise, Mom does not roll her eyes or make snide remarks when I present to her a "to do" list. She asks if I can pack up her closet, leaving a few nice outfits and her work uniforms accessible. I agree and try to hide how upset I still am about having to uproot our family.

Mom works on the weekends, leaving Leif and me to begin the arduous task of storing our lives into cardboard boxes. While packing up mom's closet, I come across a tattered white box buried deep in the back. It contains an old, yet elegant, prom dress. Curiosity getting the better of me, I dig further. Hidden underneath the dress, I find a stack of letters neatly tied with a black ribbon from someone named Drew. Digging deeper within the folds of the dress, I find a binder. I sit stunned as I realize, in my hands, is my mother's diary. A tome holding her most intimate thoughts and secrets. Taking a deep breath, I press the binder to my chest, realizing between these worn covers are the answers to many questions which have plagued my mind. I contemplate opening the binder. The need to understand mother's past consumes me. Her dedication to change today makes me question what could have driven her to put herself before her family for so many years.

Having never spoken of her past, either positively or negatively, I know nothing of my grandparents or aunts and uncles. I can sum up the facts I know about my mother in a simple paragraph.

Her name is Constance Jo Turner. As a youth, she distanced herself from her siblings, preferring to spend time alone. She once told me the only solace she found in her youth was listening to a tiny red transistor radio while drawing in a pad she kept hidden from her siblings. She considered her room a safe place away from her functioning alcoholic parents. The one lesson she tried to pass onto me was never trust your heart to anyone. It is because of this statement I feel the need to understand my mother's past. Perhaps between the pages in this binder, I will find the answers to many unanswered questions.

Hiding the diary under my sweatshirt, I slip into the bedroom mother and I share, tucking it between my mattress and box spring. Under the cloak of darkness tonight, I will find a secluded place outdoors to delve into Mom's past. My conscience warns me not to breach her privacy, but the pull is too great.

Mentally and physically exhausted from the day's activities, Mom and Leif go to bed two hours earlier than usual. Checking in on Paige one last time, I quietly shut the door to her and Leif's room. Stepping lightly, so as not to wake Mom, I quietly retrieve the binder hidden in my bed. Excitedly, I grab the flashlight from atop the refrigerator, taking it and the binder with me as I curl up beneath my quilt in my favorite lawn chair outside. I hold the flashlight in the crook of my neck as I prepare to journey with mom through the past she so carefully documented between the covers of this old tome.

After reading a multitude of entries which reveal little about her character, I stumble upon a powerful account of her first teenage hardship.

January 21, 1959
Dear Diary,

It was another horrible day at school. That bully Perry pulled my hair again, and Mrs. Holland did nothing about it. School is a lot like home, no one cares about me or even knows who I am. My brother and sisters get all of mom and dad's attention, and I am always alone in this room. At school, because I am not smart or pretty, everyone else gets attention from the teachers. I like that I am invisible at school and here. As long as people don't notice me, they don't bother me or ask for anything.

Flipping through the yellowed pages of her journal, I learn puberty had been especially kind to Mom. No longer could she hide her new, well-proportioned body. Through her writings, I learn these are unwelcome developments—ones she truly despises. At thirteen years old, she confides in her diary.

March 5, 1959
Dear Diary,
Changes to my body are making me uncomfortable. My breasts are growing too fast, and now it will be all but impossible to stay invisible. Other things are happening to my body, too. I am going to have to talk to my oldest sister. She should be able to tell me what is going on. I am scared. There is blood down there, and I don't know who to tell.

In the diary, she makes comments regarding teenage boys and their raging hormones, showing a side of my mother I had never seen prior. She had a sense of humor.

April 19, 1960
Dear Diary,
I can't help but notice puberty has been outright evil to the boys. They all have pock-marked faces with cracking voices. They are so proud of their mustaches, which are so thin you have to squint to even see them. I swear, diary, I can count each little hair on top of their lips, it's so funny.

23

Reading farther, I learn of her battle with self-esteem.

August 12, 1960
Dear Diary,
I do my best to hide my body under loose-fitting clothes. I don't know how much longer I can do this. Things are changing so fast, and my clothes are starting to fit well and are snug against my breasts and hips. I hate this. Mom and Dad don't have money to buy me new clothes, and my older sisters are smaller than I am, so I can't even wear their hand-me-downs anymore. Some boys have already started talking to me. I don't much care for the attention. You know me, diary; I like being alone. Next year, I will be a freshman and turn fourteen in May. I am not looking forward to high school at all.

She writes about a boy two years older than her. His name is Drew Brooks. According to her, he is very handsome, athletic, and popular. Clearly, she has a schoolgirl crush on him. Yet, she is uncertain about how to garner his attention. Captivated, I continue to read. Several entries help me become more familiar with who my mother and father were in their teenage years.

September 2, 1961
Dear Diary,
Drew Brooks seemed to notice me today. He has grown so much over the summer. He is as handsome as any teen idol today, and even though he was clean-shaven this morning, he has whiskers in the middle of the day. He always wears that tight T-shirt with enough chest hair poking out to drive not only me, but all the girls batty. I overheard some of the boys saying he was going to be the captain of the football team this year. He played so well last year that he made first string. We have a small team, so that isn't saying much, but I saw him. He plays football as good as he looks. I don't want

to start wearing a lot of make-up and doing my hair up nice, but I know that if I don't, I will lose his interest to other girls who do. I really like him, and not just because he is good-looking with a hunky bod. I have seen the way he treats others. Drew has always been so kind to Kyle, the little eighth grader who fell out of the back of his daddy's farm truck and ended up in a wheelchair. He always holds doors open for everyone, not only girls. He is polite and so well-mannered. I never thought I would have a chance with him, but I honestly think he noticed me today.

I can barely put the diary down. Her writings chronicle the courtship with her new boyfriend. She shares their good and bad times. There are entries reading like the steamiest of romance novels, and others describing a scorned woman hellbent on revenge. She and her beau grow apart during the summer before Mom's Junior year. Football practice, the restoration of his old pickup truck, and work keep the young couple from growing closer. Her next two entries explain when it was my mother's attitude towards life changed forever.

January 2, 1963
I know it's been almost two years, Diary but Drew, and I have been going out and I love him. With school and all, there has been little time for writing. I know that's no excuse, but honestly, I have been so happy. That is, until today.

Drew told me he needs his space. Football and other things need his attention. I asked him if we could stay together until prom as he promised to take me. He reluctantly agreed. I only have a short time to solidify our future, and I have marked my calendar. The best chance for me to get pregnant will be next month, the week of the sixteenth. I am going to have him, diary, and there is nothing I will allow to get in my way. I love him and cannot live without him. If having his baby will make him marry me, then so be it. I got off the pill two months ago, and if I know high school boys like I think I do, after prom, Drew will try to put his moves on me. This time, I am going to let him.

Her next entry adds more details.

February 16th, 1963
It was a brilliant idea for the prom committee to decide Valentine's Day as the theme this year. Though strained, mine and Drew's relationship will weather this night. The gym is all made up in red and white with hearts everywhere. I'm in charge of the photo booth and backdrop. I chose to make a large cardboard Valentine's Day card for couples to stand in front of, and it came out good if I do say so myself. Diary, the night will be perfect. It's all planned. Drew and I will go parking after the dance, and I am certain he is going to want me. I have waited for this night for two months. Drew doesn't know it yet, but we are about to become a family.

The diary details the planning and execution of my conception. My mother writes of the difficulties attending school once she became pregnant with me, and how hateful the other girls were towards her. In a small town, everyone knows your business, and it didn't take long before everyone knew my mom's "dirty little secret." Drew's parents would say how he had a future in football and not as a father. Both sets of parents agree on only one thing, a wedding would not be practical, as the couple were too young. Another entry told of my mother's defiance towards her parents' plans of giving the baby up for adoption.

April 30, 1963
I screwed up, Diary.
The baby is growing inside me, and I don't want to be a teenage single mother. This was supposed to keep me and Drew together. I am still shocked all my planning came back to bite me in the ass, but I cannot give up the only part of

Drew I will ever have. mom and dad are furious, but finally have accepted that I am keeping the baby.

After reading these passages, I come to understand I am a constant reminder of the first of many errors in judgement she would make throughout her life.

There are far more details written in her diary, some I wish I had never read. The last entry, however, explains why I have sensed such distance between her and the family.

February 5, 1964
This will most likely be my last entry Diary,
She is three months old now. She won't stop crying and always needs changing, feeding, burping, or bathing. I can't even go back to school. Drew and his family want nothing to do with me or her. Our families came up with a "solution to our problems." Drew will sell his restored truck, giving me the proceeds from the sale and all the money he saved over the summer. I only have to agree Drew will no longer be responsible for the baby. His parents will even throw in an extra thousand dollars. Both our parents try to make us believe we have a choice in any of this, but we don't. I know Drew does not want to sell his truck or give up the money he worked so hard for. All I wanted was to marry Drew and have a family. The only way we will survive any of this is to agree to our parents' demands. Sylvia Rose will never know her dad. Had I known there was no chance of us being a family, I would never have gotten pregnant. Now I am stuck with a crying and needy baby. I did not know how hard this was going to be. This baby has taken from me any chance of living a normal life ever again. I am only 16 and won't be able to attend my senior prom. I can't even go out on dates. All I do is work and take care of this damn baby. It is going to take me months to get my figure back, if I can at all. She has ruined everything. She was supposed to be the glue that held me and Drew together. Now look at me, a single mother with an ungrateful child who won't let me sleep at night.

With all that is going wrong in my life, and having no time to myself anymore, this will most likely be my last entry. God, I hate my life, boys, and most of all, babies!!!!

I close the binder and wipe away a tear. Her coldness towards me now explained. Through her words, I envision her struggles, and I understand how she was forced to deal with her own abandonment issues. After Mom leaves for work tomorrow morning, I will return the diary to its original resting place beneath the dress worn by mother to seduce my father. I will then carefully store her box of memories on the bottom of the cedar chest tucked beneath an old quilt for safekeeping.

Chapter 6

Starting over at Thirty

𝕰ach new journey begins with one step, and mine starts today. For my family's sake and to a lesser extent, mine, I am accepting Chance Marlow's generous aid, along with the stipulations he has set forth.

As a single mother, no change is easy, especially when uprooting my family because of mistakes I made. Chance insists on paying our next two months' rent in this house, and I am to give our landlord notice of our impending move. We agree I will find a new home and employment in a neighboring town. My best chance of finding a decent paying job is in a town fifty miles away. Industrial for its small size, Mathiston offers several factory jobs with health benefits. I request the night shift at the cafe to allow my days free to secure a new job and home. With the incident at Chance's house behind me, I concentrate on doing what is best for our family. Watching every morning as Sylvia Rose cooks breakfast and gets Leif ready for school, I am amazed at the woman she has become, although I am saddened she has not had the advantages other fourteen-year-old girls have had. I selfishly placed a lot of responsibility on her, something I regret but cannot change.

Once she has her brother ready for school and out to the bus stop, I will speak with Sylvia Rose regarding plans I have made for the day. I hope our conversation will be less contentious than those in our past. Neither of us can seem to forgive and forget, and our conversations inevitably end in raised voices.

"Sylvia Rose," I call out, walking through the house. Coming from the living room, I hear, "Yes?"

I see my daughter busy wrapping knick-knacks in old newspaper. "Can you stop for a minute?"

A curious look comes over her face as she sits on the arm of the sofa and responds, "Sure, what's up?"

"Sylvia Rose, you know I have been using my days to look for a new job and house."

"Yeah?" A slightly impatient tone surfaces in my daughter's voice.

"I would appreciate it if you came with me to tour this little town I found. It is important you like it as much as I do. Your input means a lot to me. If you don't like it, we will find another. I haven't found a house yet, but I have interviewed for two jobs. My boss at the café promises a glowing reference. Frankly, I imagine he is offering that because he is glad to see me go. The furniture factory I applied to first called earlier and I have an interview with them later today. I was offered a job at the children's clothing factory in Eupora too, but I cannot see myself sitting at a sewing machine all day long. When you get done here, let me know and we can head out."

A look of utter disgust takes over my daughter's face and I brace myself for the comment I know is to follow.

"You already turned down a job? Really?" My daughter turns her back to me, placing more wrapped items into the cardboard box.

"I cannot take a job I know in my heart I won't keep, Sylvia Rose. I am sorry if you don't understand that. This is my only chance to do things right for us, and taking a job I don't want will not help me reach our goals."

I try my best to use a nurturing, motherly tone with her—one foreign to us both.

"Sorry," she says, adding, "I guess that makes sense. Can't say I understand saying no to any job, as I have had only this one since I was ten and was never given a choice to say no."

The statement, however true, still cuts me to the core.

"So, you say you have another interview this afternoon?" She asks.

"Yes, that is why I need you to finish up here. We have about an hour's drive ahead of us, and I don't want to be late." Turning to leave, I add, "I can't make up for my past, Sylvia Rose. All I can do is move forward and try to become the mother my children need and deserve. I can only promise to give this all I have."

Sylvia Rose does not respond as she folds the flaps and closes the box, she just finished packing. Taping the top and setting it aside with a deep sigh, her frustration with me is evident and I cannot blame her. I only wish she could see how hard I am trying to make things up to her. Before leaving the room, I ask her to finish up and get her little sister ready to leave.

The drive to the little town is uncomfortable on account of the harsh words my eldest and I exchanged earlier. Like the trees being overtaken by kudzu vines along the highway, my guilt suffocates me. Looking over at my daughter, I notice her arms crossed as she ignores me and stares out the window. Seeing such anger within her, I wonder, will she ever be able to forgive me?

With time running short, I drive directly to the furniture factory. Approaching the receptionist's window, Sylvia Rose cradles Paige as I announce to the girl behind the partition that Mr. Hoyt Ashton is expecting me. With a disapproving look, the young girl instructs me to sit in the small lobby provided for applicants. Over the loudspeaker, we hear her page the supervisor. Mr. Ashton eventually shows up, asking me to follow him into his office. Our meeting is brief, and his only questions are, do I believe I can do the job and why would I bring my children along? I state emphatically that I can and will do the job. With no

31

desire to delve into details regarding my current problems, I simply explain, no babysitter was available on such short notice. With the interview complete, I leave his office with a sense of great dismay. The job I am offered requires sewing sofa cushions all day long. Having refused a similar job earlier, and because of Sylvia Rose's harsh statement from this morning, I can't say no to the offer. It would cause more tension in our already tumultuous relationship. I do not want the job, and I know within a month, I will most likely quit. But to appease my child, I accept the position graciously. I tell my daughter about my new job and ask her if she is interested in taking a tour of our new town. She reluctantly agrees and we drive around to get a feel for where we will be living.

After the brief tour, I ask, "What do you think?"

"I can see calling this place home," she responds with a slight smile.

I am shocked and happy to see the first positive reaction from my daughter.

The day got away from us, and we barely make it home before the school bus drops off my son. Sylvia Rose puts Paige down for a nap before preparing dinner, instructing Leif to change out of his school clothes and play outside for a while. I ask Sylvia Rose if there is anything I can do to help. Shaking her head, she politely declines my offer. To keep myself busy, I finish packing up the living room, noticing Sylvia Rose has most of the boxes stacked neatly in the corner. Removing shades from the lamps, I place them beside the closed and labeled boxes. I struggle to concentrate on what needs done in the living room, as I am preoccupied with thoughts of taking a job, I don't really want only to avoid disappointing my daughter. The more I think about the job offer I accepted, the more frustrated I become. Angry with myself for doubting my resolve, I dial the factory and request a meeting with Mr. Ashton. The pedestrian task of sewing sofa cushions all day long is one I can never see myself doing for the rest of my life. I receive a call back within the hour. Mr. Ashton agrees to meet with me the following day. I decide it is best to keep this tidbit of information to myself during dinner.

I help Sylvia Rose clean the kitchen after dinner and together we put Leif and Paige down for the night. After saying our goodnights, the peaceful darkness of our bedrooms provides comfort as my children and I drift off, dreaming of a better tomorrow.

I arrive at the scheduled time, and Mr. Ashton seems confused, asking why I wish to see him today. I express my reluctance in accepting a job sewing all day long, knowing it to be a job I will not keep. Reluctantly, he offers me one of the final two open positions at the factory. To avoid any more meetings, he asks me to follow him into the plant so I can watch the two jobs being performed and the physical stamina they require. Walking through the main factory, I see most machines are being used in tandem. I watch as the two employees work, their movements in perfect synchronization with the machine they are assigned to. Everyone on the floor seems to enjoy their job. The high decibels produced by the machines require workers to wear earplugs and communicate through hand gestures, often followed by laughter. I assure Mr. Ashton this is the job I'm meant for, and I'm thrilled to be part of the team.

Back in Mr. Ashton's office, I request the frame floor position. Shaking his head, my future supervisor looks disappointed as he points out, "By tomorrow, I hope to have all vacant positions filled. The frame floor is a physically demanding job which requires long hours on your feet. Should you accept the job, but find you are unable to perform the duties required, there will be no other positions available."

"I understand, Mr. Ashton. I can handle the job, and I appreciate you allowing me to prove myself."

Dismissively, he says, "All right then, see you in two weeks." Job secured; my next priority is finding a house for rent in this tiny town. With my current time constraints, this may be an undertaking, as I have seen very few "for rent" signs and only have two weeks to find my family a place to live, or else, I'll be stuck driving fifty miles in either direction. I decide to worry about these things tomorrow. Right now, I deserve a celebratory drink. I pull my 1969 Mercury into the graveled parking lot of the only liquor store in town. Upon entering the well-organized store, I locate a fifth of my favorite whisky within seconds. Setting the bottle on the counter, I rummage through my purse in search of my wallet. An elderly, unassuming man waits patiently. Santa Clause's doppelgänger, he has a bushy white beard, balding head, and a sweet smile which is framed by a wreath of smoke coming from his pipe. Finally able to locate my wallet, I hand the man a ten-dollar bill. He counts out my change after ringing up the sale, saying, "And twenty-five cents makes ten. Haven't seen you 'round these parts before. Ya lived here long?"

"I don't live here at all yet," I answer, placing my wallet back into my purse. "I got a job at the furniture factory today, and I'm looking to move down this way in about a week or so." I try to sound friendly but do not want to delve into my life's story right now, no matter how fatherly and friendly this man appears.

He places the bottle of whisky in a tall, thin paper bag and asks, "You got a place lined up already? We don't get many new people to the area, and I only know of a couple o' places that are fer sale or rent 'round these parts."

Noticing a sign posted just above his head and written in bold red magic marker, I say, "I see there is at least one for rent. Guess I need to write that number down and give them a call."

"Oh, ya don't want to do that. The place is not really right fer a family. It had been used as a huntin' cabin by the mayor and his friends pert near thirty years. No one's been in thar since 'the incident.'" He makes finger quotes around "the incident," and I chuckle, finding it unexpected coming from an old southern gentleman.

"The incident?" I ask, while quickly jotting the phone number on the back of the receipt he handed me with my change.

I can see his heart is obviously set on telling me the story so I set my purse back on the counter. He leans in close, and almost whispering, continues, "'Ya see, 'bout five years ago, the mayor took several huntin' buddies up thar—nothin' strange 'bout that.

Ever' huntin' season was the same. Bunch of 'em would go up thar fer a couple weekends, drinkin' and huntin'. This particular weekend, tho', was different. This time, he took Buddy Fondren. Now, I ain't much on gossipin', but ya see, it was common knowledge, 'cept fer mayor Townsend, that this here Fondren feller was spending time with the mayor's old lady, if you know what I mean. Well hon, this is a small town, and it don't take no time fer word to get back to someone. The mayor was madder'n a wet hen. Ya see, Buddy and the mayor were best friends ever since first grade. Now, I'm sure Mayor Townsend felt slighted. Lord knows I would have, but he seemed to take the news well. As ya would expect, once word got out around town his wife left him, 'cuz I guess she done got embarrassed. Well, I gotta tell ya, the ol' mayor seemed to take all of this in stride, like water on a duck's back. Didn't seem to bother him none at all. Fer five years nothin' more was said 'bout that dang affair. Buddy and Mayor Townsend would eventually mend their fences. After the dust settled, pert near ever'one forgot about it. The mayor's wife ended up marrying some highfalutin' lawyer in Tupelo. Ya see, Betsy Townsend was kind of, well… an ambitious girl. She was never satisfied liven' in this hick town, as she called it."

Weary from the day's activities, I find a more comfortable position. I rest my chin on the back of my hand, intently listening to the kindly old man's every word as he continues his epic saga.

"After some time, t'weren't long fer all the guys were headin' back up to the cabin fer one of their weekly huntin' weekends. Well, darlin', ain't no one ever been able to prove nothin', and if the talk 'round town is true, Mayor Townsend got away with murder. Now, ifin' that ain't the case, then maybe it was just a terrible huntin' accident."

Taking a long draw from his pipe, he exhales. Billowy white smoke surrounds his head. I cannot believe how much I am enjoying his story. Emotionally invested, I cannot turn away.

He continues, "As it's told, one mornin', 'bout four o'clock, a shot rang out in the old cabin. The two other fellers say the mayor was just sittin' thar like a statue when they saw Buddy lyin' face down in a puddle of blood by the ol' potbelly stove in the livin' room. Now, the mayor done went and told those fellers while Buddy was tellin' him 'bout a new fishin' spot he done found, his ole shotgun accidentally went off while he was cleaning it. Well hon, I don't know 'bout you, but I never clean my shotgun in my house at four AM. Most of us clean our guns outside while tellin' stories and drinkin' beer round a campfire just 'for turnin' in fer the night. Anyway, ain't but one person knows fer sure what happened, and that's the story he told the cops. After being ruled a terrible accident, the mayor's family done went and boarded up that old cabin and no one has been in there since."

The friendly elderly man continues, explaining old Mayor Townsend has since passed away from a massive coronary. Leaving the cabin to his brother and sister who will not sell because it sits on forty acres of prime pulpwood land. He informs me the owners are interested in renting only the cabin, along with a three-acre plot of land.

Smiling, I state, "Seems to me like this place might rent for cheap since it has such a grim history and most likely needs a good deal of work, wouldn't you say?"

"Well, if'n you are serious 'bout the cabin, be ready fer some stares from the locals, and not cuz yer so purdy. They all gonna think you're nuts fer moving into 'the cabin.'He again uses finger quotes and I giggle under my breath.

Thanking him for his time and story, I leave the liquor store with a renewed sense of purpose.

Deciding the cabin is exactly what my family needs, I place the receipt back in my purse and say to myself, "Yes, I can see calling this town home."

Chance insists on paying the first three months' rent on whatever home I find. Although the offer is generous, I'm still seeking a more affordable rate on the rent. I will use the "single mother moving to a new town" plea and, if needed, will allude to the fact the cabin has sat vacant for several years. I can't help but wonder if the owners will ever reveal the cabin's secrets. If they don't bring up the house's past, it can only mean they are trying to hide it or are ashamed. This will give me the leverage needed to get a deal on the rent.

I can't wait to get home and share my news with the family. Excitedly, I drive through the town in search of the nearest pay phone. I see one on the corner by the town's only grocery store. I pull my car over and step out, the warm summer air enveloping me as I dial the number on the back of my receipt. Adrenaline pumping, I almost drop the dime in all my excitement. I wait for the party to answer and drop the coin in the slot.

"Hello?" answers a woman.

"Hello, my name is Constance Jo Turner. I saw your flyer in the liquor store today and am enquiring about the cabin you have for rent two miles south of town. Is it still available?" I ask, doing my best to sound friendly and professional.

"Why, it just so happens it is," the kindly woman responds.

"I would like to set up a time to see the cabin if you don't mind. I just got a job at the frame mill in Maben and need to move nearer to work. I can meet you there at your earliest convenience." Not wanting to appear too eager, I try to dampen my excitement.

"Oh, you're not from around these parts?"

Her question catches me off guard. Why would it matter if I was not from this area unless she had no intention of revealing the cabin's sorted past? "No, I am not, and am a single mother of three. I hope that is not a problem."

"Hoyt did tell me he hired a new girl from out of town. Can you meet me at the Broken Arrow Restaurant on Thursday around noon? We can have a cup of coffee and talk before heading out to see the cabin. I would like to get to know a little more about you, if you don't mind, honey."

"I will meet you there at noon on Thursday," I reply.

"Well, we'll see you then. Have a nice day, Ms. Turner."

I hang up the phone, releasing a giant sigh of relief and think to myself, I guess this is home now.

A fifty-mile drive home does not seem to take as long when your mood is giddy and light. Pulling into our driveway a little too fast, my car fishtails on the loose gravel, kicking up a cloud of dust.

Entering the house, I shout in an upbeat voice, "I am home!" The kids immediately rush into the kitchen to join me. While setting the paper bag on the table, I cannot contain my excitement, as I exclaim, "Mama has a new job!"

My eldest daughter focuses on the brown bag holding the bottle.

Her disdain and disappointment are visible for everyone to see.

"Oh, don't give me that look. It's for celebratory purposes only, Sylvia Rose. You know I have to work a double shift tomorrow at the restaurant to make up for the time I have missed today. This is only to help me relax and unwind before bed."

As I prepare my drink, I detail the busy schedule I have facing me over the next few days. "On Thursday, I have to go back and look at an old hunting cabin I found for rent. I am going to have to work the two jobs for at least a week and drive a hundred miles a day. With all that is going on, I don't need to come home to a judgmental daughter. I am working very hard to get our family on the right track, Sylvia Rose, and do not need to be judged by you right now."

Upset, as I do not feel I need to justify my actions to my daughter, I leave the kitchen and go back to the room Sylvia Rose, and I share. Setting my drink on the nightstand, I lean back in my rocking chair, close my eyes, and try to relax.

The house and children remain quiet until Sylvia Rose announces supper is ready. Gathering at the table to a well-prepared meal, I refresh my drink. Once dinner is done and the younger children leave the table, I offer to help my daughter with the dishes. She declines, shooting me a hateful look. The air is thick with tension, and I choose not to engage. To avoid another argument, I excuse myself, announcing I have an early day tomorrow and need to get some rest.

Chapter 7

Mom is Trying, and it Shows

Recent events have caused a frenzy of activity and chaos. From Mom getting arrested for destroying a man's property to the hope she may have found us a permanent home; the emotional roller coaster has taken its toll on us all.

With all the positive changes Mom has made, I am disheartened to see one old destructive behavior remain. Last night, she came home and proudly placed a brown paper bag on the kitchen table. It seems she feels the need to celebrate her recent successes with a bottle of whisky. Noticing my disappointed and disapproving stare, she states calmly, "For celebratory purposes."

To me, it sounds like another excuse to hit the bottle. Everything had been going so well. It has been almost a month since she had her last drink. I was so proud of her until I saw the dang bottle. By the time I get to bed, she is sleeping peacefully. I only saw her pour two drinks tonight, but I am certain it took several more for her to become so relaxed.

With the children settled in for the night, I crawl under my covers, opening my worn out, tattered copy of Great Expectations. My eyes grow tired quickly, and I place a marker in the book, quietly setting it on my nightstand. Still upset about the whisky bottle, eventually I drift off to sleep.

Waking at five in the morning, I find Mom's bed empty and made. Her car is gone from the driveway, and the smell of coffee fills the air. I am a light sleeper, so I am shocked she left without me knowing.

Noticing the empty Mason jar on my mother's nightstand, I remove it, placing it in the kitchen sink. She is pulling a double shift today, and she will not be home until late tonight. Once here, she will find the kids tucked in for the night, and I will use the rare quiet moment to voice my displeasure regarding her drinking.

After feeding the kids, cleaning the breakfast dishes, and sending Leif off to school, I turn the TV on to keep Paige company. I will spend today packing my side of the room and boxing up the rest of Leif and Paige's toys.

The fading light of day casts a peaceful glow around the room as I pack all but a few changes of clothing for our family. Finishing a little early, I decide to give my mother a jump on getting her things together, and I carefully pack the pictures and bric-a-brac cluttering the top of her nightstand. As if to haunt me, the bottle of whisky sits on the windowsill, peeking out from behind the curtain next to her bed. A ray of sunlight catches the decanter at the perfect angle, allowing me to notice only a small amount of alcohol is missing from the newly opened bottle.

Shame creeps into my heart. I had expected it to be mostly empty, which means she'd only had two drinks. It is now that I understand I owe my mother a huge apology.

Arriving home and exhausted from pulling the double shift, Mom leans against the kitchen door frame. I made spaghetti for dinner, one of her favorite dishes. Wearily she grins, setting her purse on the table. Muscles sore from a long day, she slowly takes a seat. Placing a plate of pasta in front of her, I ask if we can have a quick talk after she is done with supper.

Fatigue apparent in her voice, she answers, "Not tonight, Sylvia Rose. I am very tired and not in the mood for yet another one of your sermons or arguments."

"No sermon or anything like that, I promise," I respond.

After Mom finishes her meal, I remove her plate as the time has come and I must now eat my own dinner of crow. "Mom, I hardly know where to start," I pause. Looking into her confused eyes, I continue, "First, let me say how sorry I am for not trusting and believing in you. When packing a few of your things today, I noticed the bottle of whiskey. I assumed it would be nearly empty. Mom, you always hear that once a drinker starts back, they don't stop until they pass out or the bottle is empty. Like an idiot, I too thought that. 'I am sorry' does not cover how badly I feel. You have been doing so well. Landing a job, finding a house, and still managing to work a double shift? I honestly don't know how you are doing all this." Hoping she can hear the sincerity in my voice, I add, "Mom, I am proud of you, and I love you."

Smiling a weary smile, she whispers, "You see, Honey, some people can change. Big changes don't happen overnight. I made a promise to be a better mother to you kids. Sylvia Rose, I can't make up for my absence while you were growing up. All I can do is move forward and not revisit my mistakes. I only hope one day you can forgive me."

I have never seen a more sincere and pleading look on my mother's face. "Mom, I admire your dedication, but I was afraid nothing had changed. I can see how hard you are trying. I am glad Mr. Marlow has given us this second chance and am happy to see these changes in you. Oh, and speaking of chance, Mr. Marlow stopped by for an update on how things are progressing. He wanted to remind me we only have another month left in this house. I told him about the cabin you found and, not to worry, things here are great. He asked me to tell you 'hello,' and said he knew you had it in you."

With our conversation ended, Mom pours herself a drink. Tonight, I will not be shooting judgmental and dirty looks her way. Her new attitude and determination to change allows me to leave those petty reactions behind.

Mom gets up from the table, reminding me of her appointment to see the cabin tomorrow. Mid-sentence, the phone rings. We look at each other, the same thought reverberating between us. Who could that be at this hour?

Entering our room, Mom sits in her rocking chair and answers. I can hear only her side of the conversation and it seems to irritate her. "Hello, yes, this is Connie," she says as a pause follows, "I can't. I have to look at a house tomorrow morning." More silence, "I will have to call you back if that's okay. Yes, I will see what I can do. Okay, bye."

I hear the phone being placed back on the cradle. "Sylvia Rose?"

"Yes?" I answer, drying my hands with the dish towel as I walk into our room. "Is everything alright?"

"Yes, well, kind of. I need to make a call or two, and the noise from the kitchen is distracting. Can you stop what you're doing for a few minutes?"

"Yeah, sure thing, Mom," I answer, with a shrug as I leave for the living room.

An hour passes, and I assume Mom has gone to bed. With a long day ahead of her tomorrow, she needs sleep. The evening grows late, and I hear noises coming from Leif and Paige's room. I tap lightly on the door frame before entering and see my brother giggling as he throws stuffed animals into his sister's crib. I gesture to him to be quiet and watch as he scurries to his bed. As I tuck them in, I kiss Paige on her forehead. Leif turns away, telling me he is getting too old for goodnight kisses. Before closing their bedroom door, I hold my index finger to my lips and whisper,

"Mom's sleeping and has a big day tomorrow, time to sleep."

On my way back from scolding my younger brother, I am surprised to find Mom sitting at the kitchen table.

"I thought you would be asleep by now," I comment.

"Change of plans," my mother responds, disappointment clear in her tone. "I have to ask a huge favor of you, Sylvia Rose."

"What's that?" I ask, trying to sound upbeat, hoping to ease her worry.

"That was Hoyt on the phone. I have to go in for my first day of work tomorrow, on a Thursday, of all things. Seems they are a man short due to an accident at the plant today. I cannot make the meeting to go see the cabin, and I just got off the phone with Chance to see if he could possibly take you to meet Cathy Townsend at the Broken Arrow. I trust your judgement better than my own. You know what you want when it comes to a home, and you will know if this cabin is right for us. Chance said there was no issue with him taking off part of the morning, and he would be glad to give you a ride to Mathiston. I fought for this job so hard, and I need to show I am a team player who can be counted on. This is last-minute notice, but I have no choice. I hope you understand."

Hearing her apprehension, I respond, "No problem, Mom. I can get Leif off to school as I always do, and I am certain Jan Blackwell will watch Paige for the few hours we will be gone."

"Well, I suggest we turn in for the night. Tomorrow is a busy day for us both. I have to admit, Sylvia Rose, I am a little frightened about these changes and how fast things are happening."

I grasp her outstretched hand to show my support. "Together, we can do this." I say, watching as my mother's eyes tear up. "We got this, Mom, or should I say, you got this. You have been so amazing, so strong and dedicated. Please don't be afraid. Together, we will get through this."

After our heartfelt conversation, Mom places the empty mason jar which held her cocktail into the sink and heads to bed. I follow closely behind with a newfound optimism bubbling deep inside.

After a late bedtime, I sleep fitfully, and morning comes too quickly. Many chores need to be completed before I look at our prospective home. My list is long, and time is short.

Surprised at how little time I take to complete my chores, I sit with my second cup of coffee, waiting for Mr. Marlow. Still worried about the long trip ahead, I make a mental list of subjects for conversation. I can ask how he has been, ask him again why he insists on helping us as much as he has, and thank him repeatedly for his kindness. My thoughts are interrupted as I hear the loud roar of a car's engine coming up the driveway. Looking out of our bedroom window, I see an old, green truck covered in dust with Mr. Marlow behind the wheel.

I thought he would arrive in his Mustang, but I am surprised to see and hear this loud truck.

Picking up my purse, I rush out to meet him.

He greets me with a cheerful, "Good morning, young lady."

I return his salutations as he helps me up into his truck. "Good morning to you."

"I was glad your mom called me last night. I was curious to see this new house," he says before placing the truck in gear.

Knowing the conversation will be strained, I answer, "I am glad too, and thank you for all you have done, Mr. Marlow."

"Chance," he replies.

"What?" I ask over the loud engine's roar. "Chance, call me Chance," he repeats loudly. "I can't do that, I just can't," I answer.

Looking over at me, he smiles and says, "I respect that."

He keeps the conversation to a minimum, and I sit and enjoy the scenery as it speeds by. It is 11:45 AM when we pull into the Broken Arrow parking lot. "Do you see her?" Mr. Marlow asks.

"Not yet. According to mom, Ms. Townsend is supposed to have blonde hair with a pageboy cut and said to envision Mrs. Brady of the Brady Bunch."

Mr. Marlow holds the door open for me as we enter the restaurant. Immediately, I spot Cathy. I explain to her that my mother had to work today, so I will be the one looking at the cabin. Then I introduce Mr. Marlow and ask to join her in the booth.

"Oh, that's a shame. I was so looking forward to meeting your mother. Pops told me a lot about her." Motioning with her arm for us to join, she adds, "By all means, please take a seat."

"Pops?" I ask.

"Yes, he owns the liquor store there in Maben." With the same breath she adds, "Well, this morning isn't going as planned for any of us. I have a last-minute meeting with a client in Eupora and cannot stay. I have written the directions to the cabin on this slip of paper. You can't miss it. My brother Charles—he goes by Chip— should be there by now and will show the cabin to you. We co-own it, so if you like it, tell him, and we can meet later to work out the details. Not meaning to be rude, but I gotta run. I am already late."

Cathy stands up, grabs her purse and keys, and waving, says, "It was nice to meet you both."

A renewed sense of excitement fills me as Mr. Marlow drives to the cabin. Positive energy always seems to surround this unselfish and helpful man. A large old oak tree stands twenty feet behind small mimosa trees which conceal the cabin from direct view of Highway 15. As we pull in, I see a blonde brick cabin with a slightly rusted, galvanized tin roof. Parked ahead sits a new Cadillac with a tall, thin man propped up against it. As we drive up, he impatiently checks his watch.

Mr. Marlow exits the truck, asking me to stay seated for a few minutes. "I need to tell him what's going on." he explains.

After they speak briefly, Mr. Marlow motions for me to join them, and introduces me to Chip Townsend, the late mayor's brother. Inserting the key into the side door of the cabin, Chip remarks, "Well, come on in and check things out." A large wad of chewing tobacco in his mouth makes it nearly impossible to understand him. We follow as he leads the way up the steps. Leaning over the handrail, he spits brown liquid into the holly bush growing against the house and wipes the remaining liquid from his chin with his sleeve.

Ew, that's disgusting, I think as we enter the cabin.

"Y'all just take a look 'round and meet me outside when you're done. We can talk business later if you're still interested."

Mr. Marlow and I take our time looking around. Having never been privy to a woman's touch, the cabin feels cold and unwelcoming. However, the rooms are large and built with solid floors, and the potbelly stove in the living room adds a nice rustic touch. With a few minor changes, Mom and I can quickly transform this oversized man hunting den into a cozy home.

I turn and ask Mr. Marlow for his thoughts on the place. He responds by telling me it does not matter what he thinks. The decision rests squarely with me.

"I like the cabin and can see calling it and this little town home. I don't believe we need to look any further."

"Well, let's go have a chat with Chip," Mr. Marlow says with a big smile.

As I close the cabin door behind us, Chip asks, "Well, wadda ya think of the old place?"

"It will do nicely," I respond.

"Okay then, let's get a cup of coffee in town and we can talk business at the restaurant," Chip offers.

I do not voice my concerns, but I am confused. When leaving the Broken Arrow, Cathy's last remark led me to believe she will handle the monthly rent and lease.

"We will follow you there," Mr. Marlow pipes in.

Neither Chip nor Cathy mention the reasons behind the cabin sitting vacant for so long. Their silence gives me the leverage I need to ask for lower rent. During our conversation, Chip informs us they set the rent at $400 a month. Even before ordering coffee, Mr. Marlow takes out his checkbook. Quickly, I place my hand over his to stop him from writing. "Wait a minute, Mr. Marlow, we cannot rent the cabin."

"What?" he mutters in surprise.

"We can't rent the cabin." My statement catches both men off guard,

"What do you mean?" Asks Chip.

"Yeah, what do you mean?" Mr. Marlow chirps in.

Confidently, I address Chip. "First, you have not told Mr. Marlow of the murder which occurred only three short years ago in the cabin."

"The murder?" Mr. Marlow stammers.

"Yes, murder. The whole town knows about it, and that is going to cause gossip. Not to mention the place is a mess, and the bloodstain by the potbelly stove will never come out. Something like that is a constant reminder someone died there. So very much needs to be done before we can ever consider it a home. I am sorry, but four hundred is too much."

Taken by surprise, Mr. Marlow looks at me, not saying a word, while Chip sits across from us, with an insulted and disgusted look on his face.

"How about—?" Chip begins to counter.

I interrupt, "How about two hundred for the first two years, three hundred for the third, and four hundred for the fourth year? It will take that long to convert it from a dusty cobweb factory with a bloodstain on the floor to a home. Now, if this does not sit well with you, I understand, but honestly, Mr. Townsend, the cabin has been sitting for three years. With the rumors surrounding it, it could be another three before you find anyone interested. My mom insists I get a good deal on the cabin or we will move to a house in Maben she has located. She says they only want three hundred a month for it, and it doesn't need cleaning up."

Not looking at me, Chip turns to Mr. Marlow. "Tough negotiator you brought with you, feller."

"Yeah," Mr. Marlow responds, unable to hide his amazement.

Turning his focus to me, Chip Townsend states, "Cathy may not be happy about this, but you do make a good argument about the cabin, and I want someone living there." Ordering three coffees, he turns to us with his decision. "Sure, why not? When do you plan to move in?"

"The first of next month," Mr. Marlow answers, adding, "I am going to write a check out for six hundred for the first three months of rent. When can we expect the lease?"

"There is no lease. We do business with handshakes in this town. I can give you the key now, if you like, and you can start cleaning the place. Rent still won't start until the first of next month."

Chip seems happy to resolve his empty cabin issue, and I am excited to know we finally have a permanent home. I again thank Mr. Marlow for his generosity and kindness before we climb into his truck. The loud drive home gives me time to daydream about this tar-papered cabin and how we will convert it into a loving and permanent home.

We arrive back at my house mere moments before Leif gets off the school bus. Running at full speed, he slips, falling on the wet gravel. Immediately getting up, he gives us the thumbs up gesture, letting us know he is okay.

Starting up his truck, Mr. Marlow looks down at his watch and remarks, "Dang, where'd the day go? I gotta run." Honking his horn, Mr. Marlow waves goodbye as he leaves the driveway.

We both wave back as Leif looks up at me and remarks, "I like him. He's nice."

Chapter 8

Our Family Prepares for a New Life

$\mathfrak{E}$xcitement fills the air as we ready ourselves for a new adventure. Having moved several boxes to the cabin on Mom's days off, the mounting tension for meeting the deadline to move out of the old house has eased, allowing our family to relax. It seems mom and Leif are as excited as I for our new beginning in the quaint little town of Mathiston.

Moving day arrives, and the entire family eagerly awaits Mr. Marlow's arrival. Having agreed to rent a U-Haul for Mom, as she has no credit cards, it will be the last bit of help he will offer. Checking to make certain we have overlooked nothing, we survey each room as our steps echo off the walls of the now empty house. A few packed boxes, which I have neatly stored in the corners, and the larger pieces of furniture, patiently wait to be loaded. We have dismantled the beds, leaning mattresses and box springs against the walls of each bedroom. With all preparations complete, Mom and I sit nervously as several hours pass. Clicking her fingernails on the side of her coffee mug, Mom releases a sigh of pent-up frustration. She has called Mr. Marlow's home about a dozen times, only reaching his answering machine. Growing angry now, she paces by the kitchen window, pulling the curtains back as she looks for the U- Haul truck to drive up. Wiping perspiration from her brow, she sits at the kitchen table, mumbling something under her breath I cannot understand.

The loud roaring of a diesel engine comes from outside. Rushing to the windows and shoving each other aside to get a peek, we are all surprised to see a huge moving truck backing into our driveway, followed by Mr. Marlow's mustang. Extremely teed off, my mother leaves the house, storming down the driveway to intercept both vehicles. Not wanting to miss a moment of this confrontation, I follow close behind.

"What is this?" Mom asks. With a broad smile, Mr. Marlow answers, "Well, I thought since you all have worked so hard getting everything ready for your move, instead of you guys having to load and unload a U-Haul truck by yourselves, I'd hire a moving company. It'll make things a lot easier on all of you."

Her angry reddened face noticeable to all, my mother stares at Mr. Marlow and after a long, deep breath, states in a loud and emphatic voice, "You should have cleared this with me first Chance. This is too much. Absolutely too much. You have already spent so much money, money I can never repay you. I know, I know, you say I don't have to pay you back and you're doing this for the kids, not me. I ask you to understand the effect this has on me. Chance, it is bad enough I cannot afford to make these changes on my own, your over-the-top gestures, though well intentioned, emphasize my inability to care for my family. This is the last straw; you gotta promise this will be the last thing you do for me or my family. I am not asking you to stop caring about my children's wellbeing. You have done more than enough, more than anyone could ever ask, and we all appreciate you. I need you to allow me to show my children, you, and the world I can be the responsible adult here."

Looking surprised, Mr. Marlow stands silent, as I admire my mother's resolve. I quietly ask Mr. Marlow's forgiveness for my mother's harsh words as we walk slowly towards the soon-to-be- vacant home.

Stopping short of the stoop, Mr. Marlow grabs both my hands, and in a fatherly tone says, "You know I am doing all this for you, Leif, and Paige, right?" I nod. "I see the changes in Connie. In less than two months, she has become a totally different woman— determined and strong enough to weather any storm. However, you, Sylvia Rose, are still a young girl, barely a teenager. You put on a strong façade, but you are still just a little girl. I am trying to give you both the tools needed to help your family get settled into a normal life and routine. With your mother now home every night, it will be time for Sylvia Rose to concentrate on her needs and personal goals. I hired this crew because I knew if I didn't, you all would be exhausted by the end of the day. Also, I have things going on today and would not have been able to help. This is my last gift to you both. Now, let's go inside to see if I can calm your mother down."

Walking through the house, Mr. Marlow notices all the packed and organized boxes lining the empty walls. "My, you have been busy," he says, looking in my mother's direction.

"You seem surprised," my mother retorts.

"No, not really, only an observation." Mr. Marlow reaches for my mom's hand.

She pulls back, rejecting his gesture. Unfazed, he continues, "Connie, I am proud of you and all you have accomplished. Please know that. The woman standing before me today is the one I wish I had gotten to know. I am glad to see and be a part of this change with you. I hold no ill will towards you, no grudges, only respect. You got this and don't need anyone else trying to run your life. I understand that now. It is time I step back and let you take control. Again, I am happy to see all this progress. I'll leave this to you and your family from here on out. I will always care for you and your family, Connie, and wish you all the best."

Softened by his words, my mother allows Mr. Marlow to get close enough to kiss her on the cheek before taking his leave.

I look at my mom standing silently with her hand on the cheek Mr. Marlow kissed.

As he shuts the door behind himself, in frustration I ask, "You're just going to stand there and let him leave? Will you not walk him to his car?"

"He doesn't want to be escorted out. The kiss on the cheek was his personal goodbye to me. We must go on by ourselves from here, Sylvia Rose."

Walking to the kitchen window, I watch Mr. Marlow back out of our driveway as a wave of sadness flows through me. Mom sits stoically at the dining room table, nursing a cold cup of coffee with a forlorn look in her eyes. I want to offer her comfort, but I'm unsure what to say. With so much left to do, we must snap out of this emotional vortex and concentrate on the move.

The moving crew makes quick work of loading our lives into the large moving van.

Filled with our belongings, the van follows closely behind as we drive to our new home. It takes less than six hours to unpack all our items and get them put in their designated places. Exhausted from the day's adventures, Mom and I tuck Leif and Paige in for the evening.

Afterwards, we both relax in our new living room. There is no need for conversation as the television emits a warm, comforting glow. The flickering light illuminates her tired face, permitting me to see my once absentee mother in a whole new light. I admire the woman sitting next to me who is showing a newfound and awe-inspiring dedication to her family.

Chapter 9

Chance Marlow's Unannounced Visit

The past several months has been hell on me. Trying to run a successful construction company and helping Constance Jo Turner and her family settle into a new home has been financially and emotionally draining. Without her eldest daughter's intervention, I would have sent my ex-girlfriend to jail. Instead, I have been able to watch Connie become the strong, responsible mother she is today. The family remains in contact with me, letting me know how things are going and repeatedly thanking me for the help I have given them. I realize they are grateful, but enough is enough already.

The family has worked hard to transform the rustic hunting cabin into a cozy home. As summer slowly faded away, Connie registered Leif for school as Sylvia Rose continues to look after the family and home. Connie reports she truly loves her new job, and all family members are content with their new hometown.

Work has kept me busy, and I haven't had the chance to visit the cabin since Sylvia Rose and I ventured there several months ago. I long to witness the transformation they have described to me over the phone. I cannot deny a flutter of anticipation as I dial Connie's number, eager to arrange a time for me to come out for a brief visit. She says Saturdays are the best day for visitors to come over because the family usually returns home around noon after buying groceries for the week. Our phone conversation comes to a polite conclusion after we settle on a time and date which works for us both.

The date agreed upon for my visit arrives quickly. Finding myself on edge this morning, for reasons I cannot understand, the usually calming and scenic hours' drive to Connie's new home is not helping to ease my tension. I am, by nature, a composed man, but this morning I find myself uncomfortably anxious. As I pull into the drive, a wave of disappointment overtakes me when I realize Connie's car is not there. Looking down at my watch, I realize it is only 11:30 AM. I settle into a green metal lawn chair beneath a pecan tree, its multi-colored fall leaves contrasting with the weathered wood of the outhouse. Despite having functioning plumbing, the outhouse is a remnant of a forgotten era, and for the life of me, I cannot understand why the owners allow it to stand. As a good 'ol country boy, and owner of a construction company, I know the dangers old and dilapidated structures present. These buildings are not only home to spiders and snakes, but they are also a danger to curious young children.

With nothing left to do but wait, I sit back in the metal chair and observe the ants scurrying around, carrying morsels of food to their mound. Some people might enjoy nature and the sounds the country offers. I do not. As boredom strikes, I decide to stroll around the perimeter of the home. Often, Connie pridefully speaks of the transformation the home has undergone. As I walk around the tar- papered cabin, through sheer drapes, my gaze lingers on the freshly dusted furnishings in each room. The cabin seems cozy and inviting. I can't help but feel proud of the family's efforts to turn this space into a home. The mid-fall season brings with it a subtle crispness to the air, and I notice some windows are open to take advantage of it. Curious about the music I hear emanating from the next window, I venture closer to investigate.

Before even peering inside, a deafening scream startles me. Stumbling back and tripping over a rotting log, I tumble to the ground, nearly smacking my head against a weathered, rusty yellow Tonka Truck left abandoned by

Connie's thoughtless son. In a state of panic, I quickly rise to my feet, pine needles and other debris clinging to my clothes.

"Who are you?" I hear. "What do you want? I am calling the police, you pervert!"

The owner of the voice is rightfully very upset, and I can tell it belongs to a very surprised Sylvia Rose. I step back, and shock leaves me unable to respond, as I wonder, what the hell? Connie told me no one would be here.

Deciding it best to reclaim my seat underneath the pecan tree until Connie gets home, I sit, nerves completely shot and more embarrassed than I have ever been in my life. The metal chair is cold as I nervously squirm, trying to find a comfortable position.

Hearing the screen door open and slap loudly on the frame, I look up to see Sylvia Rose rounding the corner, holding an aluminum baseball bat as she shouts, "Hey, you perv. I got a bat and am not afraid to use it. If you come near me, I am going to hurt you." Once completely around the corner, the young sentinel notices me. "Mr. Marlow?" she shouts. "What are you doing sneaking around our house? You almost gave me a heart attack."

As the young woman walks towards me, shame causes me to sit petrified, unable to speak or move. Seeing my embarrassment and fear, Sylvia Rose releases the bat. As it drops to the leaf covered ground, she approaches, stopping just feet in front of me as silence surrounds us.

I answer in a calm and hopefully reassuring voice, "I didn't mean to scare you. No one is supposed to be here. Your mom said you guys would be out shopping, and being early, I decided to look around. Connie and I set up this visit two weeks ago. She told me you guys would be here around noon-ish. Didn't she tell you?"

"Mom is at work. Why do you want to see her, anyway? I thought you were done with us."

"Sylvia Rose, how can you say such a thing? I still care for your family. I swear to you, your mom knows I am supposed to be here today." I pray my response is what the young woman wants and needs to hear.

A smile replaces her scowl as she shakes her head and laughs.

Reaching for my hand to help me up, she says, "Well, come on in and see the place. I guess that's why you're here, right?"

Attempting to steer the conversation away from the events which have transpired, I ask, "Where's your brother and sister?"

She answers calmly now. "Leif is at the neighbor's; Edd is teaching him how to replace an alternator on his old Cadillac. Paige is napping."

Uneasiness between us gone, I follow Sylvia Rose into the house.

The cabin is quite homey, with everything neatly in its place. The pine scented air is pleasant as she guides me through the home. Sylvia Rose tells me of her decision not to enroll in school, stating she feels Paige is still too young and needs her care. She opts to homeschool herself during the quiet evening hours, using Leif's books, lessons, and homework as a guide. She speaks of her ambition to obtain a GED.

As the tour of the cabin ends, Sylvia Rose presents me with a glass of iced tea as we casually stroll to the living room. She informs me of her mother's amazing progress, but reluctantly admits Connie enjoys a cocktail from time to time.

"I will say this," she proudly states, "I haven't seen Mom drunk or tipsy since that morning the cops showed up."

Sylvia Rose speaks fondly of Connie's love for her new job. She tells of how wonderful it is to have her mother at home in the evenings. I admire Sylvia Rose's maturity as she relays how thankful she is her brother and sister can create memories with their mother, a luxury not afforded to her. Pausing, she apologizes for talking too much and inquires politely, "So, how are you doing?"

"Oh, just work and home," I answer bluntly, not knowing what to add.

A quiet and uneasy stillness hovers over the room. As I wait anxiously for Connie's arrival, I tap my fingers against my leg restlessly. Breaking the uncomfortable silence between us, Sylvia Rose clears her throat, stating, "I know you don't want to hear this again, but I want to thank you for changing our lives. All the bills are paid, and Mom has opened a small savings account. One day, I don't know when or how, I will pay you back Mr. Marlow. You can hem and haw all you like, but it's going to happen. We are grateful for the things you have done, and I know this has been a strain on you. Until I can pay you back, please know, not a day goes by when I don't thank the Lord for all the changes in my life. Our family's transformation has been made possible through your generosity and kindness."

Her words are so pure, so honest, and so well-intentioned, I am taken aback by the maturity she shows. However, I never want her to think she or her family owes me for anything. Not wanting to hear such nonsense again, I try to make my point one last time.

"You have always been wise beyond your years, Sylvia Rose. Under the most straining circumstances, you have always presented yourself with the utmost poise. There is no need to pay back anything, young lady. What I did, I did for you, Leif, and Paige. Your mother lived with me for over a month, spending every night, never letting on she had children. After speaking with you on the phone before I brought your mother home from jail, I realized something had to be done to give you and your siblings some semblance of a normal life. Your mother's vandalizing my car and trashing my house gave me the leverage needed to strike the deal with her—one meant to benefit you. I can see it has, and you are doing well. That is all the reimbursement I will ever need."

"I am going to pay you back. N'uff said," she says in a forceful and angry tone.

Never having heard a raised voice from Sylvia Rose, and realizing this is a sore subject, I immediately discontinue the conversation. The unmistakable sound of loose gravel crunching beneath tires alerts us Connie has arrived.

"That'll be Mom," Sylvia Rose announces.

"Sylvia Rose!" we hear coming from outside as Connie stands at the rear of her car, trunk open and obviously exhausted. "Sylvia Rose!"
Rushing out, we join Connie at the back of her car.

"I need help getting these groceries into the house." Her statement is curt, as she glares at my Mustang taking up valuable space in her drive, not allowing her to park closer to the kitchen door.

As her daughter and I remove the bags of groceries from the disorganized trunk, with a look of despair, Connie remarks, "I completely forgot about today. I trust Sylvia Rose has been able to keep you company?"

"Yes, she has been lovely, thanks." I force a smile.

Following Connie into the house, I carefully set the groceries on the table. We exchange mild courtesies, and I can only watch as the two women work in unison to put away Connie's purchases.

Moments later, Leif joins us in the kitchen, hands and face covered with black grease smudges. With a huge smile, he washes his hands and face, regaling his mother with each step it took to change the alternator on Edd's car.

"Oh, and Edd asked if I wanted to go to the horse auction in Ackerman next weekend. Can I, Mom?"

Connie nods yes.

The four of us sit in the living room and talk for two hours. Leif fills me in on his school activities. Connie speaks proudly of her job and how the family loves the charm of this small town, while Sylvia Rose sits, silently listening, her bright smile speaking for her. Noticing the hour growing late, I look at my watch and announce I must leave. Connie walks me to the door, whispering, "I'll never be able to thank you enough."

"No thanks needed," I whisper back as we embrace on the stoop. Looking back at the home these two ladies worked so hard to build, I wave goodbye and laughingly remark, "Screen could use some cleaning." As I back out of their driveway, there is but one thought on my mind. Best money I ever spent.

Chapter 10

Fitting In

$\mathfrak{E}$lation and excitement wrap my family in joy as we adjust to our new lives and home. With time, our euphoric state shifts from newfound joy to a secure sense of peace and happiness.

Mom has established herself in the community and church as a hard-working single mother who lives in "that cabin" with her three children. Being accepted in the community is very important to her. "It is not a matter of religious belief," she would say. "The most important thing as a new resident of a small community is to attend church and be seen placing money in the offering plate. If you support your church and high school football team, the townsfolk will eventually support and accept you."

To truly become members of our new town, mother insists we attend Sunday services. She also makes us dress up and attend teen and preteen festivities such as ice cream and box socials. In small towns such as this, they expect everyone to heed certain, unspoken rules. Boys are to join the football team, and pretty, athletic girls are encouraged to join the cheerleader squad. The Ladies Church League expects mothers to provide a selection of cakes and cookies for the many charitable bake sales held at the church and school.

Because it gives us a nice reprieve from our daily chores, we attend church each week. On Sunday mornings, Leif and Paige rush out of the house and eagerly await the church bus to whisk them away to Sunday school. Mom and I follow an hour later. After church services, Brother Bibb hands out half a stick of spearmint gum to the children as he offers a friendly handshake to exiting parishioners, reminding them of upcoming church-sanctioned events. From the back seat of the car on our ride home, Leif gushes on about Penny Sue Tannenbaum and how pretty she looked in her Sunday dress, as Paige plays quietly with her Barbie. No words need to be spoken as Mom and I exchange a shared smile, comfortable in the knowledge we are finally Mathstonians.

We have grown accustomed to the peaceful rhythm of country living. Mom has acclimated to the structured life of a single, working mother. Leif is making friends, and Paige, well, she is growing like a weed. My responsibilities remain the same, caring for my siblings, preparing meals, and cleaning the home. This time, however, I no longer feel abandoned or overlooked as I embrace our new settled life.

With the weekend behind us, I open the cupboard to find no cornmeal, a crucial ingredient needed for tonight's dinner. The weather either makes or breaks my trips to town. Preparing for the two-mile trek, I tie my worn tennis shoes and grab Mom's wide- brimmed straw hat with the silk bow. As I step out of the house, I immediately notice the dryness of the air accompanied by a slight breeze. Mother Nature has granted the perfect temperature for a pleasant walk.

Normally, I schedule each visit to town, always leaving time to visit with the town's librarian. As this one is unplanned, today, I don't have time to bask in the cozy atmosphere of the small book depository. I will miss the diversion of leisurely looking through magazines while getting lost in colorful images of lively city streets and picturesque town squares. Unlike these tourist destinations, small towns are more modest in terms of entertainment, lacking grand theaters, renowned ballet companies, and art galleries boasting famous collections. I vow to myself to one day visit these places and experience life beyond this town's quaint borders.

My task of shopping complete, I search for a place to sit down as somehow, a pebble has found its way into my shoe. My eyes settle on the concrete bench beneath a shade tree in front of the post office. Setting down the groceries, I remove a tiny stone which has become lodged in my shoe. I take this chance to unwrap a chocolate bar (a special treat I have saved up for) as I look down Main Street and rub the sole of my foot where the stone left an indentation. I close my eyes, letting my imagination drift back to the days when this small town was first founded.

In the late 1800s, the old train depot in Mathiston, Mississippi, served as a social hub. At 6:30 PM, the townspeople would gather to catch up on the latest happenings and gossip while waiting for the mail car. Today, the rail yard sits ghostly quiet, deserted except for a few randomly scattered stacks of banded pulpwood. A dilapidated platform is all that remains of the landmark. Years of neglect have caused it to decay slowly, and now it is just a sad and fading reminder of simpler times.

Last month, I learned the brick structure standing kitty-corner from the post office is the oldest in town. Decades ago, the multi storefront building served as the major gathering place for the town's residents. Standing proud and regal, the building holds within its walls nostalgic stories time has long since forgotten.

Formerly the proud centerpiece of the town, the old bank is now a smoke-filled pool hall where young boys gather, and old men play five cent dominoes. Next door to the rundown billiard room is the town's only library, once the first restaurant in town, and the dry cleaner now occupies the old shoe store. This enormous building was the center of trade and commerce decades ago. Time and weather have taken their toll on this once majestic structure.

Replacing my shoe and shifting positions on the hard bench, my mind travels back in time to the late nineteenth century. A sepia- tinted image of Mathiston forms in my mind. The scene slowly comes into focus, and I envision gentlemen casually strolling down Main Street dressed in their Sunday finest as their wives proudly show off the latest fashions ordered from the Sears and Roebuck catalog the winter before. As the well-to-do couples walk along the cobblestone sidewalk, I can almost hear the gentle rustling of petticoats accompanied by the tapping of men's walking sticks. Close behind their affluent parents, young debutantes twirl their fragile parasols with lace gloves delicately encasing their dainty hands. As teenage boys pass, the young ladies playfully tease them. With a quick look back, they coyly peer over their shoulders, exciting the lads with a playful yet risqué wink. One girl may choose to be extremely naughty by raising the hem of her taffeta dress, providing one lucky boy a glimpse of her ankle. Once certain they have the boy's undivided attention, the young women abruptly turn away, lifting their noses high in the air as if to say, "You wish." These vivid images bring a smile to my weary face.

The shouting of a man followed by a loud car horn jolts me from my peaceful daydream.

"Use the damn sidewalk, you kids! You're going to get someone killed!" a loud baritone voice shouts.

Looking down the street, I see an enormous figure standing outside his open car door, shaking a fist to emphasize his anger. I find it funny he is using such colorful language as he is standing between the only two churches the town offers.

Suddenly aware the day has grown late; I gather my things and prepare for the trip home. The midday sun beats down mercilessly, and with each step, the shopping bag grows heavier in my arms. After the two-mile trek, I am soaked in perspiration, and I'm grateful when I see the tin roof of the tar-papered cabin shining like a beacon in the sunlight, welcoming me home. Exhausted and overheated, I rush to unpack the groceries and slip a pan of cornbread into the oven.

Chapter 11

The Road to Maturity

I remain an enigma to the townspeople. I am seen only when shopping, at church, or occasionally when I treat myself to a quick visit to the town's small library. I have spent my entire life in the shadows. Never wishing to draw attention, I keep to myself. As both my siblings are now in school, my chores have become fewer, and I spend my free time studying Leif's homework assignments from the week before. Last week, his English teacher chose Romeo and Juliet as their next book to read and discuss. My brother never brings the book home. He says Mrs. Reed plays a record of the book as the class reads along. I will have to visit the library in town today.

If I am to stay abreast of my studies, I must ask Deb if the library has a copy of Romeo and Juliet available.

Deb stamps the "due back by" card as we exchange pleasantries. She does not appear to want to talk today. Placing the book in my oversized bag, I retreat to the corner of the room and bury my head firmly in a six-month-old copy of Elle magazine. Once again, I allow myself to get lost in images depicting the latest Paris fashion show. I imagine hearing camera shutters whirling and rapidly clicking as emaciated girls parade down the catwalk in tomorrow's latest clothing lines. The small bell above the library door rings, causing me to look up from my magazine. Mr. McDonald enters the library, asking for a book his wife ordered a month prior. While searching around her desk for the package, Deb halfheartedly asks him how things are going, and I overhear him complain.

"Henry Dorn, our dishwasher, just up and left mid-shift last night. The little misses insist on me being home at night and does not like it when I have to fill in because some kid decides he doesn't want to work anymore."

Because I have less housework to do, I have been contemplating getting a part-time job. I do not wish to seem like an opportunist, but I cannot allow this chance to slip by. Excited, but not wanting to show it, I carefully place the magazine I am reading back on the table and follow Mr. McDonald outside.

"Mr. McDonald!" I yell as he walks to his car. No response. "Mr.

McDonald!" I shout again.

Spinning around on one heel, he looks agitated. I may have already blown any chance of working for him. "Can I help you, young lady?" he asks tersely.

"I'm so sorry to bother you," I say, catching my breath. "I was in the library and overheard you tell Deb you are short a dishwasher. I didn't mean to eavesdrop, honest. It's just that I could certainly use a job." Looking for acceptance, I stand there nervously and wring my hands.

"You're Connie Turner's girl, Sylvia, ain't ya?" he asks. "Yes sir, I certainly am!" I answer in my most upbeat voice.

"Well, young lady, this is neither the time nor the place to speak of a job." He turns to get into his car.

"But..." I say, raising my hand. It is too late; he has already started pulling away from the curb.

As I re-enter the library, my footsteps echo while I think of Mr. McDonald's rude words. Noticing the puzzled look on my face, Deb questions, "What were you thinking?"

"I was only asking about a job," I reply.

"You don't just run up to a prominent business owner

like that, especially Mr. McDonald. You don't know him, and he certainly doesn't know you. Few people like being approached on the street, much less by someone they don't know." Statement ended, Deb continues stamping returned books.

"But he does know me. He called me by my name."

Briefly looking up from her task, Deb interjects, "Just 'cuz someone knows your name, doesn't mean they know you. I hope you understand. I know if I wanted a job at the Broken Arrow, I would first fill out an application and use the chance to introduce myself properly to Mr. McDonald."

Taking Deb's words to heart, I excuse myself. With a confident and determined stride, I walk towards the Broken Arrow restaurant, taking my first steps on the road to maturity.

Heeding my only friend's advice, I properly introduce myself to Mr. McDonald and, with a firm handshake, timidly ask for an application. I notice a broad smile overtake his face. Using a most friendly tone, he states, "Now, that's the proper way to ask for a job, Ms. Turner."

Mr. McDonald does not believe in paper applications; he sees no need for them. Taking a pen and pad from beneath the register, he ushers me to a booth located closest to the kitchen. He asks the standard questions and jots down what he considers important information, such as my home address and phone number. Mentioning the job is physically demanding, Mr. McDonald asks if I am up for the challenge.

I answer with an emphatic, "Absolutely, sir."

Patting the top of my hand, Mr. McDonald concludes our interview. "Now, you go on home and speak with your mother about working here. I will not hire a minor unless I have the approval of their parents. Should she agree, I will call you back, and we can set up a time and date for your first day of training."

Shaking his hand and giving him my biggest smile, I remark, "Thank you, thank you sir, you don't' know what this means to me."

With a light heart and uplifted soul, I walk home. Fear and anxiety soon replace joy and accomplishment as I near the rustic cabin we call home. I am unsure how mom will react to me asking to take a job. I must be prepared to state my case clearly, something I never seem to do when it comes to speaking of things I truly want to do. To keep from stammering or looking like a fool before mother gets home, I practice my speech, laying out all my reasons for wanting to work.

Fishtailing slightly on the gravel, Mother's '69 Mercury slides to a stop, suggesting that she slammed the brakes. This behavior indicates the possibility of her being in a foul mood. Lately, her conversations regarding work revolve around a young man who wants her job and will say and do anything to discredit my mother and her work ethic. I need Mom to be in a great mood since the news I have to share will drastically affect how our house operates.

The door slams loudly.

Yup, she's in a mood, I think.

In what I can only described as Yosemite Sam muttering, my mother plops down at the dining table as her inaudible sounds continue. "Rasa frassen idiot, moron," is all I can make out of her mumblings.

I cannot bring up my news. Right now, Mom needs a compassionate sounding-board. Pouring her a quick glass of iced tea, I take the seat next to her and listen as she describes the horrible day she suffered. After explaining that she has a headache and needs to lie down, I offer to do the cooking tonight.

"That's sweet of you, Sylvia Rose. Thank you."

It's the least I can do, considering the bombshell I will drop later this evening. The kids come home, get out of their school clothes, and play outside while I prepare a simple dinner of fried pork chops and applesauce. Once dinner is complete, the children adjourn to the living room and watch TV, giving us time to talk.

Approaching mother, I simply blurt out, "I have a job, Mom!"

I tell her Mr. McDonald will call to ask for her permission before allowing me to accept employment. My schedule is to be Friday nights, three PM to close, and weekends from six AM to close. Mom readily agrees to watch the kids on Friday evenings and the weekends, stipulating that I contribute towards household expenses.

Elated, I agree to pay the bill to fill the propane gas tank when needed. As a biannual bill, I see no problem meeting this demand.

Mr. McDonald calls as promised. He and my mother speak for about fifteen minutes. As mom hangs up the phone, she calls out for me. Entering her room, she informs me I can take the job but reminds me I still have responsibilities to the kids and house.

Chapter 12

A New Routine for the Family

Since I only work three days a week, there has been little change in my routine. I still send Leif and Paige off to school in clean clothes, and the house remains tidy. The extra income allows me to contribute to items my brother and sister need for school. I now have the life and family I dreamed about in my green metal lawn chair beneath the stars and apple tree in Pontotoc, Mississippi.

Difficult times behind us, I watch as my brother and sister intricately weave themselves into the fabric of this community and become a part of the rich and colorful tapestry of small-town life. Leif, now thirteen, is a member of the high school football team, and eight-year-old Paige helps around the house without supervision. Mom secures a promotion, and her nemesis, the a-hole, as she calls him, now has her old position. According to her, his ambitions go no farther than the assembly floor supervisor. My job is going well and working extra shifts allows me to save up a sizeable nest egg. A sense of accomplishment overtakes me each time I add money to the old Maxwell House coffee container I keep hidden in the darkest corner of the wellhouse. When the time arrives, I want to move out swiftly and with minimal stress. Working at the restaurant for over a year, my desire for independence grows deep within me, becoming more difficult to suppress each day.

Last week, Mr. McDonald caught me off-guard when he asked if I have any interest in becoming the night shift grill cook. Our current evening cook, Ruth, relays to me her desire to become a, as she calls it, real chef, and has enrolled at the culinary school in Tupelo.

With a lot of experience cooking for my family, I have none when it comes to cooking for a large crowd of people. I have seen how frustrated Ruth becomes during the evening rush and am uncertain I have what it takes to handle such pressure. I realize I must try as the twenty-five cents an hour raise is too much to turn down. I cautiously accept Mr. McDonald's offer. The extensive training and encouragement Ruth provides ease my tensions and I begin to feel comfortable behind the grille. Ruth and I spend the next two months getting me acquainted with my duties and the tasks required for running the kitchen. With the end of Ruth's employment quickly approaching, I feel prepared to take over. During her last week with us, Ruth stands behind me, watching as I develop my rhythm, assuring me things will come easier with time.

Ruth's goodbye party is a sad event for all. Mr. McDonald fights back tears during his goodbye speech to Ruth. Raising a glass of iced tea, his sentiments are short and to the point. "To the best damn grill cook I know. We wish you all the best, Ruth."

Hugging her neck, I choke back tears as I tell her how much I appreciate all she has done for me.

At the age of seventeen-and-a-half, I find myself in charge of the kitchen at The Broken Arrow. I am also tasked with overseeing the new dishwasher, Carl. But most importantly, I can finally leave my dark and unsettling past where it belongs and enjoy the bright future awaiting me.

Chapter 13

Founder's Day

Mathiston is a proud town with a deep sense of community. Generations have gone to school, worked together, and raised children here. Its residents enjoy peace of mind and sound sleep as they leave their homes and cars unlocked at night, knowing theft and vandalism pose no threat to them. After several years, our family has embraced this peaceful little town. Steeped in strong Christian values, social activities are few.

The most exciting social event, which also marks the start of summer, is Founder's Day, where residents gather in the old town square to enjoy the many church-sanctioned events. After the mayor's long-winded address, the fun begins with the children's egg toss, one of many contests and competitions scheduled for the weekend-long event. Dottie Burton's pies always take the blue ribbon. At least one child gets hurt trying to catch the greased pig, and then there's my absolute least favorite event, the putrid tobacco spitting contest. Although it is a most unpleasant competition, Leif refuses to miss out, and usually places in the top three in his age category. I have no time to engage in such frivolous activities as I am scheduled to work at the event this weekend.

Working over a hot grill outdoors with humidity at eighty percent is no picnic. The first week of July this year has been the hottest on record. Ruth has arrived home from Tupelo to spend time with her loved ones, but she promises to lend a hand in our booth on Founder's Day. This happy turn of events allows me to get away long enough to check on Leif and Paige. I find my brother locking lips with Rhonda Morgan by the monkey bars as Paige plays on the swings nearby. Upset, I ask Leif why he is not watching his baby sister. Looking over his shoulder, he points and says, "She's right there. What more do you want?"

Upset, I do not have time to argue with my brother. I cast a glance her way, noticing Paige playing with other children as doting mothers supervise. Content that both my siblings are safe and enjoying themselves, I get back to work and allow Ruth a chance to get some air and walk around.

Five minutes later, Leif shows up at my booth with Paige in tow. "You embarrassed me. You take her, I am done." Leif releases Paige's hand, adding, "I am outta here."

Leaving me with no opportunity to respond, I have no choice but to sit Paige in the corner of our booth and ask her to stay put for a few minutes.

Ruth's unparalleled talent for cooking and conversing entertains our patrons. She shares stories of how she enjoys school and is still trying to adjust to the fast pace of the city. I plate fried chicken dinners, hamburgers, and hotdogs as I keep a close eye on my bored little sister. Keeping very busy, I never notice my boss's arrival.

From behind me, I feel a tug. Untying my apron, Mr. McDonalds shoos me from our booth. In his lovingly doting and fatherly manner, he declares, "You've worked hard all day, and I cannot thank you enough. Now, you go on and enjoy yourself. Ya'll need to walk around and mingle." With shooing motions and smile for emphasis, he adds, "Now go on, git."

With his blessing, I take Paige's hand as we casually stroll around the square, admiring the various hand crafts on display. We stop at the booths long enough to say hello and perhaps comment on the unbelievable and unrelenting humidity.

Paige soon eyes a group of her classmates playing near the merry-go-round. Grabbing my arm and pulling hard, she begs for permission to go play with them. I tell her that if I allow her to go, she must promise to be a good girl and behave. I can only watch as she darts off without so much as a goodbye, leaving her under the watchful eyes of protective mothers who will make certain no harm comes to the children playing on the marry-go-round.

It only takes thirty minutes to walk around the town square, and boredom sets in. It is getting late, and I walk over to retrieve my little sister. Asking the children to stop the merry-go-round, I let Paige know it is time to leave.

Not happy to see me, Paige resists and pouts. "I don't wanna go home. I wanna stay and play!" she shouts. Wiping layers of dust from her face, I let her know in no uncertain terms that we are going home. That is not what she wants to hear. Paige rebels against my authority. The heated disagreement forces me to scold her as I take her hand and guide her from the playground.

From behind, I hear, "She's a fighter."

It is a very familiar voice—one I haven't heard in a while.

This is indeed a wonderful surprise, and I am woefully unprepared for such a moment. Mr. Chance Marlow is insanely handsome. With sandy blonde hair and classic features, he is a dead ringer for John Schneider, the actor who plays "Bo Duke" in *The Dukes of Hazard*. With his God-given attributes, he remains an even-tempered and unassuming man.

Three years have passed since last our family has seen or heard from him. After many failed attempts to locate and talk with him, we assumed he had moved on to bigger and better things.

"Sylvia Rose, how are you?" Not waiting for a response, he remarks, "and look how much you have grown, Paige. you probably don't remember me." Shy, my little sister immediately steps back uncertain of who this stranger is. Bewildered, Mr. Marlow apologizes for frightening her.

"No need to apologize. She is like that with everyone." I try my best to sound reassuring.

Dressed in a light blue button-down shirt, black slacks, and wingtip shoes, he seems overdressed for a small-town shindig such as this one, and I make a wry remark about it. Laughing, he explains that he needed to take a trip to Pontotoc, and that the route takes him through Mathiston. He adds, a nice lady at the truck stop mentioned the Founder's Day celebration as he paid for his fill-up. With a big heart-melting smile, he continues, "I came to see if I could find your mom and you kids."

"Well, Mom and I had to work today. Leif brought Paige with him, and honestly, I have no idea where he's gone off to."

"You have a job now?" Mr. Marlow asks.

"Yes," I excitedly answer. "Started out as a dishwasher and now I am the evening cook. Our booth is right over there," I say, pointing towards the sign reading "The Broken Arrow."

Stepping back, as if to take stock of me, Mr. Marlow comments, "Look at you. You're now the grown-up you were trying so hard to be when we first met. I am so glad I decided to gas up here today."

Blushing and embarrassed, I find myself unable to respond. "Dang, that chicken smells good," Mr. Marlow announces,

patting his belly for emphasis.

"It's coming from our booth and is Mr. McDonald's specialty. All proceeds this year are going to James Straub, who hurt himself while working at the sawmill. The First Baptist Church promises to match every dollar we contribute." Like a blathering fool, I throw out more information than anyone needs to hear, especially since Mr.

Marlow does not know who I am talking about.

"Wow, that's so nice of your boss. Have you eaten? What say we go and buy ourselves some fried chicken dinners to support the cause?"

His joyful tone elicits a yes from Paige. Not waiting for an answer from me, my once timid little sister grabs Mr. Marlow's hand, practically dragging him to the Broken Arrow's booth.

Standing in line, we say little to each other as we step in unison, following those in front of us.

"Your boyfriend?" Mr. McDonald asks as we reach the front of the line.

"Oh no sir, nothing like that. He is a dear family friend." My answer sounds more defensive than intended.

Presenting his gloved hand, my boss introduces himself. "Hiya, I am Abe McDonald. Nice to meet you."

"Chance Marlow," my visitor says, shaking Mr. McDonald's hand. "I used to live in Pontotoc. That's where I know this one from."

Confused by his matter-of-fact statement, I think to myself, *used to live in Pontotoc?*

Established as a pillar of the community and owner of his own home and business, why he would ever leave the town he calls home is a mystery to me.

Mr. Marlow politely continues, "Well, it was nice meeting you, Abe McDonald. If you will excuse us, we need to find a place to sit before our dinners get cold."

Paige and I follow as he finds a spot for us beneath the one- hundred-year-old oak tree. Setting our plates on the table, we squirm, trying desperately to get comfortable in the metal folding chairs provided. Mr. Marlow's nonchalant attitude towards no longer living in Pontotoc unnerves me. I have questions that need answering. First, why the silent treatment for so long, and second, why would he ever leave a town where he and his family are so well respected?

We eat our chicken dinners, talking for an hour. Mr. Marlow tells of life-changing events which caused him to leave Pontotoc. While renovating an old Victorian home in Starkville, a loose clay tile shingle caused him to fall three stories. He thanks God for shrubs, which buffered his fall. Unable to work for over a year and with the recession, his business suffered. Tears well up in his eyes as he speaks of the loss of his father's construction company. The hurtful memories become too much, and he changes the subject abruptly.

Noticing a look of pity in my eyes, Mr. Marlow chastises me. "I don't need anyone's pity. I am like a cat. No matter how many times I fall, I always end up back on my feet." He also asks me to keep our conversation private. "Your mom does not need to know any of this, understand?"

Choking back tears and many other emotions, I respond, "Yes, I understand. I feel awful. I have some money squirreled away and can pay you some of what we owe you and will do anything I can to help, if you'll let me."

The glare in Mr. Marlow's eyes pierces my soul. Rather than anger, he flashes a disapproving and intense look. I grow frightened. He leans in close and whispers in a harsh tone, "Please find Leif or let Paige go back to the playground immediately. I have already said too much in front of her."

Shocked by his reaction, I am confused.

"Please, Sylvia Rose, there is a little more I wish to talk about but not in front of her. We need a bit of privacy."

Grabbing my baby sister by the hand, I ask her to get up and come with me. "I'll be right back."

Unable to find Leif, I am fortunate most of Paige's friends and their mothers are still in the playground area. I ask if Paige can join. Lois Arkin answers yes. Thanking them, I take my leave, uncertain I want to go back to Mr. Marlow. I am still frightened and not sure I want or need to hear what he is about to say.

Sitting back down, I see his demeanor has not changed. If anything, it has intensified.

"Now, you look here," His voice is demanding and firm. "Number one, none of this is to get back to your mother. Number two, I do not need, nor want, your money or help. It is hurtful you would make such an offer. You don't have two nickels to rub together, and you think you're better than me? You think you can help me? I just paid for our dinners and am in no way in dire straits. I care for you, but your statement hurts. Now, I know that was not your intent, but you need to realize, though you mean well, it's a slap in my face for you to think for one second, I would take a penny from you. The help I offered came from an honest place of concern, and from what I can see, it was worth every penny. You are all grown up, your brother and sister have adjusted to their new lives, and though you have not mentioned much about her, I know your mother is doing well. Connie is a strong woman who has proven to be able to handle whatever life throws at her. A trait I also see in you. I am doing fine. I need this to be a positive visit, not end on a note such as this. I should not have told you why I left Pontotoc, but knowing you, you would not have let it rest until I did."

The mood too serious, Mr. Marlow changes the subject, "I still can't believe how you have grown into such a lovely young woman. What I need is for you to become the strong, independent woman I know you can be. That is the only repayment I will ever accept from you. Understand?"

I understand all too well, and nodding, I choose my words carefully. Not wishing to offend him more, I answer, "I'm glad you are okay, and I'm so happy to see you again. I'm sorry to hear about your injury. Had I known, we would've at least sent a card letting you know we were praying for you and wishing you a quick recovery. Mr. Marlow, the last thing I ever want is to offend you. I will be forever in your debt. If not monetarily, I am certainly obliged to make the best of the opportunity you have given us. You have to agree we owe you that, Mr. Marlow."

After begging for his forgiveness and understanding, I am glad to see a smile replace his frown.

"Of course, I give you that, and I do accept your thanks and gratitude." Again, he reiterates his wishes. "What I have shared with you stays right here. Your mother does not need to know I no longer live in Pontotoc or about my accident, okay?"

I agree to keep his secret as he touches my hand gently, asking me to get Paige so he can drive us home. The playground is empty except for my little sister and Tommy Brooks, who are racing each other to see who can go the highest in the swings. My shadow falls over the little boy's mother, causing her to look up. We exchange hellos as Paige, noticing my arrival, slows her swing down as Tommy Brooks shouts, "I win!" "No fair" Paige laughs, "I had to stop cuz my sister is here." Saying goodbye to Tommy, she rushes to my side. The crowd has thinned, and a quick scan of the town square reveals Leif is nowhere in sight. Not one to inform me of his comings and goings, I am certain he left with Rhonda or is playing basketball with his friends.

The drive home gives me barely enough time to tell Mr. Marlow about Leif's success on the football team, mom's two promotions, and how well Paige is doing in school. Before he leaves, I thank him for dinner and the ride home and ask Paige if there was something she needed to say to the nice man.

"Thanks, mister." She says, not looking back while running towards the house.

"Sorry 'bout that. She's always in a hurry to go nowhere." Trying to sound upbeat, I am secretly disheartened by the thought it may be some time before I see Mr. Chance Marlow again. I shut the car door, and while leaning in the window, thank him again for dinner, saying how nice it was to see him. He says no thanks are necessary,

"Screen could still use some cleaning," he adds with a laugh as he drives away, waving goodbye.

Waving back, sadness envelops me, and I am surprised when a tear slowly makes its way down my face.

Once inside, I turn on the TV for Paige. The Smurfs will keep her entertained for the next few hours while I rest.

Tired, I allow myself to plop on the sofa, eyes so heavy, they close immediately. To my astonishment, Mr. Marlow's face appears vividly behind the darkness of my eyelids. Shocked by the image, I take a few long, deep breaths to calm myself. Drifting off to sleep, the image of the ruggedly handsome blonde man remains clearly etched in my mind.

Chapter 14

Gaining My Independence One Milestone at a Time

With Founder's Day behind us, the Broken Arrow's staff is back to being a happy family. My workday starts with a two-mile walk. Occasionally, someone who recognizes me will offer a ride. Other days, I am not so lucky. Having recently seen A Streetcar Named Desire, I think that, unlike Blanch, the sentiment "depending on the kindness of strangers" does not suit me. After my shift ends and I finish mopping up, Jason Bledsoe often offers me a ride home. He is here most nights to eat dinner, and afterwards, sticks around to socialize. He is a friendly boy and just has nowhere else to go. Mr. McDonald joins him in the employees-only booth from time to time, and they talk for hours.

Jason has lived a hard life. He was just a toddler when he lost his parents, and he felt the cold emptiness of being passed from one relative to the next. A troubled child, relatives would take him in, soon realizing they did not have the means or skills to cope with such an active and imaginative young boy. As a teenager, moving from one relative to another only exacerbated his troubling behavior. He began stealing cars and getting into minor legal trouble during his early adulthood. The Baptist minister saw something in Jason, taking him in and giving him odd jobs to do around his home. Jason eventually took over Mr. Otis's position as handyman and janitor for the church. He often says he is a jack of all trades, and master of none, admitting the one skill he never learned was to cook. With my responsibilities running the kitchen, I rarely interact with Jason. Tonight, as I leave the restaurant heading home, there is a nip in the air. Buttoning my coat, I hear a truck pull up behind me. I turn around as Jason honks his horn and opens the passenger's door, announcing, "Your chariot awaits, m'lady."

"Oh, I couldn't," I insist. "My house is two miles south of here. I couldn't ask you to make an unnecessary trip like that."

"I don't mind none. I have nuttin' else goin' on and it is too cold fer you to be walkin' tonight."

He has a point. It is getting cold, so I relent and climb into his truck. I am not uncomfortable around Jason; he has a manner about him which instills calm in most everyone he meets.

Jason drops me off at the end of our driveway, not wanting to disturb anyone who may be asleep. As I enter the house, the sound of ice clinking in a glass draws my attention to the dining room table where Mom sits sipping a drink. I haven't seen her do that in three years. Taken aback, I say nothing as I put my purse on the counter by the fridge. Shaking my head, I take my coat off while walking to my room to hang it up.

"Nope," Mom says. "Stay right here. We need to talk."

Oh boy, I think to myself. *This will not be good, especially because she is drinking again.*

Standing quietly, I listen as my mother goes on about the home's bills, my time away from the kids, and the dereliction of my duties as big sister and housekeeper. She rips into me about how I have deserted her and our family, stating that had she known this job was going to demand so much of my time, she would never have given me permission. She continues by demanding I pay the electric bill along with the filling of the propane gas tank outside.

"Since you are gone so long, you need to pay your share around here. You haven't dusted this house in months. You go to bed right after you get home, and the only contact you have with your brother and sister is when you get them fed and ready for school. I could hire a nanny to do those things."

Her words, and intent, are clear. I understand the drink now. She knows this conversation has a good chance of becoming a full- fledged argument.

Over the past several months, I have become self-reliant, asking her for nothing. Despite my busy schedule, I make sure my brother and sister have what they need, never forgetting they are my most important responsibility. This time, I find my mother's demands unreasonable, and I will not back down. I have been meaning to talk with mother regarding my plans for the future, but a hostile environment is not one in which I wanted to present her with my news.

"Ain't gonna happen, Mom, sorry." My words seem to fall hard on her ears. I guess she thought she was prepared for this conversation. What I am to say next is sure to sober her up immediately.

Not allowing her the opportunity to respond to my previously defiant words, I firmly and forcefully state, "I knew the day would come when you asked too much from me. It seems today is that day, Mom. It's no secret that I have been a mother and cook for the kids, a housekeeper, an accountant, and a bill payer for you. When is it Sylvia Rose's turn, Mother? When do I get to live my life?" I slap my palm on the table. "You think I owe you? For what?" Tired from my shift, I pull out the chair opposite my mother and sit.

My tirade continues. "I have been nothing but supportive of this family. I have been working to keep us together since I was ten. Or have you forgotten? Well, got some bad news for you. By Monday, I will be all moved out and in my own apartment. They accepted my deposit yesterday. It's only a few blocks from work, and the electricity and gas are already in my name. This is not how I wanted you to find out, honestly. I would prefer to have left on a more positive note."

As Mom slams her glass on the metal table, the contents spill over the rim. "You ungrateful little brat!" she yells. "How dare you think you can leave without so much as a discussion? Who the hell do you think you are? Well, missy, you won't be leaving. Not until you have fulfilled your obligations here. How do you expect me to take care of Leif and Paige once you are gone? Have you even thought about that? Have you given one ounce of thought to what effect your leaving will have on the kids? Well, *have you*?" she shouts.

I take a deep, cleansing breath. There will be no diffusing this argument. My only choice is to respond openly and honestly. "Yup, thought about that and so much more. To be honest, I just don't care. Over the last seven years, I have taken care of Leif and Paige. I have watched them grow into well-behaved and polite children. I kissed their boo-boos and disciplined them when necessary. Yes, I guess I have been more of a mother to them, but I am not their mother. You are. Welcome to the world of motherhood. I love my brother and sister, but I love me more. They need you, and it is now your responsibility to take up where I am leaving off. I know you think this selfish of me, but it's time, Mom. It's time I make it on my own. I am sorry you cannot understand, but it's the way it's got to be. My servitude to you and our family is over."

My rant complete, I sigh, preparing to stand and leave. Her heartbeat, now visible through a vein which has popped up above her eye, leaves no question now how furious my mother is with me. She stands, points to the door, and demands, "You leave my house this instant! Right now, get up, go on. Get up from this table and *leave*! You are *not* welcome here anymore."

I expected a negative reaction, but nothing like this.

Sitting motionless, I cannot believe what I am hearing, and am taken by complete surprise as she yells again, "Well? What's taking you so long? I said *leave my house now*!"

I have never seen her angrier or more serious, but I cannot leave without clothes or my few belongings. I will also need to retrieve the money I have stowed away in the dark recesses of the well house.

Trying to buy myself some time, I respond, "I am not leaving tonight. I can be out first thing in the morning after packing my things."

"Out! Now! Or I am calling the police," she seethes.

I know better than to reply when she is like this and run to my room, hastily grabbing what clothes I can and throwing them in the small suitcase I keep stored underneath my bed. She follows, repeating, if I don't leave now, she is going to call the cops and have me arrested.

Suitcase in hand, I open the door while shooting a hateful look in my mother's direction. I then see Leif and Paige standing in the doorway to the kitchen. Paige is crying, and I witness evidence of Leif's sadness silently streaming from his eyes. Reaching for the doorknob, I watch as Paige pulls her hand from her brother's, running towards me at full speed. "Please don't go," she says through heavy sobs, hugging my waist tightly. Prying her little arms from around me, I kneel to her level, and hugging her tightly, I say, "I have to honey; you heard your mother."

"Don't you lay the blame for this on me, young lady," Mom screams. "You're the one who decided to leave. I'm just helping you decide when." Her harsh tone is full of hatred.

"Mom," Leif interrupts, "can't she stay just one last night?"

Shooting an evil stare in my brother's direction, she shouts, "You stay out of this, mister. And you, Sylvia Rose, turn loose of Paige and do as I say. Leave now!"

Kissing Paige on top of her head, I pat her bottom before she walks back to Leif.

Through tears, I sob, "I love you, Leif and Paige. Remember that, please."

As I reach for the doorknob, my peripheral vision catches the blur of the mason jar holding what remains of Mom's drink as it passes beside my head. It shatters as it hits the doorframe. Things have become dangerous, so I leave, not bothering to shut the door. Quietly sneaking to the wellhouse for the last time, I hear Paige's heartbreaking cries. I can't help but wonder if I am doing the right thing.

I cannot allow this fight to distract me. Slipping around to the well house, I quickly grab the stored coffee cans from the darkest corner, emptying them in haste. Shoving the cash into my purse, I leave the cans strewn about the lawn. Fighting back tears, I stop at the end of our driveway. With one last look at my first true home, a sense of immense sorrow and loss fills my heart.

I feel guilty waking the owners of the only motel in Mathiston at one AM. After I lightly tap the bell on the counter, Mr. Ford, a shorter, dark-haired older man wearing paisley pajamas, comes out from behind the checkered curtain. Wiping his eyes, he asks mid yawn, "What'll it be?"

Barely able to understand him through the yawn, I answer, "I need a room for the night, please."

"How many people?" he asks. "Just me."

"Fill this out," he says, sliding a small clipboard towards me. "Cash or credit?"

"Cash."

"Ok," he responds, holding back another yawn. "Make it an even ten dollars. I won't charge tax since you're paying cash."

Thanking Mr. Ford, I hand him the money and apologize for waking him.

"That's why we're here. Don't you fret none about

it."

Taking a deep breath, I insert the key labeled room four into the lock, opening the first of many doors which will mark all future milestones in my life.

Exhausted from the long walk, with clothes damp from perspiration, I shower, giving the heater time to warm the small room. I have tomorrow off, and will be busy settling into my new apartment. Mr. McDonald has offered to help pick up my new secondhand furniture I purchased from the Salvation Army in Eupora. Since my mother wanted me out immediately, my plans to move out in shifts have changed and I am forced to rush my move. Having planned to take off this week and the next to move, I now must pack ninety-six hours' worth of work into the next two days. Crawling into the firm hotel bed with a lot on my mind, the loud humming of the heater eventually lulls me to sleep.

My first morning as an independent woman leaves me confused and disoriented as a peaceful stillness surrounds me. Scheduled to meet with Mr. McDonald this morning, I gather my belongings and drop my room key off at the office. Impeccably dressed and put together, Mrs. Ford takes the diamond-shaped keyring, asking if I enjoyed my stay. Nodding, I again apologize for waking Mr. Ford so late last night. I leave the motel to face my first day as a single adult female, ready to take on the world and hell-bent on making it on my own.

Having nothing planned for another two and a half hours, I walk, suitcase in hand, to the Broken Arrow for breakfast and hot coffee. A strange sensation comes over me, one I have never experienced before. It's a euphoric state enhanced by a sense of pure, unbridled freedom. The morning sun shines brighter today. The fall air is clean and perhaps even crisper. With a renewed sense of promise and great anticipation, my walk to the restaurant is a leisurely, pleasant one.

I enter The Broken Arrow and, as the bell above the door jingles; the confidence emanating from my stride and demeanor does not go unnoticed by the customers who have turned to see who has arrived. Finding my seat, I take out my copy Of Mice and Men from my purse, removing the bookmarker as I continue where I left off last. "What'll ya have?" Janice asks with her usual pleasant smile, "One egg, wheat toast with no butter please."

As soon as I place my order, I am surprised when Mr. McDonald joins me two hours early.

"Truck's all gassed up and ready to go when you are," he says before taking his first sip of coffee.

I look at him and smile. "Mr. McDonald, plans have changed, and these next few days are going to be hard on me. I cannot thank you enough for all your help."

My boss places his hand atop mine and says in his calmest voice, "I know you left home last night. Your house is next to the biggest gossip in town who I am sure was on the phone most of the night calling folks. It's already all over town how you stormed out, leaving your mother, brother, and sister, telling her off and, from what I hear, you were overheard using very foul language." Taking a defensive posture, I insist, "That's not true!"

"Look, those of us who know you know that. Those who don't, well, don't you worry none about them. Who cares what they think?" With that, Mr. McDonald patiently waits as I finish my breakfast.

Truck loaded, we leave Eupora. My euphoria drifts into a sense of calm once we near my new apartment. The only truly new piece of furniture in the apartment will be a bed, and for it, a new mattress, box spring, sheets, and comforter set.

Pulling into the parking lot of my apartment complex, I am surprised to see Jason leaning against my apartment door. My boss informs me he has hired Jason to help me move into the new apartment, as he must be at the restaurant to accept and inspect today's deliveries. Jason immediately begins unloading Mr. McDonald's truck as I unlock the door to my new home. Once the last piece of furniture is unloaded, I thank my boss and turn my attention to Jason. He lets me know Mr. McDonald has paid him for the entire day and will help in any way he can. After setting up the new bed and helping arrange my home, I offer Jason a little extra money; he refuses, saying my boss paid him plenty. I thank him again and we say our goodbyes. Tired, as the day has been a long and emotional one, I throw together a quick salad and eat while stretched out on my weird-smelling sofa. Everything from the Salvation Army always smells the same. Each item carries with it this very distinctive odor. The smell reminds me of disinfectant mixed with a hint of pine scented floor cleaner. They seem to battle it out to see which can best camouflage the embedded odors collected over many years. It is a scent one never forgets. Eventually, the smell will dissipate, but for now, it is very unpleasant. Surveying my new home, I find it comfortable, yet eerily quiet.

Living alone is not what I had expected. After a few short months, reality sets in. For years, I envisioned a utopian world with butterflies, rainbows and unbridled freedom. As an adult, I'm now seeing the stark difference between the fantasy world I had dreamed of and the harsh reality of life. Unlike people who look forward to days off, I dread it. Filling my days off with productive activities has become tedious and filled with new struggles I never considered. Grocery shopping consumes only a fraction of my time, as there is no need to plan for the two-mile-long walk or worry about bad weather. With no one to take care of, or a large house to clean, boredom has become a serious issue. The extra shifts I ask for are no help in my fight against this devastating solitude. A crippling loneliness engulfs me.

Chapter 15

It's a Little Bit Funny

I cringe as a gust of cold, damp October air hits me just before I step through the back door into the Broken Arrow. Shivering, I remove my coat and scarf and say hello to Carl as he places foil wrapped potatoes in the oven.

"Hi," is his only response as he moves on to his next task, weighing out and pressing the hamburger patties for the evening.

Today's weather will be enough to keep most customers home, most likely making for an unusually slow Monday evening.

Mr. McDonald schedules one waitress for Monday evenings. Tonight, it will be his only daughter, Christy. Back from Mississippi State University, with a completed degree in business management, she is now home for good. Interested in becoming familiar with most aspects of her father's restaurant, she wishes to have nothing to do with the kitchen, grill, or fryers.

The bell above the restaurant's door rings. Busy cutting up tomatoes and onions for the hamburger station, I am not paying attention to our first customer of the night. Having several spare minutes before Christy brings the order, I fill up the last stainless- steel container with pickles. Done with my task, I wipe my hands on the lower half of my apron. With prep work complete, I check the order window to see who braved the cold tonight. Then I step back and try to catch my breath. I spin around and crouch down, my back to the window, making sure I am hidden from sight. Shocked, I remain out of sight for several minutes.

I keep myself busy towards the back of the kitchen. My purpose is not to hide from our first customer of the evening, but to avoid any awkwardness. It becomes apparent I cannot ignore the situation as Christy comes into the kitchen to speak with me.

"The gentleman says he'll have for dinner whatever you decide to cook for him. I do not know what that means, Sylvia Rose, or even how to write it down."

She shows me her order pad with the word coffee written on it, followed by several question marks.

I am unprepared to see Mr. Marlow and feel very uncomfortable. If I choose a grilled item for his dinner, I will be visible through the order window. A dish like fried chicken or fish will keep me out of his line of sight as the deep fryers are located to the left of the order window.

"Write down half a fried chicken and baked potato," I suggest.

Christy heeds my request. Exiting the kitchen and seemingly confused, she shakes her head.

Having placed the dredged chicken in the fryer, I wash my hands. Christy comes back to relay another message, which shakes me to the core.

"I don't know who he is, but he knows you. He says he would like to speak with you when there is time."

Glaring at Christy, I firmly declare I cannot take time away from the kitchen. I must prepare for the dinner rush.

"You and I both know there will be no dinner rush, Sylvia Rose. It's Monday, and this is the first cold snap of the season. Other than him, we'll be lucky if anyone comes in for coffee. Well, except for Jason."

"Please tell Mr. Marlow I do not have time to come out and chat."

Hoping the ordeal is over, I am dismayed when Christy reenters the kitchen, this time handing me a folded order ticket and leaving the kitchen promptly. Opening the ticket, I read, *Please come join me at my table. I would like to catch up. I still care about you and your family.*

It seems I cannot avoid a meeting with Mr. Marlow, and I am quite perturbed.

Before leaving the kitchen, I catch my reflection in the mirror hanging over the washbasin. Stopping for a moment, I tighten my ponytail and wipe the flour from my cheek, still hesitant to join our guest.

No time like the present, I say to myself as I slowly walk towards Mr. Marlow's table.

"So, what's with the cold shoulder?" he asks.

"Not a cold shoulder. Look at me, a total mess with a stained apron and hair that looks as if I have not brushed it in a week. I am embarrassed. Please don't take my insecurities as a snub. I would never do that to you, I promise."

A long response to his brief question, but an honest one.

In his naturally soothing voice, he continues, "I did not intend to upset you. I am on my way to our distributor in Tupelo. Lately, the company has been dealing with messed up orders. Scenic as it is, the Natchez Trace's fifty-mile-an-hour speed limit makes the sixty-mile drive seem much longer, so I thought I would stop in for a quick bite before continuing. Not knowing your days off, I had no idea you would be here tonight. Believe me, I did not mean to upset you."

Unable to deny it is a pleasant surprise to see him, I listen as he tells of his many trips to Tupelo and how he stops in the Broken Arrow from time to time. He speaks of his job with a furniture company in Starkville and the cold, unwelcoming shoulder he gets from the owner. He credits a girl named Angie for his employment, noting he probably would not be working there if not for her. Captivated by his every word, I listen intently, yet I notice a remorseful tone in

Mr. Marlow's voice. He asks how things are with me and I share with him my latest news. Proudly, I tell him of the car I just bought and my apartment. I do not go into detail regarding the unpleasantness which occurred the night I left home. I tell him of the several unanticipated adjustments I had to make. Just then, we hear the bell above the door announcing Jason's entry. Following closely behind him are Mr. and Mrs. Ford.

Trying my best to be nonchalant, and failing miserably, I announce, "Guess it's time. I best be headed back to the kitchen— work, you know."

As I rise from his table, Mr. Marlow says, "It was great seeing you again. You really have come into your own, Sylvia Rose. I am so happy for you."

After returning to the grille, I look through the order window and watch as Chance Marlow pays for his meal and exits the restaurant. Several unexpected emotions cause me to grow uneasy.

Chapter 16

His Visits Become More Frequent

𝔉or the past several months, Mr. Marlow frequently stops in the Broken Arrow for dinner. Most times, I can break away from my duties and spend some time catching up with him. Our conversations are mostly benign as we speak of his wife and job. In response, I tell him how Leif and Paige are doing. When he asks about mom, I remind him she and I rarely say two words to each other because of the way she kicked me out.

Mr. Marlow has insisted I address him as Chance, saying he sees me as an adult and therefore I must address him as an equal. I am honored he feels that way towards me, as I have worked hard to assert my independence.

With each visit from Chance, I grow closer to him and more concerned when he mentions the emotional distance growing between him and his wife. I can see the hurt in his eyes as he desperately holds back tears. He asks about a boyfriend, and I tell him I have none. Though Jason and I have been out on a few dates, we both have decided we are better suited to be friends. I do like Jason, but his wild side is a bit much for a conservative girl like me to handle.

I am happy this wonderful man sitting across from me considers me a friend and confidant, but I feel our visits will have to end. On more than one dark night snuggled comfortably beneath my bedspread, I have found Chance Marlow occupying the recesses of my mind. I know these feelings to be wrong. For crying out loud, he was my mother's boyfriend for several months and I have known him since I was fourteen years old. How can I possibly be developing feelings for this man? Yes, he is very handsome and only six years older than I but still I must consider our past. He has proven to be a good friend and selfless man, giving of himself without hesitation.

Am I reading into these emotions more than what is there? I have never had a father. Perhaps my feelings towards him are more like that of a daughter. I only know to avoid these feelings from growing more intense, our visits must stop and our friendship end.

Chapter 17

Chance's conflicting feelings

𝕴 am a torn and broken man. An unfortunate birth defect cause physical intimacy to be unpleasantly painful for my wife, rendering love making uncomfortable and unwanted. As a loving and supportive husband, I understand and accept our marital limitations. Our friendship remains strong, as I love Angie and always will. She has taught me that love comes in many forms, a lesson for which I will always be grateful. My forced days away have become frequent, and I worry because Angie no longer says, "I'll miss you," while watching me pack for these brief business trips. Without intimate relations, I fear the physical closeness in our relationship has become strained.

Lately, I have questioned many aspects of our marriage. Recently, there has been a noticeable emotional distance between us. Her kisses goodbye now only land on my cheek as doubts regarding Angie's feelings towards me have slowly crept into my mind.

I have been visiting with Sylvia Rose at the Broken Arrow restaurant where she works. She has grown into a very lovely and independent woman. Even when she was fourteen, she carried herself with more maturity than her mother. I find myself purposely leaving Starkville in the late afternoon, putting me near the Broken Arrow around dinner time. The visits with Sylvia Rose are always pleasant, but our conversation mainly revolves around our families.

As my wife cannot bear children, perhaps what I sense for Sylvia Rose is a misplaced transfer of emotions, seeing her as the daughter I will never have, rather than a love interest. These conflicting feelings tear at the fabric of my soul, racking me with guilt. My intention was to reconnect with an old friend. Instead, I have stumbled across a much more profound connection.

I need time with Sylvia Rose away from both our jobs. I must make peace with the incessant thoughts haunting my brain and the pain lingering in my heart. Asking her out is the only way to silence my unspoken thoughts and emotions. However, I'm afraid she may misconstrue my invitation as something inappropriate.

Fall days and mild winds bring a slight chill to the afternoon air, making the drive on the Natchez Trace tolerable. Windows down, music playing, I rehearse my question for Sylvia Rose. I need the opportunity to sort my thoughts. Having only one chance to ask her for time alone, my anxiety is through the roof.

As I take the offramp to the Broken Arrow, I feel a level of nervousness that is new to me, and it causes me great discomfort. I select a table in a corner, away from the chatter of other customers. Sitting quietly, I try to talk myself out of asking her the question which has been lingering in my soul for months. She looks so busy and may not have time to come out and talk, which would render my worries pointless.

The lump in my throat grows as I watch Sylvia Rose walking towards my table. Fear and weakness overtake me.

"You look just awful, are you ok?" she asks, pulling out the chair across from me.

I lie, "I am fine, thanks."

Our normal generic conversation begins as my anxiety mounts. The tension becomes too much, and the question stumbles over my lips, landing flat and not evoking the response I had been expecting. "Would you like to come to Tupelo with me on your night off? I could take you out to dinner and we can go see that new Steve Martin movie?"

I watch as her smile fades and her complexion grows pale. Her reaction is immediate. She stands quickly, and her chair moves backwards, almost tipping over. A look of shock overtakes her face.

"Mr. Marlow, wow, I don't know what to say. I am not comfortable going out on a date with my mother's ex-boyfriend."

Disgust in her voice causes me to think quickly to save face. Practically whispering as not to cause more of a scene, I state, "Oh gosh, I am sorry. Please sit. You misunderstand." It's a lie, but I feel the need to put her at ease. "I am not asking you out on a date. Well, I guess it sounded that way. I am asking to spend time away from here so we can talk and avoid the accusatory whispers in the background. A chance to get to know one another beyond this place. I see no reason we cannot share dinner and a movie as friends. We are friends, aren't we?" Hoping these words are more acceptable, I flash a forced smile.

Touching my shoulder, she answers, "I am so embarrassed, jumping to conclusions like that. Of course, we are friends, and I have not been to see a movie in so long. I would enjoy meeting you in Tupelo. Hey look, orders are coming in, and I need to get back to the kitchen. You have my number. Call me and we can arrange a time and place to meet next Wednesday evening."

Paying for my meal, I exit the Broken Arrow as I try to navigate the strange new feeling of being "just friends" with Sylvia Rose. I am, however, filled with delight at the prospect of spending time with her in an informal environment. These thoughts cause an intense uneasiness in my stomach. Needing to focus on my drive to Tupelo, and tomorrow's meeting, I force these concerns from my mind and file them away to be dealt with later.

Chapter 18

We Are Friends, Nothing More

Using the hotel lobby phone, I notify Chance I have arrived. As planned, he takes me to T.G.I. Friday's, and then to a movie. It ends up being a calm and relaxing evening for us both, and we talk of things beyond our work and families. I appreciate the opportunity to discover the individual behind the thoughtful and compassionate gestures from years ago. I listen as he describes his duties as the furniture store's only outside sales representative. He, in turn, feigns interest as I grumble about a botched food delivery at the restaurant.

Still fresh in my mind is our last conversation and how my reaction to his question regarding going out made the color drain from his face. He caught me off guard and I reacted defensively, as I often do when approached with uncomfortable situations.

After dinner and the movie, our evening ends with a brief hug as I thank him for the wonderful meal and discussion. *Stone cold fox*, I think while watching him walk through the hotel lobby doors. I try to shake the thought as I start my 1962 Pontiac Star Chief I lovingly refer to as my yacht on wheels and drive home.

Leaning against the back of my apartment door, my skin tingles with delight as I replay each moment of our perfect evening in my mind. His inviting smile and gentle demeanor, combined with effortless conversation, gave the evening a feeling of intimacy. We conversed with flirtatious ease as sparks of electricity flew between us. The coy banter and laughter between us created a romantic atmosphere, making the evening feel more like a date than a night out with a friend. I know this reaction to be inappropriate. As a friend, I should be supportive and offer solace when he speaks of his marital issues. However, during recent conversations, I have felt oddly jealous when he speaks of their relationship.

The next several months find me spending at least one of my days off with Chance. I look forward to our time together. However, emptiness consumes me the moment we part, causing unsettling emotions within me. Having never given myself time or permission to explore what makes me happy, I second guess my decision to allow Chance to become such a large part of my life. I find my heart aches, my soul feels empty, and I yearn for him once we say goodbye. These new emotions send chills that creep up and down my spine. Chance Marlow is very handsome, kind, and generous. He is a tender man who forces nothing, allowing me to be free and imperfect in his presence. He has become my best friend, confidant and, unfortunately, more. It is the "more" which causes me angst. I force myself to remember he is indeed a married man, one whom I have looked up to for years. I am certain he still sees me as the fourteen-year-old girl he met so many years ago.

Last week when we attended the flea market in Tupelo, a vendor had an incomplete set of Franciscan Desert Rose China which caught my eye. Picking up one of the old plates, I checked the price, and immediately set the dish back down. My expression must have been telling because, without hesitation, Chance paid for the set of dishes, explaining I was to consider them a belated housewarming present.

With tears of joy, I leaned in and kissed him on the cheek, whispering, "You shouldn't have."

"I couldn't let anyone else buy the dishes after seeing how much you liked them," he answers.

He showed no sign of being bothered by my

impromptu kiss, and our day continued without incident. Obviously, Chance is content with our friendship as it stands. I am the one who has developed unhealthy emotions I must suppress.

If I allow this relationship, friendship, or whatever it is, to proceed, it will ultimately cause us both pain.

I am fortunate Chance has not noticed how I truly feel about him. I will use my next few days off to come to grips with my unexpected emotions and this complicated relationship in which I have allowed myself to become entangled.

With nowhere to really go, I use my time off to relax and truly enjoy my apartment. Able to clear my mind and think rationally instead of with my heart, I decide that complicating my life with a long-distance married boyfriend is not for me.

I am not upset or unhappy with my decision to end things with Chance. He is a friend and presents himself as nothing more. However, I know myself well enough, and eventually, I will do or say something stupid like kissing him on the lips, or heaven forbid, saying, "I love you," at an inappropriate time. Unwilling to risk either scenario, it is best I end things now.

I do not see Chance again until Thursday evening. He takes a seat at his usual table, ordering a single piece of apple pie with a slice of cheese melted on top. Plating the pie, Christy passes it through the order window, saying, "You know the deal, a melted slice of cheese."

I place the slice of pie under an aluminum dome with a pat of butter for reheating, asking Christy to tell Mr. Marlow I will be out shortly.

Scraping the melted cheese from the grille, I remove my apron and join Chance at his table. He flashes me his million-dollar smile, which always melts my heart. I hope what I have to say does not upset him.

"Chance, we need to talk, but here is not the place. Can you meet me at my apartment tomorrow, preferably mid-afternoon? It's homecoming night for the high school, and we are expecting a large crowd here this evening. The football team has done well all season, so tonight will be hell on all of us."

My simple request doesn't appear to be what he wants to hear, and he asks, "Is something wrong? Your mom? Brother? Sister? Are you ok Sylvia Rose? What's going on? You can tell me."

"Family is fine. Just need time to talk to you away from here. I have a lot of prep work to do before the crowd shows up, and I must get back to the kitchen. Will you be able to stop by my apartment tomorrow afternoon?"

"Sure, I'll be there. I do wish you would tell me what's going on."

Leaning in close, I whisper in his ear, "We'll talk tomorrow, don't worry."

With prep done, Carl and I wait for the crowd. Neither of us are looking forward to the unruly kids.

At 10:30 PM, young boys, girls, and a few sets of parents acting as chaperones flood the Broken Arrow. From the moment they enter, a loud ruckus ensues. We watch as mothers helplessly attempt to quiet their overly exuberant sons and husbands. Carl and I take a deep breath, preparing for the night from hell.

Unable to stand idly by and watch as the waitresses grow increasingly frustrated, Carl exits the kitchen, and in a loud voice which takes everyone by surprise, yells, "Shut up!"

The crowd does not immediately settle down, causing Carl to once again yell out. This time, however, he places both pinkies in his mouth, letting out the loudest whistle I have ever heard. "I said shut up!" he shouts even louder. "These ladies are trying to take your orders. If you all don't settle down, Sylvia Rose will shut the kitchen down, and I know you don't want her to do that. So, be quiet, let these women take your orders, and behave for Christ's sake."

At the end of the night, having served all the customers, the waitstaff fall into the employee booth. At half past twelve in the morning. The whooping and hollering dissipates, finally allowing everyone to hear the jukebox in the background. Stepping out from the kitchen, I see the restaurant looks like an F5 tornado hit it. With only cleanup remaining, I help Carl get caught up on the dishes. From the doorway, I hear, "Hey sis?"

I look up to see my brother, Leif. "I have bussed most of the tables for ya, but I gotta go. Penny wants to go to the Blue Hole, and you know I can't say no to her."

I thank Leif for his help and wish him a good night.

Locking the front door after one AM, our entire crew begins the arduous task of cleaning up after the celebration. Worn out, Carl and I take out the last bags of garbage at two AM.

I arrive home late, and exhaustion keeps me from my bedroom. Too tired to shower, I lay on the couch, telling myself it will only be for a minute. My conscious thoughts end there.

Loud banging wakes me. I sit up, rubbing my eyes. The knocking continues. Mind foggy and body sore, I make my way toward the annoying, repetitive sound. In a hoarse voice, I yell, "I'm coming, I'm coming, for Christ's sake, stop with the banging."

As I open the door, the sun pours in, momentarily blinding me as I hear a familiar voice.

"Are you okay? I've been knocking for fifteen minutes."

Unprepared for a visitor and certainly not ready for the serious conversation I want to have with Chance, I mumble, "Good morning."

I am shocked to learn twelve hours have slipped away. Desperately, I try to shake the fog encapsulating my mind. With the overpowering smell of stale cigarette smoke, fried potatoes, and grilled hamburgers permeating from my clothing, I ask to be excused to shower. After I hand Chance the TV remote, he comments, "Must have been quite a party last night. From the looks of it, they wore you down."

"You have no idea," I mutter, closing the bathroom door.

Although we have been friends for years, I still feel nervous leaving him alone as I prepare to freshen up. The shower's soothing heat eases my tension as the steam helps clear my head. Knowing he is in the next room patiently waiting makes me nervous and I cannot understand why.

Stepping from the tub, I quickly wrap a large towel around myself and rush to my bedroom. Once appropriately dressed, I enter the living room, taking a seat in my wingback chair as Chance lowers the volume on the television. I am certain he has noticed a distance in my demeanor, so I am not surprised when he starts the conversation by asking, "So, what's this all about, Sylvia Rose?"

"Chance, I don't know how to say this. Having practiced this many times in my mind, it has never come out sounding right. I guess the best way is to just say it." Sighing deeply and with a tremble in my voice, I continue, "Chance, I can't see you anymore."

The bluntness of my words linger in the air, sounding much harsher than expected. It is far too late to retract them. "Say what?" His voice is loud and angry. "What have I done to upset you? What did I do or say to make you feel this way? Why, now, do you want to close the door on our friendship?"

With the hurt prevalent on his face, I can barely look this wonderful man in the eye. But he deserves answers.

"Well, that's it, our friendship. Good Lord, this is going to sound so cliché. Chance, it's not you, it's me." I cringe the very moment the phrase rolls off my tongue. "Must I say it? I thought I could be just friends with you, but I can't. I know having deep feelings for you to be inappropriate on many levels. My having to admit this to you changes everything. There is no way I can allow our friendship to continue."

Silence dominates the mood of the room as we sit looking at one another, neither stirring.

Finally, Chance readjusts his position on the sofa, eyes filled with fire and glaring as if I were the Devil incarnate ripping his soul from his body. Visibly upset, Chance leaves the room, making his way to the kitchen. Several minutes pass before I sense his trembling hand on my shoulder. I see a man visibly in pain, one hurting so deeply he can no longer hide the tears streaming from his eyes.

Pulling up a dining room chair beside mine, he offers his hand. Trembling, he squeezes mine softly; a deep sighs precedes his words.

He apologizes for leaving the room so abruptly saying he needed time to gather his thoughts. He tells of his marriage and how it is one of convenience, but still a commitment he cannot abandon. I know this to be true of his nature and would expect nothing less. Explaining in vivid detail about his wife's physical condition, he says Angie was a virgin and unaware of the severe pain sex would cause until the night of their honeymoon. He insists his initial reason for wanting to meet in Tupelo was to catch up and perhaps rekindle our friendship.

His head falls gently onto our interlaced fingers as he continues, "I understand the many reasons you might believe we cannot continue to see each other. I can find but one reason for us to continue our friendship. You came short of saying the three words which could change everything. So, you leave me with no choice."

Raising both our hands to his face, he gently places the back of my hand against his lips and, with a soft kiss, continues, "Sylvia Rose Turner, I say with great honesty and conviction, I love you. I admired the young, determined fourteen-year-old girl who tried so desperately to keep her family together. That is what and who I saw when we first met. Though I admired your tenacity and strength, I could not see you in any other light. Today, I see you as a strong and vibrant woman any man would be proud to know. When we met in Tupelo for our first 'friend date,' I grew closer and closer to you. Two months ago, I had to admit my feelings for you have taken over my head and heart. Each night, when I close my eyes, I see only you."

He pauses for a breath and continues, "What else can I say? I lay all my cards on the table and share my emotions with you, unabashed, unpolished, and from the heart. I bare my soul to you. If I am wrong to admit my love, so be it. We both know a relationship between us to be taboo. Fate introduced us for a reason. I believe that with all my heart and soul, and to be completely honest, I can't fight this any longer. Which begs the question, where do we go from here?"

Patiently, he awaits a response. I can give him none. Chance Marlow spoke the words I thought I longed to hear. I cannot believe he has voiced a desire for me, and I am overwhelmed with emotions as I contemplate how a relationship between us might work. Too much is preying on my mind. Chance has admitted he loves me, however pleasantly unexpected, is also unfair as I decided only yesterday we could no longer be friends.

Breaking the awkward silence between us, I ask for a few days to contemplate this new wrinkle. He agrees, mentioning the time has come for him to leave. Walking towards the door, Chance raises my chin, forcing me to look at him. I try desperately to avoid his stare, not ready to see the love reflecting so deeply in his crystal blue eyes.

"Please know I do love you, Chance," I say, wiping tears from my eyes. "I need time to think. There are so many things to consider. You have a settled life back home in Starkville, and I have one here. Obligations to your marriage will make any relationship between us difficult, if not impossible. I, too, can't fight these feelings I have for you. A week, that's all I ask. Give me one week to make heads or tails of this and come to a decision we both can live with."

Kissing the tip of my nose, he brushes the hair from my forehead and simply says, "I gotta run. Take all the time you need. We can continue our talk when I stop by here next Tuesday evening after get off work. Until then, just know I love you, Sylvia Rose."

We embrace, and with one quick gentle kiss, I close my apartment door. Through the peephole, I watch as he drives away. With my back against the cold metal door, I slowly slide to the floor, tears flowing down my cheeks like rain. Head buried in my hands, I sob uncontrollably. *Now what?* I think, *can you allow yourself to be the "other" woman? Can you live with yourself if you pursue this? Dare you allow yourself to experience a love so wrong? With our unconventional past, can we even have a future?* These thoughts play over in my mind as I sob deeper than ever before.

That evening, sleep eludes me as my mind vividly replays our visit. Feeling emotionally unsettled with an aching heart, I toss and turn until I eventually tire enough to drift off.

Getting very little sleep, I do not greet the morning so much as acknowledge its arrival. Having today off work will allow me to calm my mind and process the emotions running through me. With little motivation to complete my daily chores, the couch beckons. An hour of lazing about on my back solves no problems. I cannot allow self-pity and doubt to control this day. Removing myself from the couch, I decide to ease my heart and mind. It is time to make a list.

I sit at the dining room table as the smell of fresh ink on paper motivates me to complete two lists. The first will detail all the reasons why a relationship between Chance and me is unwise, while the second list's purpose is to persuade me that a relationship between us is workable. An hour passes and after much deliberation, I am Done. The answer stares me in the face. I can no longer deny it. The list representing the cons is far longer, whereas the nearly empty page of pros contains only one reason to pursue a relationship with Chance.

Well, there you have it, choice made.

I push away from the table and crumple the handwritten list into a tight ball. With a sense of triumph and pride in a job well done, I deposit it into the kitchen garbage with a self-satisfied smile. Uncertain how Chance will respond to my decision, I nervously await our meeting on Tuesday.

Taking a rag and can of furniture polish from under the kitchen sink, I dust all my wooden surfaces. As if the good Lord himself was sending a message, a Barbara Mandrell song plays on the stereo. I stop cleaning as a line in the song grabs my heart.

"If loving you is wrong, I don't want to be right."

When the song ends, I'm met with an awkward silence as I realize how unrealistic the lyrics sound. Why am I even considering putting myself through an affair destined for heartbreak? I am smart enough to know that no one comes out unscathed in these situations.

The crumpled list in my trashcan relays the same message. Any fool can read these signs. I can only hope the wonderful man whom I truly love will understand my decision.

Chapter 19

Choice Made

After an abnormally busy Tuesday night at the restaurant, Carl and I are exhausted. Home by ten, I pull up next to a beautiful blue Cadillac. Recognizing the car and driver, I unlock the door, leaving it ajar for Chance to enter. Placing my purse and keys on the dining table, I turn to see him sitting on the sofa as if he has been here all evening.

"Comfy?" I ask sarcastically. "Yup," He answers smugly.

"Would you care for tea? Coffee? Water?" "Nope, just you," He answers coyly.

I choose to sit in my wingback chair instead of on the sofa. We both sigh deeply, neither knowing how to start the conversation.

"So…" Chance sighs, as he slaps his thighs with the palms of his hands.

"So…" I mimic.

Jumping right to the reason for this visit, Chance interjects, "Look, I am not one to pussyfoot around, you know that. We have to get this over with. I will respect your decision and abide by your wishes."

Not wanting to just dive right into it, Chance leaves me with no choice. I tell him of the song which caught my attention and how it spoke of love and a married man. The lyrics ask, how could one person invest so much of herself into a man she can never truly have? He nods as if he understands, though I know he cannot. I tell him with every fiber of my being; I did not want to be involved with someone who is married, and how unfair it would be, to both of us. With tears in my eyes, I now must admit to suppressing my emotions, feeling it would have been improper to confess them.

However, it is time to speak of things I have so desperately tried to deny.

"I love you, and I am certain we can make this work. There are a million reasons why being together is wrong, and only one to justify such a relationship. Love, Chance, love is why this can and will work. I fell in love with you the afternoon we ran into each other on Founder's Day, and I am tired of fighting it. I know what I am getting into. No holidays with the man I love, no waking next to him every day. Had you not been clear and honest about your relationship at home, my decision would have been to end our friendship. I cannot bear the thought of you being denied the physical intimacy you deserve. Chance, I know you are hers first, and you have responsibilities there, but I can no longer pretend I do not love you. I have a choice to remain alone or take a leap of faith and follow my heart."

Chance rises from the sofa and, without hesitation, kneels by the chair I am occupying. Looking up into my tear-filled eyes, he asks for forgiveness, telling me he never meant for this to happen. I believe him, as I too, never intended for our friendship to go any farther. Chance then grasps my hand, and our tears fall uncontrollably while we hold each other close. Through his muffled sobs and tight embrace, our hearts race, beating as one.

Chapter 20

The Taboo Affair

Over a year has passed, and I have grown accustomed to Chance's routine. Obligations in Tupelo, Memphis and his wife in Starkville give us only a small window of time together. Chance arranges his schedule, so we share Tuesday and Wednesday evenings. He spends the rest of his time in Starkville with his wife. We never speak of his visits back home. There is no need.

As for us, we both adore going to flea markets, yet we despise malls. He is an excellent cook and enjoys dishing up culinary masterpieces as beautiful as those pictured on the cover of Bon Appetite. I, however, cook comfort food— southern dishes designed to stick to your ribs. We enjoy watching the same shows and never argue over control of the remote. I rarely find myself lonely or missing him. I cannot explain it, but it seems as if he is always here. The teddy bear he gave me holds his scent and keeps me warm at night. He leaves small notes for me to find, reminding me of his love.

As I am an inexperienced lover, Chance is patient and understanding. Through his gentle hands and loving, yet firm touch, in time, my trust builds. The emotional walls which have kept me from completely giving myself to another, crumble beneath his soft and caring touch. I now understand how a woman can lose herself in a man's love.

Winter's rapid approach is no longer deniable. Coat weather has arrived. Tonight, Chance asks me if I want to go for a walk on the Trace and enjoy one of the several scenic hiking paths the park offers. This time of year, the chilly breeze carries with it the fresh scent of pine, which lingers in the air a little longer. Bundled up tightly, we climb into his car as he drives the short distance to the Natchez Trace entrance. As he parks, I grab the paper bag I placed in the backseat earlier for collecting decorative pinecones and vibrantly colored leaves the fall season so graciously provides.

Turning to look at me, Chance smiles. "Well, come on lady, we got some walking to do."

Mother Nature generously provides a perfect romantic setting. Chance and I bask in the scenic background as my soul soars along the crisp night air. I walk by Chance's side, taking his arm for support and holding on tightly. Occasionally, I lay my head on his broad shoulder. The night is perfect. Orange, red, and brown oak leaves crunch beneath our feet as we enter the Old Trace Segment Trail, a preserved portion of the Old Trace which takes only five minutes to walk. Not there for exercise, I pick up several pinecones and colorful leaves to decorate my apartment for the upcoming Christmas season. We say nothing during our stroll along the path. We need no words as he grips my hand. Reaching the trail's end, we sit on an old bench as we take in the magnificent fall sights, watching leaves float gently to the ground. With a wink and smile, Chance announces it is time to go home.

In the cozy sanctuary of our apartment, the warm glow of candlelight dances across the room. The soft melody of our favorite song envelops us, creating an atmosphere of pure enchantment. As we settle down on the couch, the world outside fades away, leaving only the two of us in this moment. As we nuzzle close, our eyes meet with an intensity that speaks volumes. Chance draws me close and lost in the moment our lips meet. We share a long fervent kiss, igniting the embers smoldering fiercely between us.

Lovingly, Chance looks in my eyes as he gently takes my hand, tenderly leading me to the bedroom. Anticipation builds with every step we take, fueled by a mix of excitement and nervousness. Our bodies yearn for each other's touch as we enter this intimate space filled with love and longing.

His touch, so gentle and loving, I feel light as air. Guiding me down on the bed, I softly release a loving gasp as he slips beside me. My heart pounds as if it wishes to escape my chest and fly free. In the depths of our passion, time ceases to exist. Our bodies move in perfect harmony, guided by the intense desire that consumes us both. Every touch, every caress ignites a fire within us, fueling an insatiable hunger for one another. As his lips travel along my skin, leaving a trail of voltaic kisses in their wake, I feel a rush of warmth coursing through my veins. The intensity of our connection is overwhelming, as if the universe itself aligns to bring us together in this moment.

Dawn approaches as our bodies slowly surrender to exhaustion. Even as sleep claims our physical beings for a brief respite, our souls remain intertwined in an infinite bond, transcending time, and space.

Chapter 21

Following in Mother's footsteps

Two months have passed since our magical night together and I am finding it difficult to concentrate. There has been an unexpected development which is certain to alter life as I know it. I ask myself many times how I could allow this to happen, especially considering my past. If anyone knows better, it should be me. How am I to tell Chance? How will he react to this news? I know I am not handling it well. A mother, a single mother at that. There is no one to blame other than myself, and the sound of my life shattering around me echoes so loudly in my ears.

I am extremely hesitant to have this conversation tonight. Choices will need to be made; none will be easy. Nervously I await Chance's arrival, wringing my hands, frightful of how this evening will end.

My heart stops as I hear keys jingle and watch the deadbolt turn. My next memory is of Chance kneeling beside me, patting my cheek gently as he asks if I am okay.

Light-headed and cheeks flushed, I look up at the chiseled face I adore. His expression looks worried as he asks again, "Babe, what's wrong? What's going on?"

With a hand behind my neck and his other arm bracing the center of my back, Chance helps me sit upright while I shake the haziness from my brain. This is not how I pictured the evening starting. I hoped to have time to bring the subject up subtly. Now he knows something is wrong and I need a new strategy.

After helping me up and into my chair, Chance sits quietly as I gather my thoughts. Uncertain how to proceed, I sit stoically as we both stare at one another in angst-ridden stillness.

Unable to take the stifling atmosphere any longer, I ask him to get me a drink.

"Iced tea?" he asks.

As he prepares our iced teas, I use this opportunity to formulate a cogent opening line of dialog.

Reentering the living room, he holds out a glass. "Here you go."

As he reclaims his seat on the couch, he asks, "Wow, what's going on, Sylvia Rose? Whatever it is, it must be serious. I have never seen you look so upset and anxious."

"You have always been able to read me like a book," I respond, while joining him on the sofa. "I-I don't know where to start, Chance. I have not had a decent night's sleep in the past two months. I thought I knew, but I wasn't sure. This past year has been so wonderful. I never believed I was worthy of love, you know, because of my past. Then you came along and admitted your feelings for me, and I told you of mine too. You see, Chance," I stop there, realizing I am rambling and making no sense. I draw in a deep breath, allowing clarity to return.

Hang on, I tell myself, *you can do this.* Turning to face Chance, I continue, "Okay, okay, here goes."

"Here goes what? Sylvia Rose, for God's sake, say what you need to. This is driving me nuts."

"I am pregnant!" I blurt out.

"You're what? Are you sure?" His shock is obvious.

"Pregnant, Chance, yes, I am sure, I am preggers, knocked-up, with child, however you want to say it. We need to talk seriously about where we go from here. First off, I am not getting an abortion, we will take that off the table right now. I will not put the baby up for adoption, either. As the father, you have some say-so in how this goes, but remember, it's my baby, my body, and my choice."

I look for comfort in his eyes but see only fright, confusion and possibly anger. Chance bolts to his feet. "Oh God, I can't have a child, not now. Perhaps in a few years, but not now. I don't have enough money left to support a child, Sylvia Rose. Angie's and my bank accounts are intertwined. She is my wife and aware of every penny I spend. How do I explain child support to her? We simply cannot have a baby. That's all there is to it, Sylvia Rose. We just can't."

Frustration mounts as I now spring from the sofa, angry and upset with his reaction. I draw closer to him as there are points I need to make without interruption. Like the drill sergeant in *Full Metal Jacket*, I get up in his face and, poking his chest, I bark an order. "Sit down Chance." As he sits, I continue, "okay, I'm not sure what you did not understand, but I will go over this again." Standing over him and angry with his response, I restate my words from earlier, "Number one, no abortion. Number two, no adoption. Number three, my body, my baby, my choice. I hope I am being perfectly clear."

"Very," he answers, continuing, "however, there are many things here to consider, Sylvia Rose. Your health, job, and finances. Can you afford a baby working as a short-order cook? You have never been selfish, and now is not the time to put yourself before the welfare of your child. Do you want the baby to grow up like you did? You know how hard things were for you. Think of the baby, Sylvia Rose, and what's best for it."

What happens next takes us both by surprise.

Angrier than I have ever been, I slap Chance across his face, instructing him to leave immediately. I cannot look at him now. His words cut me to the core. His statements were self-protecting and contradict everything I thought I knew about him. I become infuriated, unable to believe he has the gall to suggest we wait until I am more rational and calmer before discussing the matter farther. Enraged, I push him out my door, slamming it with all my might.

How dare he tell me to calm down? I would rather never lay eyes on him again. Taking in a cleansing breath, I stomp off to my bedroom for a long, muffled cry into my pillows.

The next few days are stressful, unsettling, and nerve-wracking. Chance's circumstances will not allow him to be part of our child's life in any tangible way. However, I mistakenly allowed myself to believe he would be happy we were having a baby together.

With the decision to end things with Chance, I carry on as I always have, to ensure the best life for myself and the unborn child I'm carrying. I have always been a determined woman, trusting in my strength and perseverance. My many years of caring for my siblings have prepared me for what lies ahead.

By the end of my shift today, I am emotionally and physically spent. I open the door to my apartment to a few unwelcomed surprises. The strong, fragrant aroma of roses fills the air and soft music plays in the background. The room is dimly lit, and for a moment, I am frightened. Barely able to make out the figure sitting on my couch, I grow angry knowing the last person I wish to see right now is lurking silently in the shadows.

Seething mad, I shout, "What are you doing here?"

He does not reply as music continues to play.

"I need my key back. If I was not completely mad at you before, I certainly am now. How dare you invade my privacy like this? Chance Marlow, I need you to leave right now. I am tired, and it has been a long night. I have too much on my mind to deal with the likes of you right now."

Acknowledging the roses, yet falling short of thanking him for them, I again ask what gives him the right to barge into my home, uninvited. I remind him we already said all the words we need to, leaving us with nothing more to discuss.

The shadowy figure rises slowly and walks towards me, head lowered. Quickly turning on the floor lamp beside the sofa, I barely recognize him. Unshaven, unkempt, and looking ten years older than he had a few nights before, the broken man looks at me, at first saying nothing. A moment later, from his lips stream an apology directly from his heart and soul. Words so elegant and poignantly stated, I am unsure how to react.

"About the other night, you caught me off guard. You, yourself, have to admit that was quite a bombshell you dropped. I can't apologize enough for bringing your mother's past into this. I know how much it must have hurt, and I am deeply sorry. There are a few truths we must face. I cannot get a divorce right now, and this cannot come at a worse time. Mr. Segal plans to open stores in Tupelo and Columbus. Angie will manage the one in Columbus, meaning a move is eminent for us. I will try to help you with the baby. However, visits will be sporadic at best. I respect your decision to keep the child and honestly, I am glad you are. Again, I apologize for my comments regarding adoption. No one on this Earth has proven to be a better mother than you. After you threw me out, I had a lot of time to think and realize how very much I hurt you. You deserve better. All you need to do is let me know what it is you both need, and I am there. You are not alone in this Sylvia Rose; you know I take care of my responsibilities. I do love you, with all my heart and soul, and always will."

Having allowed him to speak his mind, it was my turn once again. His heart will surely break when he hears what I have to say.

Nervous, I reveal my plans to go to Tupelo and look for work there. I inform Chance of my decision to leave Mathiston before the baby bump shows, telling him I want everyone, including my mother, to believe I am leaving for a better job in a larger city, not because I am knocked up. I reject Chance's offer of financial support. My pride prevents me from ever taking anything from him again. I tell Chance of my undying love for him, promising our unborn child and I will be alright. In my most tender voice, I apologize for the way we must part. I compassionately state that seeing him again would be too much to bear, and I hope he accepts this must be our last goodbye. Not wanting a part-time father for my child, I have no issue doing this alone. I remind him I have faced difficult times in life and have always survived. This time will be no different.

Sitting silent for a few minutes, Chance vows never to forget me or the child he will never know. Once again, he asks for forgiveness, explaining he will love me always, and wishes things were different.

Knowing there are no words to ease our heartbreak, I rise, taking Chance's hand as we adjourn to our bedroom one last time. Holding one another, we take turns drying the other's tears. He tenderly kisses me as I press my ear firmly against his chest, listening one last time to the heart I foolishly thought would be mine forever.

We hold each other for hours as our love echoes throughout the room carried along the invisible waves of our heartbeats. That evening, two hearts break silently in the dense darkness of night. Chance Marlow and I share our final intimate moments, neither one wanting the relationship to end, both knowing it must.

After hours of extremely passionate lovemaking, we lay in bed whispering how much we will always love one another.

Chance speaks of his love for me and the child and how those feelings will last forever, promising to never forget the memories we have built together.

Unable to stop the passing of time, Chance must now take his leave. As he reaches for his clothing, he cannot keep his emotions in check. With tears in his eyes, he says his heart is being ripped from his chest. He kneels at my bedside and holds my hand, saying I am the only woman he has ever completely loved. Although neither of us wants the morning to end, reality sets in.

Once dressed, I take Chance's arm and walk towards the front door. Our hands slowly slide apart as the man I love kisses me goodbye. Stepping beyond the apartment's threshold, I can only watch as the father of my child slips away. He blows a kiss, and I mime catching it. I hold it close to my heart as the last part of it breaks. Slowly closing the door, I wonder what will come of me and the fatherless child I now carry.

Chapter 22

A New Day

Extremely tired due to lack of sleep after Chance's departure, I spend the remaining early hours of the morning in a hot bath, sobbing occasionally as I plan my day. Last Tuesday morning, Deb allowed me to take a week-old copy of The Dispatch, Tupelo's daily newspaper. I plan to sit down with my coffee this morning and comb through the classified ads in search of a job.

Sitting at the dining room table, I circle three jobs listed under the hospitality section of the classifieds. The Steak and Egg on North Gloster sounds interesting and right up my alley. Emphasizing it is a twenty-four-hour eatery, the advertisement makes certain the reader understands the shifts that need to be filled are afternoon and evenings. The eleven to seven shift would suit me best, allowing me to balance both jobs while looking for a place to live in Tupelo. I hope to accomplish my goals before the little secret in my belly shows.

Standing back from the full-length mirror, I survey the loose- fitting pair of jeans and blue and white striped blouse, thinking at first, they might look acceptable. I attempt to justify my ensemble by smoothing out the wrinkled jeans, thinking, *it's good enough for a short-order cook interview*. Failing miserably to convince myself this outfit will do, I remove my jeans and put on pantyhose and the navy-blue skirt I bought to attend a school play Paige was in six months ago. Using the fabric straps from the neck of my blouse, I tie a neat bow and slip into my best pumps.

With its clean lines and bright colors, this ensemble gives off an aura of strength and poise, which is perfect for making a positive first impression. As I grab my purse and keys, I decide I must elevate my mood. It is imperative I put forth a professional façade.

Surprised to find limited parking at the restaurant, I exit my yacht on wheels. I take a quick glance in the side mirror, to make certain my makeup has not run. It is midafternoon, and the restaurant is empty. Taking a seat on the stool closest to the cash register, I notice only one employee. Steam envelops her face as she looks up, brushing a rogue strand of hair from her face. The sponge she is holding falls into the sink with a splash as her annoyance increases with my simple request for a cup of coffee and an application.

I leave a one-dollar tip, which I find to be generous, but a nasty look from the employee says otherwise. Handing her the completed application, I ask, "Do you know when they will be interviewing?"

"No idea," is the only response I receive.

A sense of defeat washes over me after submitting applications to several businesses in Tupelo's bustling commercial district, and I am met with nothing more than handshakes and a promise of being called back.

Growing tired and depressed, I want to go home, but my stomach alerts me that a meal is in order. Taking the hint, I find a nearby deli. I know exactly what I want—a Reuben and a big pickle. Finding a nice, quiet corner to enjoy my meal, I overhear a conversation two tables away from me.

"Did you hear?" one girl asks her friend. "Simmie quit the Lamplighter's Den last night. Walked right out without saying anything. He told me he was tired of the B.S. from the overbearing manager and bitter old waitress. I don't know where they are going to find a better chef." Her table mate only nods while sipping her soda.

As a short-order cook, I am underqualified for a

chef's position, but I want to at least try.

From the book tethered to the metal shelf in the phone booth, I scan the yellow pages with my finger. Under the "Ls", I find the street address and phone number for the Lamp Lighter's Den Restaurant and Bar. Checking to see if anyone is looking, I tear out the page and drive to 363 E. Main Street to submit my final application of the day.

With only one car in the parking lot, I fear they may be closed. Walking closer, I see one table occupied, and am encouraged by the sight of people inside. Disappointment follows as I find the doors to be locked.

As the young couple I saw at the table through the window exit the restaurant, I catch the door before it closes behind them. After my eyes adjust to the ambient lighting, I am shocked to find myself in the middle of a scene taken directly from the glamorous magazine photos I would get lost in as a young girl. The pristine white china glimmers in the room's light, contrasting with the luxurious burgundy linen napkins folded neatly in the center of each porcelain plate, creating an elegantly chic display. Crystal water goblets and spotless flatware complete the tables' visual appeal. I find myself taken aback by the aura of class and sophistication the room exudes.

An older woman is setting the table recently vacated by the young couple who unwittingly let me in. Intently focused on the task before her, and without looking up, the gray-haired woman speaks in a gruff tone. "We're closed."

"Oh, I am not here to eat. I would like to see the manager, if possible."

"Not here," her tone shows great frustration and is unfriendly.

Not wanting the trip to be a total bust, I plead, "Can I ask when he or she will be in?"

"Don't know for sure. He leaves right after the lunch

rush, and we don't see him again until the first customers come in for dinner. What is it you want exactly?" She now approaches, exhibiting a forceful demeanor.

"Well, I would like to see about applying for the job as a cook on the night shift here. I heard through the grapevine one may be needed."

The woman's mannerisms are intimidating, and I become frightened as her tone grows volatile. "If you want a job here, maybe you can get one as a maid over there in the hotel, 'cuz you ain't getting one here, that I can promise you. No offense, missy, but you don't have the class to work here, and I will make certain Mr. James doesn't consider you for any position." She says this with great condemnation and disgust.

Unceremoniously ejected from the restaurant, I take the advice just shared with me and decide to submit an application next door. Smoothing out the wrinkles in my skirt and checking to make certain the bow on my blouse is straight, I approach the building with determination. The automatic doors to the hotel open, welcoming me in as a plume of stale cigarette smoke uses this chance to escape the lobby, finding its way to freedom. As I approach the front desk, the clerk's monotone voice asks, "How many nights will you be staying?" And then, in the same breath, adds, "Smoking or non. We are about at capacity due to the regional bridge tournament we are hosting this week, so best you decide now."

While taking a long draw from her cigarette, the twenty- something year old girl looks up from her computer monitor long enough to impatiently expel her smoke-filled follow-up question. "Well, do you know which room you want? Don't have all day."

"I am not here as a guest. The nice waitress from the restaurant next door suggested I apply here—said you may be looking for a maid."

"Oh, did she now?" Great sarcasm is obvious in the

desk clerk's voice. "Well, that took some nerve on her part. Don't know what makes her think we are understaffed here. She has no right sending people in here to bother me all willy-nilly like that."

"I am just here asking for an application, okay? I did not mean to upset you." Failing to keep my disappointment in check, I turn to leave.

"For all the good it'll do you, I will get you the paperwork." After handing me the two-page application, she resumes the activities which I have so rudely interrupted by my unwelcomed presence.

Sitting on the loveseat closest to the front desk, I pull a pen from my purse, filling in the blank spaces of the application.

"You aren't going to do that right here, are you?" The clerk asks in a nastier tone than earlier.

"Well, if not now, when?" I ask, adding, "I don't live close by and will not be able to bring it back tomorrow."

My explanation falls on disinterested ears. "Whatever," the rude clerk snidely remarks.

After ten minutes, I complete the application, and as I make my way to return the clipboard, I notice a different woman behind the desk. Younger than my mother, but older than me, she wears a neatly pressed uniform and maroon crisscross tie that provide an elegant yet sophisticated first impression. Looking up from the desk, she smiles, asking, "May I help you?"

Presenting her with the completed application, I answer, "Yes ma'am, I filled this out and was wondering if I could leave it here with you."

"Of course you can." This woman speaks with such a warm and welcoming tone, my tension eases and I can finally relax and stand before the woman more confident and self-assured.

After looking over my application, she leans

towards me.

"Really?" she asks, "maid? And by the way, it's housekeeper. Don't you ever let any of my girls hear you refer to them as maids." Her tone is joking, yet, in a way, not.

"Thank you. I will keep that in mind." I respond.

"Sylvia, is it?" She asks. "It's absolutely none of my business, but a housekeeping job here can be physically demanding and a little thing like you may not be able to handle the workload. I am not judging, mind you; merely suggesting perhaps housekeeping is not where you belong. You seem like you would fit better behind a desk. Mind if I make a change here on your application?"

"Not at all," I reply. "If you think I am qualified for such a position."

"Says here you have several years' work experience, not in a front desk capacity, but there is something to be said for a hard- working young woman. I'll just make that change here."

Thinking the conversation is at an end, I turn to leave.

"So, you prefer Sylvia or Sylvia Rose?" Stopping only feet before reaching the automatic doors, I turn around and answer, "Whichever name will grant me an interview."

She motions for me to come back to the front desk. In compliance, I approach. "That's cute, but I truly would like to know what to put on your temporary badge."

For a moment, I excitedly ponder her question. A new job, city, and life deserve a new, more businesslike name. "Just Sylvia," I answer.

"Well, Sylvia, we need a night auditor, and I believe you may be the perfect fit for the job. I will review your application, call your boss for a reference, and if all goes well, you can start here in a week or so."

She smiles, offering her hand to shake. In response, I enthusiastically thank her for this opportunity.

In no real hurry to get back to Mathiston, the terrible traffic on the way home does not bother me. My mind replays the events of this afternoon. If not for the rudeness of one old lady, the day may have been a complete waste. Because of her attitude, I stepped out of my comfort zone, perhaps helping me to land a new job.

With the long, tiring day behind me, and an even more difficult one ahead tomorrow, I enjoy a quick siesta on the sofa, its soft cushions inviting me to stay. Forcing myself up after a few hours rest, I prepare a quick meal and retire to the bedroom. Having gotten precious little sleep the night before, and with tomorrow being a workday, I quickly succumb to a deep, much needed, restful sleep.

This morning, I wake to no fanfare or expectations of beautifully wrapped, wish fulfilling gifts beneath a Christmas tree. No stuffed stockings or smells of roasting ham or turkey fill my small apartment. The pinecones and leaves which adorn my windowsills evoke sad memories of mine and Chance's last walk on the Trace. It is another workday, nothing more. After a quick bowl of instant oatmeal and a cup of coffee, I bundle up to prepare for the day ahead. I plan to be an hour early today, as I need to come up with a believable reason for leaving Mr. McDonald's employ. He, and the entire staff, have always been a source of joy and comfort in my life, and they have accepted me into their large and diverse family, no questions asked. Until this moment, I was unaware how hard my news would be for everyone involved.

My car gives me problems this morning, and it floods as I try to get it to start. I no longer have any hope of showing up early for work. Temperatures dropped last night, and my land yacht does not respond well to changes in weather. Waiting for the gas to drain from the carburetor, I rehearse my speech to Mr. McDonald, going over talking points in my head.

Number one, I need to concentrate on my future and

education. Number two, job opportunities in large cities are many and will allow for work at night while attending school during the day. Number three, because of personal issues I do not wish to bring into my work, it is best I attempt a new start.

Arriving on time, with not a second to spare, I immediately begin my prep work. As expected for Christmas evening, we have only two coffee drinkers and Jason visiting with us tonight. A sense of unease accompanies the silence dominating the restaurant. The atmosphere is eerily still and most unsettling. Sounds normally unheard when the restaurant is full, now echo loudly throughout the building. The steady drips from the coffeemaker. Each step Christy takes in the dining room as she prepares for this evening's customers. I can even hear the heavy sighs coming from Mr. McDonald as he stands flipping through the receipts from the morning shift. A cold chill runs along my spine as Carl enters through the back door. He doesn't speak a word as he puts on his apron. Nothing about this afternoon seems normal. The tension in the air is so thick, I can hardly breathe.

The distant expression on Carl's face and in his eyes tells the story. I think they know, all of them, but how? The answer comes sooner than expected as his daughter flanks Mr. McDonald while they walk towards the kitchen. Anger overtakes the faces of the father/daughter team heading my way. In complete fight-or-flight mode, I hide inside the walk-in cooler, quickly shutting the door behind me. Paralyzed in fear, I stand in the far corner of the walk-in, shaking uncontrollably.

"Sylvia Rose!" Mr. McDonald shouts. "Sylvia Rose Turner, you come out of there this instant!" His voice is louder and more demanding with each word. Tremors and fear keep me from moving, as I hear three bangs on the cooler door. "Young lady, you come out here right now or I am coming in there! You can't hide in there all night!"

He is correct. I must accept the inevitable and confront the problem head-on. Palms sweating and heart racing, I prepare to face the people I love. With my head lowered, I sheepishly open the cooler door. Mr. McDonald asks me to join them in the employee booth.

As we sit, the kind, fatherly figure stares at me with hurt and disapproving eyes. The conversation is heartbreaking. Mr. McDonald tells me of the call he received from the Tupelo Western Hotel and how they wish to hire me. He asks me why I would choose to leave. In my defense, I list the reasons I had come up with the night before. He does not understand my need for moving on, no matter how hard I try to explain. Christy says she understands why and can't help but admit a pang of jealousy, as her future was determined years ago. After our long discussion, Mr. McDonald excuses me as we all go about our nightly routine.

As the next several days pass, and while working both jobs, I secure an apartment between the difficult work schedules. With Carl now trained to take over the grill, a sense of bittersweetness fills me as I say goodbye to my coworkers at the Broken Arrow. Emotionally charged, it is a day I will remember fondly and with great love. On my final night, after the restaurant closes, I am surprised with a going-away party. I can never understand these types of gatherings, as the word "party" indicates fun and joy. Tonight, neither is present. My boss hands me an envelope holding fifteen-hundred dollars collected from guests and employees.

Failing miserably to voice my gratitude, I hold the envelope close to my breast, unable to control my tears any longer. For the second time in as many months, my heart is being torn from my soul.

Chapter 23

Flying Solo

Once I understand the expectations of my new job and learn to navigate the nuances of the city, I realize life is the same no matter where you call home. Nothing has really changed. I go to work, keep up with my financial obligations, and adjust to the recent changes occurring to my body as the baby grows. Getting used to new people and city life is not as taxing as I feared.

I am surprised that learning numbers and spreadsheets comes naturally to me. Computers, however, are a different story. My ignorance regarding modern technology shines through, becoming more obvious during the training session. Ruby, my boss, guides me gently through the process. She is kind, understanding, and patient, reassuring me, she, too, had great difficulty adjusting to the hotel's new computer system. Once secure in my abilities, I work my first solo shift. The night goes smoothly until the printer runs out of toner. Ruby forgot to show me how to change out the cartridge and paper. After turning the printer on and hearing satisfying clicks and whirs as it comes back to life, I can celebrate my personal victory after an hour-long battle with the printer. Having made a mess of the floor and counter, I spend the last hour of my shift vacuuming and wiping all cabinets and counters clean. When the next shift employee arrives, I hand her the guest list containing our occupied and vacant rooms. Looking bewildered, she asks, "It's not Palm Sunday, is it?" Staring blankly, I am uncertain what she means. To clarify, she points to her forehead, saying, "Looks like an ash cross on your forehead."

Taking my compact from my purse, I am embarrassed. She is being kind. I look like a chimney sweeper with black smudges covering my face. Embarrassed, I answer, "Toner mishap."

If last night is anything to go by, this job will be full of activity.

As with most jobs, it takes time to slip into a comfortable rhythm. Settling into a new sleep schedule, I can feel the baby comfortably stir inside me as we adapt to our new life.

August days in Tupelo can be uncomfortably humid, and nights are not much better. Nearing the end of my pregnancy I am feeling sluggish and zapped of energy. Going to work nightly is presenting a challenge. I place my keys and purse next to the register, asking my co-worker Candace about her day. She explains it has been an unusually slow afternoon, with one exception. A man in room four-twenty seems to need something from the front desk every hour. She tells me he has called for extra towels, asked where a good Mexican restaurant was, and if there is anything interesting happening in Tupelo this weekend.

"It's terrible, Sylvia Rose. He doesn't ask all his questions at once and keeps calling with new ones. He seems lonely. You are going to have your hands full with this one." She adds, "Please understand, I don't mind talking to him. He's cute, and the accent— wow, I can't place it, but it's sexy as hell. But I gotta warn you, Juanita is getting real pissed about having to make so many trips up there."

I tell my co-worker to go home, enjoy her weekend, and not to worry; I can handle the pest in four-twenty. A little overheated, I sit for a minute before gathering the day's receipts for the night audit. Candace notices I am not my normal, jovial self and asks if there is anything she could do for me before leaving. I decline her sweet offer, and we say our goodnights.

No sooner has Candace walked out the doors than the phone rings. As warned by my co-worker, it is indeed room four-twenty. Although Candace had said she could not place his accent, I had no trouble. It was reminiscent of a Louisiana chef I had watched on television years ago. In his unique Cajun accent, the gentleman asks if there are any "Do Not Disturb" signs at the front desk. I explain we keep those on the housekeeper's carts. Almost as if on cue, Juanita Rodrigues walks by, and I say, "What luck. I have a guest in room four-twenty who is asking for a 'Do Not Disturb' sign."

Throwing her hands up, she retorts, "*Dios, podria habre pedido eso cuando estuve alli la ultima vez.*"

"Yeah, I know, right?" I reply. "You speak Spanish?"

Knowing everyone complains about their job here, I am certain some phrases Juanita says in Spanish from time to time are not for virgin ears. To ease her mind, I tell her no and assume she says something like, "Why didn't he ask when I was up there the last time?"

"Close," she laughingly says. Pushing her cart to the elevator, she presses the up button, humming a tune I cannot place.

I print out the guest roster and return to the office, the sound of the printer rings in my ears as I open the audit program. I would like to complete it by 3 am as I am nauseous. The baby is kicking especially hard this evening. The pain is moderate but noticeable. To combat the issue, I find a comfortable position and rest for a few minutes, allowing the pain to subside. I am also embarrassed this evening. The little one inside is pressing on my bladder, causing a few unexpected leaks. Tonight, I had to pack extra panties and pads for protection.

The front desk phone rings.

Instinctively, I know it is room four-twenty. Because they are sometimes lonely and bored, certain guests do not sleep well in strange cities. They will remain awake, finding reasons to call the front desk to hear a friendly voice.

"Front desk, how may I help you?" I ask.

It appears the gentleman has forgotten a few necessary toiletries and asks if there is a convenience store nearby, as he did not remember seeing one on the drive to the hotel. Mustering my remaining patience, I explain that there is a 7-11 close enough to walk to from the hotel. I remind him the hotel provides toiletries and various other items in vending machines near the lobby. He apologizes for the intrusion and thanks me for my time. I respond in the scripted words taught by our boss.

"Please don't hesitate to call if you need anything else. At the Tupelo Western, we are here to provide our guests with the hospitality you have come to expect."

Hanging up the phone, I say to myself, "For heaven's sake, please hesitate. "

As the night nears 3 am, I am almost finished with the night audit. I prepare to print the final report and notice the power is off on the printer and it is low on paper. I press the "on" button to allow the printer to warm up. As I bend over the machine to secure the paper, without warning, urine trickles down my leg. Embarrassed, I have little choice but to visit the lady's room and change. Putting out the "Please Ring Bell For Service" sign, I make a mad dash for the lady's room. I wipe the liquid from the inside of my leg and feel a trickle of wetness against my thigh. There is no color, only a sweet odor. Remaining confused, I place my soiled panties in the baggie I had packed earlier. Mom had said when her water broke, it gushed out, warning her I was on my way. She had suggested it would be the same for me. My doctor told me leaking was to be expected, also suggesting my water would break like mom had described. After I wash my hands, a sharp pain causes me to grab my stomach. I need to get back to the front desk and hope the pain passes.

As I return from the bathroom, the phone rings yet

again. "It's friggin' 3:30 in the morning. What can anyone possibly want now?" It's against my nature to say things like that out loud. I begin to wonder what's wrong with me. "Front desk, how can I help you?" I ask with a grunt.

It is the lonely guy in room four-twenty, asking if I have quarters for the vending machines. I tell him we do. Thanking me, he hangs up before I can go through the company's goodbye spiel.

My pain is growing more intense and at frequent intervals. I am no doctor, but I feel certain my baby wishes to make its debut. My body is telling me it is time, and I call my boss, letting her know I cannot complete my shift, as the baby is on its way.

Through labored breaths I listen as she says, "I am on my way. Hold tight." The call ended; I hang up the phone relieved help is on the way.

In anticipation of Ruth's arrival, I reach for my purse and keys as an indescribable pain causes me to slide out of my chair and slip onto the floor. Doubled over, I am forced into the fetal position, fearing this baby will arrive before my boss.

Chapter 24

Foster Recalls Our First Meeting

This is only my second time staying at The Tupelo Western Inn and Convention Center. I much prefer the Metro Inn on the other side of town, but since the company is paying, what's a fellow to do? As I unpack my suitcase, I notice my shaving kit is missing, and call down to the front desk to ask if there is a convenience store nearby. The friendly clerk explains there are vending machines in the lobby stocked with such items. Tired, and wanting to turn in for the night, fear of oversleeping floods my mind, so I decide to get the items I need now instead of waiting until morning. Reaching in my pocket for loose change, I realize I have none. I will have to bother the nice front desk clerk in person for the quarters needed to buy shaving cream and a disposable razor. I am certain by the end of all of this, the clerk will consider me quite the pest.

Fluorescent lights hum as I step off the elevator in search of the vending machines the nice clerk described. Unable to locate them, I approach the front desk for the quarters I need and to ask for help. As I near the desk, I hear muffled sobs, but there is no one in sight. Curious, I lean over the counter to see a young woman clutching to an office chair. The eerie green light of the computer monitor illuminates her tear-stained face. "Are you ok?" I ask. "Is there anything I can do to help?"

"I'm okay," she whispers, but her eyes betray her as they tell me of the pain she is hiding. Knowing her statement to be false, I spring into action. Instinctively, I jump over the counter and kneel beside her while trying to assess her condition. It is then I notice her pregnant belly, and it becomes clear she is in labor. For the life of me, I cannot understand why a pregnant woman is working this close to her due date. Unsure of what to do in this kind of emergency, I still want to help and comfort her. Having seen this scene play out on TV, I offer her my hand to squeeze each time she has a contraction. She takes me up on the offer and practically wrenches my hand from my wrist.

Ouch! I yell inwardly, not wanting her to feel worse. I ask if she has called her doctor, how she plans to get to the hospital, and if she has informed her husband. In a weakened voice, she tells me her supervisor has contacted the doctor and she should arrive any moment now. Then she let out an ear-piercing yell. Unable to wait any longer, I decide to take this damsel in distress to the hospital myself. I gently lift her in my arms as she flails around in protest, but I have no time to argue.

It is then a housekeeper serendipitously walks by and immediately rushes to the front desk clerk's aid. She asks if there is anything she can do, and I reassure her everything is under control, and I am going to take this woman to the hospital. The Hispanic woman tells me her name is Juanita and offers to watch the front desk until their boss arrives.

As I turn to leave with the distraught mother-to-be in my arms, a woman barrels through the automatic doors. With quick, long strides, she makes it to the front desk, haphazardly throwing her purse and keys down.

"Sylvia, are you alright?" she asks. "I am being kidnapped by a strange man and am in great pain. How do you think I am?" the mother-to be grunts through painful breaths.

As this is no time for introductions, I address the latest addition to our circle of drama, stating my intention is to take the young woman to the hospital. In protest, she continues to flail around, nearly causing me to lose my grip and I almost drop her to the floor. The extremely animated young woman shouts, "You can't let him do this!" "Sylvia, you have to let this kind man take you to the hospital. I need to stay here and complete the night audit and cover your shift. I cannot leave right now. We can call you an ambulance instead, if you like, but to be honest, it doesn't appear you have time to wait."

With a heavy, pained sigh, the mother-to-be finally relents, falling limp in my arms as I carry her to my truck waiting outside. I rush the frightened woman to the hospital; she is writhing in pain and states that she is nauseous. *"Great,"* I think to myself, *"this night just keeps getting better."*

As we arrive at the emergency room, I gently lift the woman from my truck and place her in an abandoned wheelchair sitting just outside the ER's automatic doors. Rushing to the counter, I shout for a doctor. The nurse calmly directs us to the maternity ward, explaining the emergency room is not equipped to handle the birthing process.

With directions memorized, we approach the front desk of the maternity ward. Meeting us halfway, a nurse rushes up, asking, "How far apart are the contractions, dear?"

"About fifteen minutes," the mother-to-be responds.

I am handed a clipboard containing forms which need to be filled out. I try to explain I do not know this woman well enough to fill out any legal documents, and we only just met twenty minutes ago.

Laughingly the nurse retorts, "Well, looks like you two are going to learn an awful lot about each other in just a few minutes. I need these filled out." Tapping her finger hard on the wooden clipboard, she continues, "you two decide how best to accomplish this." I look at the young woman, who is desperately trying to hide the pain she is going through. It is obvious she is hurting too much to fill out any forms, so I offer to transcribe while she dictates.

With the forms complete, I take them to the nurse at

the front desk. Unsure of what to do next, I walk to the side of the wheelchair. Kneeling next to her, I ask how she is doing. Thanking me for all I have done, she introduces herself. "I am Sylvia Turner. Sorry we had to meet under such circumstances." With a painful tone, she grunts, "you truly are a thoughtful and kind man." I blush, unable to respond as I am shoved out of the way by two large orderlies. Quickly pushing me aside, they help Ms. Turner into a hospital bed, as she cries out once again in great pain.

"It's time," the nurse states. "We have to get you to the delivery room, sweetheart."

I can only watch as they wheel her toward the double doors labeled, "Delivery."

Through what seems to be an intensely painful grunt, I hear, "Hey, room 420, what's your name?"

"Name is Foster Broussard," I say, watching as the double doors close behind the young woman and attentive staff.

Chapter 25

Two New People Enter My Life

No well-intentioned advice, sage words, or secondhand stories can prepare a first-time mother for the incredible, life- changing experience of childbirth. Physically drained, exhausted, and unusually weak, I feel a wave of dizziness overcome me. Hours later, I'm handed a fragile seven pounds six-ounce infant tightly swaddled in a white blanket. Her nearly transparent pink skin and tiny, fragile hands and feet render me speechless. Her little mouth opens, expelling an enormous yawn, and I cry as she wraps her delicate fingers around my index finger. Gazing lovingly down at my precious miracle, it is clear she is as exhausted from this ordeal as I.

"I will love you always," I whisper, kissing her forehead softly. "She's perfect," the nurse says, as she gently removes the new arrival from my arms. "What is her name?"

"Tara Hope Turner," I answer with a fading smile as I drift off to sleep.

An hour later, I wake to see Ruby quietly holding my baby. "She's beautiful, Sylvia," she says, placing the newborn in my outstretched arms. "She is going to be a fiery one with all the red hair."

"Shoot," is my first thought. "Red hair, just like her grandmother." I was hoping it would be blonde like Chance's.

"So, you're the one who has been kicking so hard," I say, looking down at my gray eyed, redheaded little beauty.

Ruby asks if I am ready for visitors. Disheveled and worn out, I answer with a quick, "No."

"Too bad," she says with an evil grin. "You have company."

Expecting to see my mother, I am surprised when I hear a familiar accent instead. "Howdy, little ladies."

Walking through the door with tastefully arranged flowers in either hand, the stranger from last night holds yellow roses in one vase, and red in the other.

Growing upset and confused, I ask myself, *Why is he here*? "Figured since your middle name is Rose, I should bring you flowers, t'were'nt sure the name of your new one, but got her roses too."

I notice a sweet kindness in his voice as my annoyance fades, allowing my defensive walls to lower.

"She done pert near wore you out, I am sure. Bet a purdy thing like her has a name to match."

"Tara Hope is her name. I will call her Hope for a myriad of reasons."

"That's a rat purdy name," he says, as he sets the arranged roses on the windowsill.

"Hey, where's my purse?" I ask.

"This gentleman gave it to me yesterday. It's in my car, safe and sound," Ruby answers.

I cast my gaze towards the man standing at the end of the hospital bed, his tall silhouette illuminated by the fluorescent lights. "I thank you for all you did, Mr. uh, Foster, is it? Thanks for the flowers and visit, but I am sure you have other places you need to be."

Taking my hint, he responds, "Well, it is nearly checkout time at the hotel, and I have appointments. I wish you well, Ms. Turner, and we'll be seein' you uns again, I am sure." With a big grin, he pats my one bare foot sticking out from under the sheet.

Taking his leave, he holds the heavy door open as Mom, Leif, and Paige enter. My first thought is, *Great, more company I don't want*. I watch in horror as my mother turns around, slapping the man exiting my room, hard on the cheek.

"What the hell?" he yells out.

"Oh, God, Mom, no! Why did you do that?" I shout.

In a firm tone, my mother reveals the reason for assaulting a man she does not know. "I don't care for men who show up for their child's birth, but do not want to have anything else to do with the life they are responsible for bringing into this world."

Spinning around to address me, she continues, "Now, you look here, Missy, you don't need him. You have a family who will look after and support you and this baby."

Looking at the man with the bruised face and ego, I humbly apologize for my mother's insane actions. "I am so sorry, sir; please forgive my psycho mother. I have no idea what has come over her."

My apology falls on deaf ears as the man makes a hasty retreat from the now crowded hospital room. Turning my anger toward my mother, I explain that the person she struck was a stranger, and only through his kind heart and actions did I make it to the hospital in time.

Not responding to my statement, Mom tells me her visit will be brief, explaining she cannot afford to take off an entire day's work. The visit with mom, Leif, and Paige takes less than half an hour. Mom makes a snide remark about my now being a single mother, and perhaps I can better understand the stress I put her through.

This crude remark causes my boss to throw a disapproving look toward my mother.

Before she leaves, I explain to my mom that I am nothing like her, telling her about the college student who has moved in to help take care of Hope while I am away at work, and how the connection between us has already grown into a strong sisterly bond. Ruby confirms that she has met the student, and the young girl's maturity, intelligence, and dedication to my well-being impresses her. My boss assures my condescending mother that Hope will have every advantage life offers. In a disapproving tone, Mom says goodbye, as she grabs Paige and Leif by their arms, rushing them from my room.

Ruby gets up to leave as the hospital staff brings in my lunch tray. I ask her to stay, as my appetite has abandoned me. She declines my offer politely and excuses herself, saying she will be back tomorrow.

After the stressful interaction with my mother, I am thankful for the solace a visitor-free room provides.

Ruby is my only visitor the following day, and she helps with our discharge from the hospital. Upon release, the doctor hands me a prescription for pain, suggesting I stay home from work for as long as needed.

Chapter 26

It is Time to Return to Work

𝕴 am eager to return to work. Patricia not only takes care of Hope's infant needs, but she is also a responsible and caring young girl. Much to my surprise, I see this young woman is tunnel focused on her career goals and not interested in the party lifestyle some college students enjoy. We three have become a family, finally making this apartment a home.

With Patricia's help, I have returned to work sooner than expected. Starting out at three days a week, I have finally been back full time since last Monday. Preparing to leave for my shift at the Tupelo Western, I check in on Hope one last time. She and Patricia have long since gone to bed and are both resting well. Not adjusted to Tupelo's winter yet, I reach for my heavy coat and scarf. Grabbing my purse and keys from the kitchen counter, a blast of cold air rushes in as I open the front door, causing me to shiver and forcing a muffled "Brr" from my lips. I descend the three flights of stairs. Hurrying to get out of the icy wind, I slide into my car, slamming the huge metal door as I blow on my hands for warmth, noticing there is no light illuminating the car's interior. Tomorrow's chore will be to get a new bulb for the overhead light. Unfortunately, trips to the parts store have become more frequent these past few months as minor things have broken or needed replacing on my old yacht on wheels. Last month the fuel pump stopped working, and the month before, the starter solenoid went out. *At least this is a quick and simple fix,* goes through my mind, as I insert the ignition key. With a turn, there is no response. As the starter solenoid is new, I don't know what else might cause this trouble. Sitting motionless with my head on the red steering wheel, I fight the urge to cry. I exit my car, making the tiring trek back to the apartment and call AAA, work, and a cab. The towing company gives me a window of fifteen to thirty minutes before they can arrive.

As I make the call to work, Candace, the lead clerk for the afternoon shift, answers, saying she will be glad to stay over and cover for me. I thank her several times for understanding and gently place the phone's receiver back on the cradle, quietly exiting my apartment so as not to wake the two girls. The tow truck is pulling up behind my car as I reach the stairs landing. Not wasting any time, the driver hooks to my car and leaves. In less than two minutes, the cab pulls into the apartment complex's parking lot. Entering the obnoxiously yellow car, I straighten my coat and place my purse on the cold, slippery vinyl seat.

"Where to, lady?" the cabbie asks.

After I give him the address, we sit in silence, punctuated by the ticking of the meter loosely secured to his dashboard. I arrive forty- five minutes late, apologizing profusely and thanking Candace once again for the huge favor of staying over and covering for me.

"Forget about it," she says, adding there have been a couple last minute check-ins and warning me Juanita is not in a good mood this evening.

Grabbing her clutch and jacket, she turns, and with a smile, says, "Oh, I almost forgot, the guy who was in four-twenty, you know the one, is in room three-twenty-six tonight. He called down, mistaking me for you. I told him you are running late."

"Oh, him," I respond. I thank her once again for staying over and wish her a good night.

Sitting at the computer, I enter my password and copy this evening's guest list to the computer for printing later. Someone walks by the front desk, and without looking up, I bid them a good evening as the desk phone rings. Instinctively, I know who it is, and am surprised to sense a flicker of anticipation rise within me as I wait to hear his voice. Picking up the receiver, I answer. "Front desk, this is Sylvia. How may I help you?"

"Yes, this is Foster Broussard. I was wondering if I could request a wake-up call for 5 am."

"Certainly," I answer cheerfully. "I will set that for you now." "Oh, I didn't mean an automated, impersonal wake-up call from ya'll's phone system, but a call from a real person. Makes the day easier to face hearin' a live voice over a danged ole robot, don't ya think?" he asks pleadingly.

"Mr. Broussard, our company policy does not allow your request for a personal wake-up call, therefore I must set it through our phone system, or you will have to set the alarm clock we provide for our guests on the nightstand." I am certain he could hear the disappointment in my voice.

As I hang up the phone, memories flood my mind regarding Mr. Broussard's and my first meeting. I think back to when he picked me up in those big, brawny arms of his, the unmistakable scent of Sailor's Spice aftershave emanating from him. I remember how odd it seemed he would put on aftershave before buying the toiletries he was coming down to purchase that evening several months ago.

My shift continues unabated, as does the night audit. Using my down time to clean up around the front desk, I hear the printer noisily spit out pages of the completed report and tabulations. Audit done; I notice the clock sitting beside the cash register. It reads 4:45. My mind wanders back to Mr. Broussard, remembering all the kindness shown by him while we were in the hospital. The roses he brought to Hope and me the next day, and the cards he sent to the hotel, wishing us both well. I convince myself, with all he has done for me, the least I can do is grant his request for a personal morning salutation.

At five AM, I cheerfully place the requested wake up

call. "Good morning, Mr. Broussard. This is your friendly front desk clerk giving you the wake-up call you requested."

"Thank you," is the only response I hear from room three- twenty-six as a dial tone follows the click of the receiver.

How rude. I go out of my way to disobey company policy and all he can say is, "Thank you?"

Near the end of my shift, Mr. Broussard bolts to the front desk to check out. Out of breath, he announces, "Room three-twenty-six, checking out." Leaning over the counter, he whispers, "I didn't mean to be rude. You said it would be one of those robot calls. Wasn't 'spectin to hear you. You went and caught me off guard. I am truly sorry. Please know, I am not a rude person."

"Please, don't mention it," I whisper, adding, "I am serious. Please never mention it, ever. I could lose my job because I called your room. Should anyone ever find out, my boss will have no recourse but to fire me. She is strict when it comes to company policy, especially when clerks decide to call guest's rooms."

"I am sorry to cause you such stress."

Hearing deep concern in his voice, I ask him again not to mention it, and in the same breath, raise my voice as I change the direction of our conversation. "Checking out?" I ask, using our company's script. "We hope you enjoyed your stay at the Tupelo Western Inn and Convention Center."

"Sure did," he replies in his all too sexy Louisiana accent.

After completing his check out, I file the night audit ledgers away and clock out. As I have no car this morning, I opt to have breakfast at the Waffle Hut less than a block away, after which I can use the pay phone to call a cab home.

Because the temperature is still cold, I button the

collar of my new winter coat as the wind cuts through me like a knife.

In the parking lot of the Waffle Hut, is an unpleasant surprise. A baby blue, step side pickup truck, which is all too familiar. Considering Mr. Broussard is a regular at the hotel, being seen in the same establishment as him may prove unwise. The rumor mill at work has been in full force lately and I wish to keep from becoming a topic of discussion. A stiff gust of wind prompts me to put my worries to rest and enter the restaurant.

A loud, "Hello," from the Waffle Hut staff alerts the patrons a new customer has entered. From a distant corner, sitting at the counter, I notice a newspaper slowly sliding down to reveal Foster's face. Sitting next to the only vacant seat in the restaurant, Mr. Broussard flashes his warm smile. Being the consummate gentleman, he pulls out the chair for me.

"Well, fancy meeting you here," he says in a cheerful voice.

Apologetically I say, "I am sorry, this is the only vacant seat left in the place. I don't mean to crowd you."

"Shucks, you ain't crowding, if'n you sat anywhere else, I would have gone over and did my best to convince you to join me for breakfast. After all, you went the extra mile for me this morning to start my day off on the right foot."

As genuine as he is being, I grow upset at him once again, mentioning my indiscretion. With frustration prominent in my voice, I remark, "Look, I asked you to please not mention the call. You never know who is within earshot. I work with two women who are gunning for my job. Night auditor pays more than the other shifts because of the knowledge needed and the late hour of the shift. I cannot afford to lose my job to some ambitious teenager because of one stupid mistake I made."

Mr. Broussard drops his head and, looking like a

148

scolds puppy, promises never to speak of the incident again. Thanking him, I order coffee and a waffle. Finding my appetite has deserted me, I pick at my waffle, only consuming two bites.

With an awkward silence mounting, Mr. Broussard comments, "I come in here a lot—don't think I've ever seen you in here."

I explain my reason for being here is because my car broke down last night and I wanted to warm up and have a little breakfast before the walk home. Not looking up, I dig in my purse to find a quarter for the pay phone. Pulling out a dollar bill, I ask the waitress for change, explaining I need to use the phone.

"I'll take you home, Ms. Turner. I don't mind at all. Please allow me to give you a ride and buy your breakfast. It's the least I can do to make amends for the thing we must never discuss again."

Considering the lateness of the hour and chilly morning air, I am in no mood to argue, and graciously accept Mr. Broussard's offer.

Uneasy about accepting a ride from the kind man, I climb into his truck. After fastening the seatbelt, I thank him again for his kind gesture. He responds with a simple, "You're welcome," and our conversation stalls.

To break the awkward silence, I ask, "Mr. Broussard?" "Foster, please," he interjects.

"Foster, what brings you to Tupelo so many times a year?"

"That would take some time to explain. Unless we can talk over coffee at your place, the answer will have to wait." There is a bit of playfulness in his banter.

"Well, my baby may still be asleep and, to be honest, explaining the presence of a stranger to Hope's nanny would be a bit much first thing in the morning."

"I understand," he replies, and in his voice, I can tell he truly does. "Hey," he continues. "I will be working here in Tupelo all week. What would you say to a ride to work each night? You live so close, it truly is not an imposition."

The cab of his truck once again falls silent as he awaits my answer. Hesitantly, I accept, reminding him my coworkers cannot see us entering the hotel lobby together as rumors are sure to fly. He agrees to drop me off in the parking lot of the restaurant so I can walk across the street to the lobby. During the short ride home, I find myself over analyzing my current situation. He is simply offering me a ride and asking for nothing in return. Glancing over at him as he concentrates on driving, I see warmth and compassion in his eyes. He is a proper southern gentleman offering assistance, nothing more. Instructing Foster to pull into spot fourteen, I thank him for the ride. He seems surprised when I take him up on his offer to give me a lift to work. After I ask if he has pen and paper so I can write my number down, he motions to the glove box, saying, "Should be something to write on in there." Pulling an ink pen from the unused ashtray, he adds, "You may have to scribble with it a bit to get it to work, but this should still have ink in it."

I write my number on an old receipt found in the glove box. With a smile, I hand him the piece of paper. "This is my number; you can call tonight after 8 pm. The next two days are sure to be busy, depending on what needs to be fixed on the land yacht."

Exiting his truck, I walk up the three flights of stairs, looking back just in time to watch as his truck exits the parking lot.

Removing my coat and scarf, I see my six-month-old daughter with her breakfast strewn atop the tray of her highchair. With more of her breakfast on her face than in her belly, I can see that she has been making today's feeding no simple task for Patricia. I watch as she pushes the spoon away from her face. Lately my little girl has become combative at feeding time and my heart goes out to Patricia.

"Are you okay, Ms. Turner? You're running late and didn't call. We were starting to get worried."

I tell Patricia about my car and how it would not start again last night, which caused me to call a cab. Kissing the top of Hope's head, I leave the two girls. After a much-needed shower, I join my baby girl in the living room. Towel drying my hair, I ask Patricia if she needs help cleaning the kitchen.

"No, that's ok, I got it," she answers.

Little blue Smurfs on the television screen have captured my daughter's attention as she giggles and points to the animated characters. Desperately trying to stay awake, Hope nods in and out. The moment her head hits her chest, she jerks herself awake—it's a battle she cannot win. Within minutes, she is sleeping comfortably on her favorite blanket.

Anticipating a call from the auto shop, I force myself to stay awake. An hour later, I cannot fight sleep any longer. I say goodnight to Patricia, gently taking my child from her playpen. After placing my bundle of joy in her crib, my bed has never looked so inviting. Laying my robe on the back of the vanity chair, I kick off my slippers and sprawl out on top of the comforter. As I doze off, for the second time in my life, I see the image of a man as clear as day. This time, however, it is not Chance Marlow's face, but Foster's. Taken aback and slightly unnerved by this vision, I force the image from the back of my eyelids, mentally pushing it to the deepest recesses of my mind, enabling me to slip from a twilight state into a much-needed deep sleep.

I hear Patricia whisper my name. "Ms. Turner?" She shakes me, and this time, I hear a forceful, "Ms. Turner?"

I roll over, placing my back towards the young girl who is trying to wake me. "Let me sleep." I grunt.

"Ms. Turner," she whispers, shaking harder this time. "I think the mechanic is calling about your car. You asked me to wake you. If you like, I'll take a message."

"Wait, what?" I blurt out in a raspy voice. "I'm up, I'm up," I say, sliding my feet into the slippers by my bed. As I shuffle off towards the living room, Patricia takes our now wide-awake bundle of joy from her crib.

"Hello?" I ask, picking up the phone's receiver from the tabletop. "Ms. Turner, please?" the voice asks.

"This is she."

"Ma'am, this is Duvall's calling about your 1962 Pontiac." "Have you found out what's wrong with my car?"

"Yes ma'am, it seems like you are going to need a new wire harness. Finding one for a car this old is going to take a while and cost you about three hundred dollars. There is also a rear main seal leak, and the rings and main bearings in your engine are shot. This motor could use a complete overhaul."

No matter how true the words are, I am unprepared to hear them. I know my car is old and needs repair, but ever since Hope's birth, it has been difficult to save money. Needing time to consider my options, I decline the repairs for now, explaining I need to mull this over. The impatient mechanic tells me they are busy and need an answer no later than Friday. Despondent, I hang up the phone and immediately go to my bedroom. Thoughts churn as tough decisions run through my mind. I cry, uncertain what to do.

Hearing three soft taps on my bedroom door, I turn toward the noise. Backlit by the hallway's light, I see only the silhouette of Patricia as she holds Hope. "May we come in for just a minute?" She asks.

"Now is not a good time, Patricia." I sob, using my pillowcase to wipe the tears away.

"Please Ms. Turner, it's important."

"Ok," I say, propping myself up with the many

pillows on my bed.

"Ms. Turner, since you do not charge me to live here, or for groceries, I have been able to put away a great deal of my financial aid. You can use as much of it as you need to fix your car. It costs a lot to take a cab everywhere, and Tupelo has one of the worst public transit systems I have ever seen. Please let me help."

Trying desperately to hide tears, I feel my heart ache and swell at the generous offer made by this thoughtful girl. "Sit," I say, patting the bed.

She and Hope join me.

"This is my problem, and I will take care of it. I cannot, nor will I ever, take a dime of your money. That is money you will eventually have to pay back with interest. It's a sweet offer, Patricia, but I cannot accept. I'll get through this. My entire life has been one struggle after another, and I always manage."

"I wish you would let me help, Ms. Turner, but I understand."

With a hug, Patricia takes Hope into the living room, shutting the bedroom door behind them. Alone in the darkness once again, I discontinue my pity party from earlier. It's more of a revelation than a decision. I realize we need a car with modern features. Something much newer and safer than my boat on wheels. Excitedly, I fling open the bedroom door, announcing, "I've decided we're getting a new car!"

Eagerly, I dial the shop, telling them to repair the wire harness and nothing more. With the manic highs and lows of the morning behind us now, I make one final trip to my bedroom. Covering myself with the comforter, I drift off to sleep, allowing the rest of the afternoon to slip away slowly.

My hand falls hard on the top of the alarm clock as

the unwelcome and annoying *beep, beep, beep* wakes me. Mustering the courage to rise, I shake the fog from my brain and spend the first part of my evening going over my checkbook, paystubs, and bills. I need a clear picture of my finances and how much I can afford to pay monthly on a car note and insurance. Being prepared to face an overexuberant salesman is paramount.

After an hour of number crunching, I decide $250 a month is affordable. Closing the manila folder with my financial information, I see Hope stirring in her playpen. Now able to hold herself up with the padded railings, she carelessly bounces up and down, giggling for no reason. Looking over at my little girl, I smile, telling her we will be alright now.

Worries of acquiring a new debt cause a sensation far more intense than butterflies in the pit of my stomach. "What ifs" control my thoughts. "*What if I cannot afford a used car? What if I buy a car, go in debt by thousands of dollars, and, God forbid, lose my job?*" These terrible thoughts cause the discomfort in my stomach to grow.

Chapter 27

An Unexpected Turn of Events

Hours of agonizing over my finances exhausts me. Allowing myself a temporary rest, I veg out in front of the television. Slipping into a blissful state of calm, I sigh deeply as I watch my little girl sleep peacefully in her playpen with her hind end in the air. Needing to settle my nerves, I stretch out on the sofa. No sooner do I close my eyes than the ringing of the phone startles me, canceling any hope for rest today.

"Hello?" I ask.

"Ms. Turner, this is Foster Broussard. You asked me to call you after eight this evening. May I stop by for a few moments? I have something to ask you."

I agree to meet him downstairs so as not to upset the household.

I knock on Patricia's door, apologizing for the interruption. She agrees to watch Hope while I meet with Foster briefly. She asks for no details or explanation, for which I am grateful, as I have none to give.

Bundling up, I am grateful for the chilly night, which is giving me a good excuse to wear a knit cap to conceal my unbrushed hair.

Foster pulls into spot fourteen. Rolling down his window and not waiting for a hello from me, he says, "If I don't ask this now, I am never going to." He pauses. "Will you go out with me?"

Unprepared for this question, I shiver in the cold, clutching the collar of my coat. I fight every instinct to say no. and to my chagrin a cloud of cold vapor escapes as the words, "I'd like that." drift through the open window of his truck, dissipating the instant they hit the warm air inside.

"Great, I'll call you later and we can set up the details."

Speeding away, Mr. Broussard leaves me standing in the frigid air, unable to speak as I stare blankly into nothingness. Wondering how I allowed this to happen, I shake my head, thinking, *Why in the world would I agree to this? With all I have on my plate, am I seriously ready to go out with someone?*

The next few days are tumultuous. With my broken-down car and Hope's sore gums, all signs point towards canceling the date I have agreed to with Foster. As I try to console my child over her newly emerging tooth, the phone rings at a most inopportune time. Hoping it is the shop calling to say they repaired my car early; I find myself disappointed, as the person on the other end of the line is Foster Broussard.

"Ms. Turner, what would you say to a night out for drinks and conversation at a nice quiet bar I know on North Gloster?"

Never having been a bar person, I pause for a moment. "Mr. Broussard, I am not much of a drinker, and tend to be intolerant of people who imbibe in the consumption of alcoholic beverages."

I didn't mean for the statement to sound holier-than-thou, but there it is, hanging in the air like a deflating helium balloon.

"Oh, I don't drink often, either. It's a nice piano bar I know we both can enjoy. Every bar sells virgin cocktails containing no alcohol. I especially enjoy this bar's virgin Piña coladas. You in?"

Even knowing he was going to call, knowing he was going to ask this question, I find myself unprepared to answer.

"Hello? Are you there?" he asks.

Stifled by insecurity and doubt, I cannot respond.

"Hello? Hello? Are you still there? Ms. Turner, are you okay?"

His voice is loud enough for Patricia to hear from the kitchen, and she dashes into the living room, grabbing the phone from my hand, quickly coming to my rescue. "I am sorry, she dropped the phone. Her daughter is crying in the other room." She lies for me as I sit petrified.

"Is she okay? Are they ok?" I hear him ask.

"Yes, they are fine," my wonderful roommate answers. "Here she is now." Handing me back the phone, she smiles and gleefully bounces down the hall, her hair swishing behind her. "I just saved your butt."

Truth be told, she had. "Hello," I answer. "I'd be glad to join you Foster, but tonight is my last night off and I am not sure Patricia can watch Hope for me."

From her doorway I see Patricia, both hands clinched to her chest, nodding her head, signaling she indeed would watch Hope.

I pause. "It seems she can, so I'll see you when you get here." "Sounds great, I will be there at 10 pm with bells awn." His Cajun accent lands hard on the last word in his sentence.

"Okay, I'll see you at ten," I nervously reply while attempting to put the phone back on the cradle several times.

Having not been out on a date since becoming a mother and the breakup between Hope's father and me, my nerves and anxiety are through the roof. I honestly don't know how to behave on a date anymore. Foster is a nice man who travels to Tupelo sporadically on business, but his home is in Louisiana. I agreed to a date because of those reasons. He is a safe friend to go out with as he lives so far away, and I need not worry about dates becoming a regular occurrence.

157

Sensing my apprehension, Patricia joins me on the sofa. She gently touches my shoulder and says softly, "You haven't been outside this house except for going to the store and work. You, of all people, deserve a night out. Why are you making such a big deal out of this? It's not like he is asking you to marry him." Patricia falls silent, seeing my reaction to her statement. "Oh, my God. You don't just like him—you really, really like him, don't you?" she asks.

Glancing down at the floor briefly, I lift my gaze and nod to Patricia. Not wanting to, I must finally allow myself to admit I am indeed attracted to this man.

It then occurs to me that the choices I am making are becoming more disastrous each day. My past relationship preys on my mind constantly. I allowed myself to become involved with a married man, a relationship which proved unhealthy and unwise. Having known all the facts beforehand, I still allowed myself to become entangled in the web, which was Chance's life. Throwing caution to the wind I allowed my emotions to overtake logic. I wonder, *have I not learned anything from my past mistakes?*

In the few conversations we have had, Foster reveals his home is in Baton Rouge, Louisiana. Because of his job, he travels along the east coast, and in his own words, rarely makes it back home. I ask myself; *do I truly want to get involved with a man who is unavailable on so many levels*? Patricia has brought to light a truth I have been denying. I admire his work ethic and the compassion he shows for others, which I witnessed through his willingness to help a pregnant woman whom he did not know. With his good looks, charismatic charm, and gentle nature, he is an ideal partner for any woman.

Could I be mistaking his kindness as a romantic interest? Am I projecting my feelings onto him? Tension leaves my body as I remind myself this is just a pleasant evening out with a nice guy.

I am ill prepared for my upcoming date, and I have

given no thought regarding outfit or hairstyle choice. I'm blessed my roommate is taking this date more seriously than I. Patricia has set two outfits on my bed for me to choose from. Both, she believes to be my finest. A navy-blue, backless cocktail dress which fits me well, and my sexiest low-cut red dress.

Choosing the more subdued blue dress, I accent it with a faux pearl necklace and matching earrings. I dust off my dark blue pumps and grab the white clutch resting on the top shelf of my closet. Transferring the contents of my purse, I am almost ready.

Leaning against my bedroom door frame, Patricia comments, "My gosh, you made the perfect choice. The entire ensemble, head to toe—wow, Ms. Turner, you look great." She pauses, "except…"

"Except?" I ask.

She rushes behind me and French braids my hair. Stepping back, I admire her work, agreeing the hairdo accents the outfit flawlessly.

Kissing Hope's forehead, I silently creep out of my bedroom. I tell Patricia I'll be home before midnight.

Nervously, I pace by the front window, occasionally peering through the peephole in the front door. I watch as Foster's truck pulls into the parking lot and announce to Patricia I am leaving. Descending the stairs, a calm flows through my body. I am oddly at ease. Foster chivalrously holds the passenger side door open for me, and as I settle in, he leans over and gently secures my seatbelt, planting a sweet kiss on my cheek. "You look absolutely stunning," he says.

"Thank you," I reply in a shy, quiet voice.

Starting his truck, he turns and asks, "You ready?" I nod. "Away we go," he says playfully.

It takes only five minutes to reach the bar, and he parks close to the entrance. I reach for the door handle.

"Now, you wait one hot minute, lady," he orders. "I may not be much, but I am a gentleman, and we are on our first date. You will be treated like the lady you are, and I will have none of this woman's lib stuff tonight."

Foster opens my door, holding his hand out for me to grab as he gently helps me from the truck. On Cloud nine, and swooning from his gallant gestures, I feel the ground beneath my feet turn marshmallow soft and nerves cause my knees to grow weak. I gaze upward, becoming lost in his eyes as he holds the door open, and we enter the bar.

Escorting me to a vacant table, Foster pulls out my chair, asking me what I would like to drink. Unfamiliar with the offerings of a bar, I timidly asked him to choose a drink for me.

"Alright, m' Lady, your wish is my command," he says with a broad smile.

I watch as he walks away, and for the first time, I notice his form-fitting blue jeans showing off a nice rear end. Waiting for my date to return, I peruse the bar, taking in the warm, friendly, and inviting ambiance. Foster has chosen an enchanting place for our first date. Arriving at our table a few minutes later with a frozen drink in each hand, he asks, "Strawberry or banana?"

"Strawberry please."

Setting the pink cocktail on the table, Foster takes his seat. We listen as relaxing music flows from the piano, adding to the chic atmosphere. A well-dressed young man sits at the glossy black instrument, which has become an extension of his soul. I am certain each patron can sense his every emotion while his hands glide effortlessly along the black and white keys. Surprised by the sweet taste of the daiquiri, I wonder why anyone would choose to ruin it by adding alcohol. We listen as mellow tunes pour from the baby grand piano. The young musician announces he is going on break after playing five requests and one of his personal favorites. He thanks the crowd before disappearing into a dark corridor. The bar falls quiet for a moment before murmurs from private conversations replace the once beautiful sound filling the bar. As we have spoken very little, Foster tries to ease my nerves.

"Sylvia, I am just as nervous as you." I am amazed how quickly this man's gentle voice calms my nerves. Murmuring continues in the background as our conversation lingers. In the dimly lit bar, Foster looks into my eyes, and I sense a warmth radiating from him I hadn't noticed before. Not wanting to read too much into it, I smile, hoping he, too, can see my admiration for him.

"This won't do," he says. "It's way too quiet in here." Standing and pushing his chair under our table, he kisses me on the cheek, adding, "Be right back."

He strides towards the vacant piano and my confusion mounts. I watch as he pulls the little bench from beneath the large instrument. I panic, worrying we are about to be asked to leave when management notices what he is doing. Once seated, his fingers fly up and down the piano keyboard. I sit completely shocked as Foster plays a few chords. I recognize the first few bars of the melody he is playing. Leaning forward, he speaks into the microphone. "This is for the lovely lady over there who said yes to a first date and took a chance on this old country boy."

The crowd slowly falls silent as he sings, "Some say love. It is a river…."

Thunderous applause fills the room when Foster completes his song. Joining his adoring fans, I stand and clap loudly as well.

Receiving pats on the back, he returns to our table, apologizing for any embarrassment he may have caused.

The rest of our evening is pleasant. Our conversation is one- sided because I speak of Hope and Patricia and how grateful I am to have them both in my life. I ask him to share more about himself. The enigma, which is Foster Broussard, answers cryptically, "In good time, my lady. All in good time."

Lost in conversation, we hear, "Last call. Last call for alcohol." "Oh my God, is it that late?" I ask.

"I guess so," Foster answers, and in the same breath, asks, "would you like another daiquiri?"

"No, no," I answer. "I should have been home hours ago. Hope is getting a new tooth, and I am sure her crying is keeping Patricia awake."

Standing to leave, I continue our conversation, telling Foster I have a big day tomorrow. With my decision to buy a new, used car, I need to prepare for salesmen who naively believe women know nothing of cars or sales tactics.

It is 2:30 am when we arrive at my apartment. Foster exits his side of the vehicle and opens my door. Gazing deep into my eyes, he catches me off guard, leaning in and gifting me with a short, yet respectful kiss. Swooning, I accept his gesture of affection and with my heart pounding I wish this sweet, gentle, man good night.

Enjoying my euphoric state, I ascend the three flights of stairs to my front door. Humming the tune Foster sang for me earlier, I allow myself to fall backwards onto my bed, expelling a deep, emotional sigh. A spark of romance tingles deep within my soul as the sensation of physical desire envelops my body, rekindling an inner warmth I feared had long since deserted me. Replaying the evening over in my head, I allow my heart to share in this newfound joy dominating my senses.

The sensible and cautious me wonders what secrets lie hidden in the man from Louisiana's mysterious past, while the hopeless romantic me asks, *who is this handsome and wonderful man fate has brought into my life so randomly?*

Chapter 28

A Very Productive Day

Last night, amidst the enchanting melodies of the piano bar, I left my worries behind. We engaged in the usual generic first date banter. Foster did not delve into the intricacies of his job or private life, nor did I. Before saying our final goodnight, he did offer to go with me car shopping. I accepted without pause, embracing the opportunity to spend more time with him.

I have a tight schedule this morning. At 10:30 am, Foster will arrive to take me to the dealership. Patricia will be home in an hour from her morning classes, and I will be glad to let her know Hope's teething pain seems to have lessened.

Like clockwork, Patricia arrives on time. We chat briefly as she peeks her head into my bedroom to check on Hope. "Oh," she remarks. "A man called last night—didn't say who he was but left a number for you to call back. Says it's about your car."

Picking up the slip of paper near the phone, the note asks that I speak with someone named James and call between 9 and 11 am.

I dial the number and listen as it rings several times. Impatiently, I consider hanging up because of the busy day I have planned when I hear, "Hello, Duvall's auto shop."

"Good morning. This is Sylvia Rose Turner. I am returning a call from James regarding my 1962 Bonneville Star Chief. The message said to call between nine and eleven."

I hear the voice yell, "James!, James! It's the lady with the old Pontiac."

After waiting a few moments, a heavy breath utters, "Hello, Mrs. Turner?"

"Yes," I answer curtly.

"Ms. Turner, I would like to talk to you about your 1962 Pontiac. I know my boys have explained to you what all is wrong with your car. Mark tells me you have approved the wire harness repair only.

We will, of course, complete the repair as you request. However, Ms. Turner, your engine needs a complete overhaul. If you're lucky and keep oil in it, I give it maybe a year tops."

I interrupt. "I am not able to afford an overhaul. Not that you care, but I have a toddler at home, and I work nights. I don't make a lot of money and can only afford to get the car running well enough to trade it off."

I try to sound strong and decisive.

"Ms. Turner, that brings us to the reason I called last night. Not meaning to pry, but I would like to know where you bought the car?"

"I purchased the car from an elderly gentleman in Mathiston Mississippi." I grow confused about where the conversation is going.

"That's what I thought," He replies. "Ms. Turner, if possible, I would like to buy this car before you put any more money into it. You see, this is the first car my father bought brand new off the showroom floor. He was a postman in Mathiston and saved up for years to buy his first new car. Oh, how he loved this car. I grew up riding in the back seat with my sister. Now, it needs a lot of work, and to keep you from having to fix the wire harness, I am prepared to offer you three hundred dollars to take the car off your hands."

Hearing the excitement in his voice, I use this opportunity to explain it is the first car I purchased and has seen my daughter and me through some rough times. I sense his desire to reclaim a sentimental item from his youth, giving me an advantage in negotiating a better offer. I inform him I need to keep my land yacht until I save enough for a down payment on another car.

"Ms. Turner, if you continue driving the car in this condition, it may throw a rod. If that happens, you will have to replace the original engine with a rebuilt one, and this car will never again be a numbers matching car. Please reconsider."

His pleading tugs at my heartstrings, and I can honestly tell he loves this car as much as I do.

"I cannot sell the car for less than one thousand dollars. The dealership has already offered twelve hundred in trade-in value."

A lie, but one I can live with. I need a cash down payment for my next car, one which will not deplete my savings.

"The car is simply not worth that much, Ms. Turner. You know what they say, *when you trade a car in, you're giving it to them and buying theirs.* They would knock off nearly that much, anyway. I have five hundred dollars cash in hand right now. It is the best I can do considering all the work the car needs mechanically. I would not even offer you that much, but since I can get the parts wholesale, it will not cost me as much to repair as it would the average Joe."

He is all business now, and I can tell he is serious about his offer. "Tell you what, since you love my old land yacht as much as I do, you got yourself a deal. I will be there in less than an hour with the pink slip. Goodbye." At the top of my lungs, I shout, "I sold my car!" Now a down-payment won't empty my bank account.

Patricia joins me in the living room and gives me a congratulatory hug, sharing in my excitement. Hope cries due to my exuberant outburst and we release our embrace.

"I'll go get her," Patricia says, flashing a huge smile,

which rivals mine.

A knock on the door alerts me to Foster's arrival. In my excitement, I forgot to check the time. Grabbing my coat from the rack, I rush out, and from over my shoulder, I shout, "Mr. Broussard is here to take me to the dealership, back soon."

With his keen eye, Foster notices my beaming demeanor and asks me, "Why the good mood?"

Telling him about the morning phone call regarding the sale of my yacht on wheels, I ask if we can stop by the auto shop before heading on to the dealership. He agrees to my request, and it is then I realize, in my haste, I forgot to grab the title to my car. I ask Foster to excuse me before running up the stairs to retrieve the paperwork for my car. Patricia meets me at the front door with title in hand.

"Here ya go," she says, a smile still plastered on her face.

After I cram the slip of paper into my purse, Foster drives me to the shop and waits patiently as James and I complete our transaction.

At the dealership, I decide on a white Civic with only forty-eight thousand miles. Foster has remained quiet until I announce my choice.

"But it has all those miles. Have you thought of buying a new car? If money or credit is an issue, I can loan you the money or co- sign for a new car for you."

His offer is genuine. However, I take offense, as this is my responsibility. I will not have a man believing he needs to rescue me. Foster sits quietly reserved as he looks out the window while the salesman and I complete the paperwork for the loan and registration. With a handshake, the finance clerk presents me with my new car keys. My joy is short-lived as I turn to see hurt and disappointment in Foster's eyes. The silence between us speaks volumes. My heart sinks after seeing how my actions affected him. I have always been my own woman and refuse to be seen as naïve or dependent. Strong women intimidate most men, and I now see that Foster falls into that category.

Leaving the showroom, I watch as Foster briskly walks towards his truck. Placing his vehicle in reverse, my heart sinks as he prepares to leave without so much as a goodbye. I have bruised his ego and am uncertain how to deal with this situation.

"Wait!" I yell at the top of my lungs. "Wait, Foster! Please don't leave!"

He hits his brakes, causing the tires to screech loudly. I run to his truck, motioning for him to roll down his window.

"I didn't mean to upset you, but you must understand I am an independent woman and overreacted to your offer. All I can say is that was never my intent."

"No harm done, little lady; I understand." He continues, "I am sorry, but I have to go. I have a few classes to teach this afternoon and evening. Maybe I'll see you tonight at work."

I walk toward my purchase, feeling no excitement or joy when I turn the key and open the door.

The drive home was not as pleasurable as I had hoped. I wanted to enjoy my new car, but the way Foster and I parted made that impossible. Somberly entering the apartment, I am met with a very excited nanny asking about the type of car I bought. I tell her we will talk soon, but for now, I am tired. Dismissively, I pat her on the shoulder as I trudge to my bedroom. Tonight, I work, and must try to sleep. As I close my bedroom door, darkness fills the room and the very depths of my soul. I cannot erase from my mind the hurt look I saw on Foster's face this afternoon,

He was only trying to offer help, yet I treated him with the same indifference as the man who sold me the car.

Shrouded in despair and regret, I bury my face deep in my pillow, crying softly, not wanting Patricia to overhear. Eventually I fall asleep, yet I do not rest.

Chapter 29

Foster's Job Demands More

Lately, Foster's job responsibilities have kept us apart for months at a time. When he finally comes into town, he seems preoccupied with the seminars he must teach. The long hours have also taken a toll on him. Our date nights have turned into quick lunches or an hour or two spent at the Metro Inn on the other side of town. It appears our relationship has become a burden and obligation. I am feeling more like an inconvenience than a girlfriend.

When we finally find time for meaningful conversation, he talks of the added workload and all the new states added to his route and already tight schedule. Yesterday he hinted he is thinking of resigning. I don't want to encourage him to quit but am shocked to find myself hopeful for our future after his mentioning the possibility of quitting his job. I must admit lately I have sensed an emotional disconnect growing between us.

Yesterday, after our intimate encounter at the Metro Inn, Foster told me of a call he received from his corporate office. His company added the state of Texas to the already vast territory he covers. Foster warns me he will have to spend even more time on the road and trips to Tupelo will be few and far between. The haunting look in his eyes frightens me as he relays this horrible, unwelcomed news. I can control sobbing out loud, yet am unable to stop the tear, which freely runs down to the tip of my nose. This wonderful man reaches over to catch the teardrop with the tip of his finger, and I grab his hand. Looking deep into his worried eyes I whisper, "somehow, we'll get through this Foster, I don't know how, but we will manage."

Today's lunch at Harper's Deli will be our last for months to come. After paying the check, Foster slips me a yellow piece of paper from a legal pad. "This is a list I made last night," he says, sliding the slip of paper closer. "It is a list of pros and cons regarding continuing with this company and the mounting responsibilities being forced upon me.

They are compensating me well, not only for my time on the road but also for my hard work teaching those lengthy seminars, nearly doubling my pay. All good reasons to stay with the company, however, there are but two reasons I am considering announcing my resignation. As you can see on that list, those reasons are you and Hope." Unable to hold my tears back any longer, I rise from the table and make a hasty retreat to the women's room. I do not want my reaction to influence him.

With the faucet turned on, I look in the mirror as I splash water onto my red puffy eyes while choking back the words I want to scream at the top of my lungs. I fight the urge to raise my fist and curse God for letting this happen. *How can he allow me to be so happy for all these months and then take it away like this? How can fate be so cruel?* Taking a tissue from my clutch, I dry my eyes before leaving the restroom, knowing I must appear supportive of Foster's decision.

Chapter 30

Decision Made

𝕿he woman I love, the strong woman I admire so, returns from the restroom, eyes puffy and red. My announcement has caused her great pain, and that is something I will not tolerate. Sylvia has always been a pillar of strength and femininity. A prideful woman, she rarely wears her heart on her sleeve, sharing her emotions with only those closest to her. Now my girlfriend's swollen eyes speak volumes; therefore, she need not say a word. Attempting to flash me a smile, I can see how visibly upset I have made her. Seeing this reaction from her convinces me that no job or salary is worth causing the woman I love this much pain. As we exit the deli, I place my arm around her waist, gently pulling her close. I look down into her sorrowful eyes and whisper in her ear, "I cannot bear to see you like this and will accept no more states being added to my schedule. The two women in my life must remain my top priority." With an approving smile, she places her head on my shoulder as we walk towards my truck.

I normally enjoy lunches spent with Sylvia. We make small talk and hold hands across the table, flirting shamelessly. This afternoon, however, was stressful and I vow to never allow such a thing to happen again. I will submit my resignation once I complete my current assignment. I love my job, and leaving it will not be easy, but sometimes in life tough decisions must be made and now is that time for me.

Checking my email one last time before leaving the worksite, I notice a reply to my earlier communication. The message is short and succinct. "Be by the phone in your hotel room at six pm eastern standard time." It came from a private account and there was no salutation or closing signature of any kind. I have met the CEO of the company and exchange emails daily, but this address is unknown to me and cannot be found in our database. I am not happy as I now must telephone Sylvia and let her know I will be running late for my playdate with Hope. After a brief conversation, disappointment is prevalent in her tone as she says goodbye before hanging up.

Already tense from the day's activities, I sit nervously on the side of the lumpy bed at the Metro Inn in Tupelo. I opted for this hotel as I did not want to interfere with Sylvia as she tended to her duties and responsibilities at her job. It turns out to be an excellent decision, as this unusual turn of events may change my entire future.

It is well after six pm and the phone has yet to ring. I tire of sitting on the side of this uncomfortable bed and decide to lie down instead, turning the TV on to provide a distraction and maybe perhaps to relax me a bit. It takes only minutes for me to fall asleep.

My head is foggy as I wake from my unintended nap. Wiping my eyes to get a better view of the red numbers on the digital alarm clock beside the bed, I notice it reads ten pm. I become annoyed, realizing I have slept too long. Not only did I miss valuable time with Sylvia, by being forced to wait here for a call that never came, but it has also deprived me of a visit with Hope. "This is unacceptable!" I say rather loudly, as if there is someone else in the room to hear. I immediately call down to the front desk to check to make certain the phone in my room is working. The nice clerk assures me their phone system is operating properly. Now wide awake, I call the Tupelo Western Hotel and Convention Center. I am surprised to hear Jaunita answer the phone. She informs me Sylvia is busy checking in a guest but will call me back at her earliest convenience.

After thanking her I place the receiver back on the cradle and turn my focus to the annoying late-night show playing on the television. Lost in the mundane monologue, I am jolted by the ringing of the phone. Picking up the receiver, I answer, "Hi hon."

"Well, hello to you sweetheart," a bass filled voice replies.

Embarrassed beyond words, I explain I was expecting a return call from my girlfriend. The voice on the other end assures me he understands. He then chastises me for not taking a room at the Tupelo Western which the company has pre-paid for and my decision to resign. In response to his remark, I simply state, "I listed my grievances in the email I sent this afternoon." The owner of the company's tone mellows and becomes almost apologetic. "Mr. Broussard, we truly understand the stress you have been under lately. We have put a lot on you due to an unexpected uptick in business.

Please understand, we are trying to hire more field reps and your resignation will only make that task even more difficult. We are stretched so thin already. We simply cannot allow you to resign."

I explain there is no amount of money they can offer that will change my mind. I reiterate the stress of being on the road, the lack of rest and a near deadly accident on the way from Houston to Austin have all helped me realize life is more valuable than this job. The owner 's tone grows even more apathetic, begging me to reconsider. My heart breaks knowing the impossible situation in which I am leaving them, but my mind is made up.

As I am about to hang up the phone, the boss asks me if I will meet with him and my supervisor at The Tupelo Western the day after tomorrow. He lays a guilt trip on me saying if I am to leave them like this, the least I can do is look them in their eyes and voice my grievances in person. He says the company deserves nothing less. I agree to his terms, mainly just to get him off the phone. I have spoken my piece and do not wish to tie up the line any longer, as I am expecting a call from Sylvia.

I write 2 pm Wednesday on the pad next to the phone and wait for Sylvia's call, which by 3am has not arrived. I understand how busy the night audit can be for Sylvia but find myself feeling slightly disappointed as I roll over and call it a night.

Chapter 31

The Rejection

Ⅰ wake up Wednesday morning as a heavy cloud of discontent looms. I have ordered a western omelet from the room service menu, as I do not want to deal with idle chit chat with a waitress or the noises of a busy restaurant. I eat my breakfast in solitude as I mentally prepare for the day.

As the bathroom fills with steam, I hold my head under the shower head as hot water brings me to life. Palm against the cold tile wall and in deep thought, I reach for the shampoo bottle. While washing my hair, I hear the phone ring. Hoping it is Sylvia calling, I open the shower curtain and slip on the cold tile floor beneath my feet. With eyes burning from shampoo suds, I rush to the phone, which at this point has quit ringing. I wipe the suds from my eyes, cursing under my breath, and notice the blinking red light atop the phone. I dial "0" and the front desk clerk relays a message to me, "Please call Sylvia at home."

After Sylvia catches me up on the activities of her night and how Hope is doing, she wishes me good luck with my meeting. Before hanging up the phone, she promises to support any decision I make regarding my resignation.

Encouraged by my girlfriend's support, I return to my task of getting ready for the day. I use the towel I am holding to wipe the condensation from the mirror above the vanity noticing I need a shave. Once I complete the task, I notice how tired I look. The past few months have taken an undeniable physical, mental, and emotional toll on me. The bags under my eyes should be enough to convince my bosses that quitting my job is in my best interest.

After dressing, I pack my small bag and check out of the Metro Inn, thanking the clerk for a wonderful stay, even though it was not. I throw my small suitcase on the passenger's side floorboard of my truck, setting my new laptop computer on the bench seat. I am ready to get this meeting over and done with.

To my surprise, both my bosses are sitting in the lobby of the Tupelo Western Inn and Convention Center. Checking my watch, I am thirty minutes early as planned, as I hoped arriving early would give me time to prepare mentally before meeting with them. I can see that will not happen now. I walk towards them as they rise with arms outstretched for handshakes. After we exchange pleasantries, I follow them towards a conference room they reserved. Almost in unison, the three of us place our briefcases on the large oblong table before us. Motioning for me to sit, the owner of RedStick clears his throat as he pulls out his chair. My boss, however, remains standing, which confuses me immensely.

I feel nervous with the thick silence dominating the room. The click of the brass latches on his briefcase adds to the drama unfolding before me. My supervisor takes from his case a printed version of the resignation letter I emailed to them two days ago.

Pushing it towards me, he speaks not a word. It is then the owner of RedStick Technologies opens his briefcase, handing a rather overstuffed accordion file to my supervisor. My boss pulls his chair out now and sits, drawing in a deep breath before speaking. I did not know an already deathly silent room could grow quieter, but it does, as tension and apprehension mounts.

"Mr. Broussard," my boss begins. "I have placed before you the resignation letter sent to us Monday afternoon. We are giving you the opportunity to reconsider the request." I forcefully push the copy back towards him. My nerves, which are now completely shot, will not allow me to utter a word.

He takes a labored breath, and continues, "we realize the heavy workload we have put on you and our other field rep, and we apologize for that. The sudden demand for computers in offices nationwide caught us off guard and put our company in a difficult situation. I want to thank you here and now for all you have done to keep up with the demand. You have always been an exemplary employee and one we cannot lose." He pushes the resignation letter back towards me. "Foster, we cannot accept your resignation at this time. I hope you understand."

Shocked at his audacity, I sit motionless for just a moment. As I seethe in anger, I stand, pushing my chair back with the back of my knees and it rolls, bouncing off the wall behind me. "You have some nerve!" I shout, "it's there, in black and white. I resign and that is final. The workload has gotten to be too much, and I cannot allow this job to contribute to the decline of my health and become a detriment to my private relationships. I am sorry, my decision is final."

"Are you quite done, Mr. Broussard?" The owner of our company asks. "If so, please roll your chair back over here, have a seat, and listen to what we have to say. If your answer is still no, we will take your resignation under serious consideration."

His unmitigated gall has me upset, yet curious. Both men take turns explaining the company's newest strategy on how they intend to rectify the field rep shortage we have. My supervisor hands me the overstuffed accordion file presented to him earlier by the owner of the company. In a calming voice, he asks me to look the contents over, study them, and reply with an email with my thoughts regarding their proposition.

This company has been good to me, and I feel obligated to at least consider the situation my leaving the company will cause. I agree to do as they ask, explaining I

will be back in touch in about a week or less. We shake
hands as we leave the lobby of the Tupelo Western. I have a
lot of material to go through. It appears the company was
honestly concerned with the workload they have placed on
the only two field reps they have. I am now more conflicted
and uncertain than I had been earlier.

Chapter 32

The Job Offer

I dedicate four days to thoroughly reviewing the overstuffed accordion folder provided to me by my supervisors. After carefully examining all the information, I now understand the reasons behind my bosses' desire to convince me to remain in their employ. Management's intention is for me to oversee an office they have recently leased in Cincinnati, Ohio. This folder contains documents detailing their strategy for this location, which will serve as the central hub for dispatch operations and headquarters for all instructors and field representatives. Essentially, the plan is for Cincinnati to become the focal point of RedStick Technologies, while the current office in Baton Rouge will primarily handle record- keeping and payroll tasks. Given the significant implications of this new opportunity and the offer from my bosses, there is much to weigh and consider. My priorities have changed, so I can only accept the job if Sylvia agrees. As I had chosen to resign, this new offer will have to be agreed upon between myself and the most important people in my life, my girlfriend, and her beautiful daughter.

I know Sylvia well enough to understand she will never allow herself or her daughter to stand in the way of my aspirations. I grapple with my feelings, torn between my love for them and the prospects which now lay before me. Whichever avenue I choose to take will alter the course of my life.

On Tuesday evening, I take Sylvia to our favorite restaurant. The cozy ambiance and familiar surroundings offer a backdrop for the conversation I need to have with her. As she sits across from me, I share the complexity of my dilemma and explain the intricate details of the offer made to me by my employer. I stumble over my words as I try to convey the turmoil I am feeling.

My beautiful fiancé listens attentively, her eyes reflecting a mixture of emotions. She promises to support any decision I make. Her words are quite sincere, but her eyes betray her, showing a deeper concern. I also see sadness within them. She appears to be struggling with her emotions as much as I am.

Amidst our conversation, there are unspoken sentiments as a pivotal moment approaches. I have carried a felt box in my jacket pocket for the past several weeks, a symbol of the question I long to pose to the woman I love. It takes all my courage as I slowly pull the box from my pocket while Sylvia continues to speak, her voice soft but resolute.

"You know Foster," she begins, her eyes now locking onto mine, "this might be exactly what you were hoping for. You said the constant traveling for work has taken a toll on you, and finding a new place to call home could be the fresh start you have been needing. I have heard great things about Cincinnati, Ohio and I have no doubt you will thrive there."

Her words hang in the air, causing me to rethink what I was just about to ask her. I slowly release the felt box hidden in the palm of my hand. As it drops to the bottom of my pocket, my heart sinks as well. Unexpectedly, her matter of fact and blunt statement reveals a perspective I had not anticipated. Have I misread our relationship? Misunderstood the depth of her commitment?

A wave of disappointment settles over me as I realize my assumptions have led me astray. The romantic scene I had meticulously planned has unraveled in an instant. Instead of a grand romantic gesture, I must recoil and reconsider. My girlfriend's reaction to our conversation leaves me confused.

As the evening draws to a close, I realize our future has become clouded with uncertainty. I envisioned a life shared with Sylvia and her daughter, yet she mentions my starting over in a new city may be a good thing. She does not use the word "us", which would have shown her desire to join me. My heart grows heavy tonight, and the felt box in my pocket mocks me as doubt now runs through my mind and fills my heart.

Chapter 33

I Cannot Stand in His Way

$\mathfrak{I}$ am anticipating a pleasant romantic evening shared between myself and the man who holds my heart. However, as the evening unfolds, Foster reveals an unexpected situation. One which has sown a seed of doubt regarding the path of our relationship. I cannot enjoy the romantic ambiance and soft music the restaurant provides, as a sense of uneasiness emanates through Foster's words. Over our amuse-bouche, he explains how the traveling required for his job has grown tiresome and old. He further voices concern regarding the limited time he now has for himself and us. As the waiter sets hot soup in front of us, Foster takes the napkin from his lap and tucks it into the collar of his button-down oxford shirt, while telling me he submitted his resignation last week with plans of moving to Tupelo. His goal was to find work here, allowing him to spend more time with Hope and me. I listen intently as the idea of having him closer stirs an undeniable allure within me.

With the main course of our meal over and my refusal to view the dessert cart, we order espressos as our end of the meal treat. It is then he drops the bombshell I could never have expected. He discloses his employer refused his resignation as they want him to manage an office in Ohio. He calls the new job offer an unexpected wrinkle and from the look in his eyes, he expects my support. I cannot let him see my heart ache as I realize my biggest fear may soon come to fruition. For months I have been in fear of our relationship ending. His trips to Tupelo have become sporadic, leaving me lonely, allowing doubt to grow within me. Despite my inner turmoil, I must wear a mask of encouragement. I know in my heart I cannot stand in the way of his aspirations.

We both are out of words on the drive home. There is a great tension in my neck and with my mind reeling, I exit his truck. Upset, I forget to give him a kiss and hug before parting ways. "Hey, lady!" he shouts, "not even a kiss goodnight?" Embarrassed, I turn around and run to his side of the truck. He opens the door, and I lay my head on his chest after we kiss. His heart is racing, matching mine beat for beat. "There is a lot to think about," I say as I look up into his beautiful eyes. "I am worried Foster, I won't lie, but will support your decision, whatever that may be." He sighs heavily as he releases me, and I step back. "Don't you fret none," he says. "Things always work out for the best; we must believe that." As I turn towards the stairway to my apartment, his words echo in my mind, but do not calm me. I watch as he pulls from the parking lot. With a heavy and confused heart, each flight of stairs to my apartment becomes more difficult than the last. Our home is dark and quiet as Hope and her nanny are sleeping. My head spinning, I retreat immediately to my bedroom.

Morning arrives later than expected, as Foster's words from last night kept me from restful sleep. It takes all my physical and mental strength to get out of bed. Pressing errands need to be completed before work tonight. I hurry through my morning routine and before leaving; check on Hope, finding her sleeping peacefully in her playpen.

On my way to pick up my paycheck, I stop at the grocery store and post office. Lost in thought regarding Foster's new job prospect and its implications, I do not notice the traffic light turn red. The crunch of metal rings harshly in my ears as I notice steam coming from the hood of the brown sedan in front of me. A young man holds his head as he lets loose a few choice words that would make a sailor blush. The Police soon arrive to clear the intersection. Before leaving, they gift me with a traffic ticket for speeding, running a red light and failure to control my vehicle. *A little excessive*, I think, but now is not the time to argue. The young man and I exchange information and I again attempt an apology, which is ignored.

Returning home, Patricia immediately notices my disheveled appearance. Seeing the bruise on my neck left by my seatbelt, she lightly reaches out to touch it, and I jerk away instinctively. Taking the grocery bags from my arms, she asks me if it hurts and I tell her no, recounting the accident and assuring her I am physically unharmed.

After we finish putting the groceries away, I excuse myself and retreat to my room, desperate for the sleep which had eluded me the night before. Several hours later, I wake groggy and sore. It takes a while for me to muster the motivation needed to rise from my bed. Half-awake, I head to the kitchen for a cup of coffee and notice Foster quietly sitting in the living room. Shaking off my drowsiness, I ask in a hoarse whisper, "why are you here?" He explains he had called when I was asleep, and Patricia informs him of my accident. Worried, he felt the need to check on me. Annoyed, but grateful he is here, I join him on the sofa, thanking him for the concern, assuring him I am alright, albeit a little bruised. He reaches for my hand and grasps it softly, asking me to please forgive the intrusion. The devotion in his eyes speaks volumes as he continues, "I love you so much, so of course I had to come over." I assure him there is nothing to forgive and kiss him on the cheek. The last thing I need now is an overprotective boyfriend, so I mask the pain emanating from my side with a forced smile.

Foster's concern over the accident is clear. He says he allowed worry to fuel countless scenarios in his mind regarding my condition and how serious the accident could have been. He then says something odd, "it made me really think Sylvia." I attempt to ease his fears, labeling the incident as a minor collision. He meets my statement with a strange reaction. I see anger overtake his normally loving eyes. As he rises from his seat and with great concern, he speaks with an unusual intensity in his voice, declaring, "Okay, that's it!" Taken aback by such a strange response, I sit, mouth gaped open, not sure what to expect next. He continues, "I see a fork in the road, which direction we go from here depends on you."

He announces there are a few options to consider. One being to refuse the job offer, stating, "I can get an apartment and job here in Tupelo so I can be close to you and Hope. If I take this job out of state, and you remain here, our relationship will surely suffer. I would constantly worry about you both. No matter what, I need to be near my girls." Contrary to his nature, Foster's words are surprising, filling me with a mix of shock and elation. While I love him deeply, I cannot let him give up such a significant career opportunity because of worry over Hope and me. The selfish side of me supports his wish to stay in Tupelo, however, my rational side can never allow that to happen.

Foster has never been a man who acts on impulse, and I can sense the rest of our conversation will be quite serious. Taking a deep breath Foster continues, "dating long distance has become an issue for us and is no longer an option. Hence my offer to move to Tupelo."

Sitting back down on the sofa, he continues, "I am ready to leave Baton Rouge and move here permanently, so we can continue dating, or we have a second option. The other evening, at the restaurant, there was something I wanted to ask you, but I chickened out. Your answer to this question will decide not only my future, but ours as well. It will determine the road on which we will travel. A yes from you means we move to Cincinnati as a couple. A no means I move here, find a job, and wait until the woman I love decides we can become a family." Looking deeply into my eyes, Foster reaches for my hand. I remain silent, trying desperately to process what he is saying. I watch as he drops to one knee in front of me. He pulls a small box from his pocket, slowly opening it and presenting me with an exquisite ring. Foster tells me it was his grandmother's, and he wishes for me to have it. The stone and setting cast a rainbow of hues against the black felt, leaving me breathless. Still unable to respond verbally, I can only watch as Foster prepares to place the ring on my finger, promising to love me and my daughter always. "Sylvia, my love, my muse, my heart and soul, will you marry me?"

In complete shock, I cannot respond. Knowing yes means moving to a new city, and no means remaining here in Tupelo, the pressure is almost too much. I try to form words but cannot. *Yes*, my brain shouts, while my jaw remains clinched, stopping any words from escaping. As my boyfriend kneels beside me bewildered by my silence and waiting for my answer, a question forms in the back of my mind. *Are you ready to uproot your life yet again?*

A storm of emotions lies behind Foster's eyes as he patiently awaits my answer.

Amidst a flurry of hopes, fears, and uncertainty, "yes Foster," finally rushes from my lips. As I watch a tear slowly journey down this wonderful man's face, my voice echoes, "yes Foster, I will marry you." Looking down as his trembling hands gently slip the uniquely beautiful ring onto my finger, I swoon. Noticing this, he draws me to his broad chest and time briefly stands still, as the rhythmic beating of his heart banishes any doubt I may have had earlier.

After our emotions settle, I notice the lateness of the hour. In a panic, I realize it is time for me to prepare for work and ask Foster if he wouldn't mind driving me tonight, adding I will secure a rental car tomorrow. He agrees, mentioning he will leave the Metro Inn tomorrow morning and check into the Tupelo Western, giving us more time together.

Chapter 34

Accepting the New Job Offer

𝔑ot expecting to "pop the question" this evening, plans have drastically changed from what they were mere hours ago. Now engaged to be married, the meeting scheduled for tomorrow with my bosses will no longer be a somber last farewell. Instead, the tone will be upbeat as I announce a change of heart regarding my resignation. After an emotionally charged evening, the ride to the hotel was quiet. We both have a lot to process. Pulling under the hotel's canopy, I give Sylvia a kiss as she exits my truck. I watch as my fiancé makes her way to the front desk, thinking to myself, *how in the world did you get this lucky?* The drive to the Metro Inn was uneventful and for the first time in many months I slept well.

After finally locating a parking spot in the unusually full lot, I am surprised to notice a spring in my step as I approach the lobby of the Tupelo Western. The automatic doors slide open, and the scent of freshly brewed coffee beckons guests to enter. I wait patiently while Sylvia completes her change of shift duties. Once she is alone behind the desk, I approach to check in to the room my company has reserved for me. Sneaking in a coy wink, my new fiancé hands me the key and flashes me her adorable smile.

Entering my assigned room, a red-light flashes atop the phone. Calling down to the front desk, I ask for my messages. "There are three identical messages," the morning desk clerk says in a cheerful voice. "They ask that you call your boss in room 128 as soon as possible." I quickly dial my boss's number and inform him of the life altering change which has occurred, explaining that as of a few hours ago, I am an engaged man. Asking me what that means exactly to him and our company, I tell him it means a move to Cincinnati is in my near future. Ecstatic to hear the news, he asks me to meet him in his room at 9 am.

At 8:50 am, I call down to my boss's room to confirm our meeting. He acknowledges we had a 9 am meeting but states he overslept and asks me to give him an hour to gather the paperwork necessary to complete my promotion.

At 9:45, I become bored and head down to my boss's room. I find his door ajar.

"Knock, knock," I say before entering his unkempt room. From a distance I here,

"Yeah, come on in Mr. Broussard."

My boss sits at a table with his attaché case open and paperwork strewn across the makeshift desk. He motions for me to join, asking if I would care for a cup of coffee or soda. I reply with a polite "no thank you." Artie, our human resources director, raps on the door, not asking to enter. He settles himself on the edge of the bed once we all exchange greetings and handshakes. A focused businessman, my boss states he wishes to get on with our meeting. Seeing my opportunity to interject, I take it.

I lay all my cards on the table, not holding anything back. Engaged now, my priorities have shifted, and I must think of everyone. I require more time for relocation than they are offering. Yesterday afternoon, they were quick to give me an ultimatum, and now I voice mine. Either they give me the extra month I ask for, or they fire me right now. Hesitantly agreeing to my request, the next topic of discussion was my first visit to Cincinnati. I am told they have already reserved for me a room at the Hyde Park Western in Oakley, Ohio. Artie advises me to look around Hyde Park for an apartment, informing me the neighborhood reflects the status of an up-and-coming executive. My boss reiterates how grateful the company is that I have accepted the responsibility of setting the new office up properly. Artie chimes in,

"We understand there will be kinks which need to be worked out, and various other issues will certainly arise. Your ability to lead and teach will serve you and the new office well. You have a certain Jana Sequa needed to motivate people, Foster. We need your unique talents for this huge undertaking. We are asking a lot of you; however, we know you can handle this and will have the new flagship office operational in no time. Now, all we need is your John Handcock on the dotted line and we all can sleep much better tonight."

Pushing the contract towards me, Artie hands me a pen.

I sign the paperwork and am handed a thick folder containing the "playbook" for opening the new office. As I shake both bosses' hands, I can't help but feel a mix of excitement and nervousness.

I check the front desk to see if Sylvia has left and am not surprised to see she has gone for the day, leaving me unable to report how the meeting ended. I take the rest of the afternoon to pack my belongings and contemplate all the sudden changes occurring. Choosing not to leave the hotel today, I dine from the vending machines down the hall from my room. Disappointed not to have heard from Sylvia, I assume she had a busy day. To battle a severe case of cabin fever this evening, I go to the convenience store to pick up a magazine. The hotel lobby is full of soccer moms. As the television blares and children run unsupervised around the lobby, I become rather uneasy. Walking into the elevator, I'm not surprised to see sticky little fingers have pushed all the buttons. Disappointed I could not see Sylvia and frustrated over the rug rats running around, I enter my room, locking the world out for the rest of the evening.

Later, I reluctantly leave my room, hoping to have the chance to speak with Sylvia before going to bed. Nearing the front desk, I see the "please ring bell for service" sign. My fiancé is apparently too busy for idle chit-chat. I accept my fate and decide to call it a night.

Chapter 35

My Introduction to Cincinnati

𝕿he gravity of our situation hits me hard this morning. With everything happening so fast, Sylvia nor I have had time to process what a move to Cincinnati truly entails. Time and circumstances have not allowed me to inform my fiancé about this trip I must take to Cincinnati. I am not happy we haven't talked or said goodbye properly.

Concentrating on my responsibilities in the new office will not be easy. With so many events unfolding simultaneously, I barely rested last night. The eight-hour drive to Cincinnati will be quite tiring, and I'm looking forward to resting once I get to the Hyde Park Western in Oakley.

There is light traffic on this Saturday morning, allowing me to enjoy the scenery as it passes by. With all the different issues preying on my mind, the hours pass quickly. Breathless, I drive over the Ohio river while looking at the most magnificent skyline. Having never been to Cincinnati, my AAA trip packet tells me I am only fifteen minutes away from Oakley. Eagerly, I pull into the hotel's parking lot, register, and settle in for the evening. It is five o'clock and much too early to call Sylvia. Having picked up a sandwich and chips during my last fuel stop, I need not leave the room tonight.

Calming myself with a quick shower, I lay in bed and turn on the television, hoping to drown out the noise coming from the room next door. Weary from my journey and the emotional highs and lows I've been through; I fall asleep as soon as my head touches the pillow.

A loud bang from outside my window wakes me from my deep slumber. I sit up, rub my eyes, stretch, and yawn. Not fully awake, and with blurred vision, I cannot see the time displayed on the alarm clock. My new fiancé will certainly be upset with me for not calling. Washing my face in the basin, I look into the mirror and state,

"You've done it now mister, she is going to be so mad at you." With face washed and clear vision, the clock reads ten PM. I slept over four hours. It is too late to call my future wife; she has already left for work. Disappointed with myself, I sit down at the round table by the window of the hotel room and study the map AAA gave me. My new office is downtown, and this area is close to that location. Prior to going into the office on Monday, I will drive by the address tomorrow to familiarize myself with the roads and parking situation. Once done with downtown, I will spend the rest of my day touring Hyde Park. Artie has spoken highly of this area of town, so I owe it to him to at least consider the area as a place to live.

After planning out my route and daily activities for tomorrow, I look at the clock again, which reads 10:30 pm. The red numbers torment me, reminding me I have failed as a fiancé. Not wanting to call Sylvia at work, as she hates it when I do, I walk over to the vanity and retrieve my watch. Securing it on my wrist, I notice it reads 9:30 pm. And that's when it hits me, Tupelo is an hour behind Cincinnati. I reach for the phone as my fingers race across the keypad, punching in her home number.

She answers with a perturbed, "Hello?"

"Hi hon, I am sorry for calling so late. I was tired from the drive here and fell asleep. I hope you can forgive me."

"Yes, the drive was okay. I am here safe and sound."

"No, I have not had a chance to get a good

192

impression of Cincinnati, but wait till you see the skyline when driving in. It's breathtaking."

"I love you too. Have a good night and don't work too hard." Before ending the call, Sylvia details an uncomfortable encounter with Patricia. She emphasizes the importance of a serious conversation between all of us. I assure her we will talk everything out when I return.

She makes kissy noises and, in the same breath, says she is running late and needs to go. We say our goodnights and hang up. Sighing deeply, I lay back down on the lumpy hotel bed, hoping to fall back to sleep.

Chapter 36

Preparations and Adjustments

We never got to say goodbye before Foster left for Cincinnati. Working at night can cause schedule conflicts with a boyfriend who lives on a normal schedule. I have time now to reflect on the dramatic changes occurring in my life. In my excitement, I accepted Foster's proposal, failing to consider the emotional toll it would take on Patricia, the one person I rely on most. She is someone I consider so much more than a nanny or friend. In the past two days, I have noticed her mood take a drastic turn. She remains attentive and loving towards Hope but avoids me at all costs. I can hear her in her room, but her silence towards me is heartbreaking and deafening. The air between us, tense and heavy. When I try to get her to talk, she turns away, refusing to look me in the eye.

With the recent rift between Patricia and me, and all that has happened, a conversation with my fiancé once he returns is paramount. We have many topics to discuss. I cannot leave my job without giving two weeks' notice. Telling Ruby of my impending departure will break my heart. Her tutelage has provided job skills which will benefit me the rest of my life. She had faith in me and has proven to be a dear friend. I am certain she will be extremely angry, and I cannot blame her.

I need a plan. My top priority is to make sure Patricia will live comfortably and complete her studies without worry.

Looking at the clock on the kitchen wall, I notice

Patricia is running late. I grow concerned. Tonight is a work night and I need her home soon. Pulling a pen from our junk drawer, I tear a page from a notebook Patricia left lying on the counter. Uncapping the pen, I revert to my standby method of problem solving and begin my list.

1. Patricia's living arrangement.
2. Apartment lease.
3. Pen a carefully crafted two-week notice conveying heartfelt appreciation to Ruby for all she has done for me.
4. Find boxes.
5. Discuss with Foster the move and how it is certain to affect all involved.

And, last but not least,

6. Never let on how nervous you are about uprooting your life once again.

The list seems manageable, but there is more to it than meets the eye. It signifies dramatic change. For years Tupelo has been my home, and with one impulsive yes, I decide to place Foster's ambitions before my own. With a lot to contemplate, I place the folded list in my purse, hearing the metallic jingling of keys as the deadbolt turns. It is Patricia, and she is over thirty minutes late. I say hello asking how she is, receiving no response as she rushes by, closing the bedroom door behind herself.

An hour later, Patricia enters the kitchen, and while throwing together a sandwich, asks, "What exactly are your plans, Sylvia?"

"Now that you are here, I am going to lie down and sleep before work." I answer.

"Oh, okay," she replies, "so, you have nothing else to say?"

A chill creeps up my spine when I hear the hostile

tone in my nanny's voice. I have really upset her, and it seems as if she is ready to talk. I join her in the kitchen, and taking her hand, I say,

"Look, I am so sorry you're upset. There is so much going on right now with Foster, my job, Hope and yes, believe it or not, I am thinking of you too. I'd like to discuss this, but I haven't worked it all out for myself yet. I love you like a sister Patricia, and know you are worried, but you don't need to be. Once Foster is home, we will come up with a plan to handle this. Please understand, I am only doing what I think is best for Hope. She really needs a strong male figure in her life."

Patricia becomes angry.

"For Hope, or is it for you, Sylvia?" Her accusation hurts, but I do not respond.

"How can you just up and leave me like this?" she asks.

"When I moved in, you promised you were done with men, and implied I was going to be with you and hope until I graduate. What am I supposed to do now? Where am I to live? Did you or your precious Foster give any thought to how this wonderful life-changing move for you both will affect me? I am so stressed out I cannot concentrate on an essay which is due tomorrow. Your life is rolling along perfectly and mine is falling apart." She pauses for effect and adds, "Gee Thanks."

The hurt in Patricia's eyes and voice is too much. I leave Hope in the living room with her nanny and run to my room, falling on my bed as I sob uncontrollably. Hearing Hope cry, I pull myself from my bed to check on her.

Walking into the living room, I find Patricia cradling Hope. Their cheeks pressed together, both are crying, and my waterworks start right back up. It appears we all need this emotional release.

Once we regain our composure, I ask Patricia to put Hope back in the playpen and sit with me at the dining room table. Taking her hand again, I tell her she is my sister, in every sense of the word, and I will never intentionally do anything to hurt her or cause her stress. I admit to accepting Foster's proposal without forethought and ask her to forgive me. To ease her worries, I add, "we will come up with an amicable solution for all concerned." I tell her how hard it is going to be for me to leave Tupelo, not because of the job, or the city, but because we are leaving her behind.

I assure my little sister/best friend and nanny; Foster, and I will not leave until we address all her worries.

She looks at me with a distant stare and responds, "I wish hearing all this made me feel better, but it doesn't. I am sorry, it just doesn't."

Her saddened eyes touch my heart as she rises from her chair and says, "I love you like a sister too, Sylvia. but this is totally unexpected. Not knowing what's going to happen next is freaking me out." Touching me on the shoulder, she suggests I put this out of my head for now and go rest.

As she prepares to leave for her room, I rise from my seat and there, at the corner of the dining room table, we exchange an emotionally distant, but understanding hug. With a heavy heart, I head to my room for an overdue nap before my shift tonight.

Chapter 37

So Much to do, So Little Time

$\mathfrak{F}$oster has only been gone for a week, and I miss him terribly. Patricia remains agitated regarding our uncertain future, adding to an already stressful atmosphere here at home. I do my best to console her, but frankly, I am not handling this well either. Our anxiety grows each day. Until Foster and I talk, I can do or say nothing to ease Patricia's well-founded trepidations. I can only reassure her that things will be okay, and this all will work out and I beg her not to worry so much. My words fall flat, and I understand why.

Foster is driving back to Tupelo today. I want to surprise him by meeting him at the hotel. He told me he will stay at the Metro Inn. Elated that my fiancé is coming home, I sit in the parking lot of the hotel, watching as his truck finally pulls beneath the canopy. Unaware of my presence, he exits the hotel a few moments later, keycard in hand. After parking, he grabs his bag and hastily enters the hotel. I follow quickly behind.

As he waits for the elevator, I shout, "Foster!"

He looks back and instead of the happy oh my God there she is reaction one would expect; I am greeted by a pair of rolling eyes accompanied by a deep sigh.

His mannerisms and reaction cause my blood to boil. This seemingly indifferent demeanor and lack of warmth in his greeting makes me wonder what is going on. A loud ding draws our attention to the stainless-steel doors in front of us. They open quickly, but Foster chooses not to enter the moderately full cabin. Instead, he remains behind as it carries guests up to their respected floors.

Turning around, he asks in a snarky tone I do not appreciate, "What are you doing here? You said you had so much to do. I don't for the life of me understand why you would show up here unannounced."

"To meet my husband to be." I answer, "to give him a proper welcome home and I thought...... to surprise you."

"Last goal, accomplished," he remarks in a matter-of-fact tone.

"Foster, why the anger?"

"Not angry, just not ready for a visit with anyone. Sylvia, it has been a long drive. I am tired and would have preferred time to rest and gather myself before seeing anyone. Look at me, I am a complete mess. You would never allow me to see you in this condition."

Knowing for a fact he has seen me in an even worse condition, I do not argue and simply ask if we can go up to his room and talk. He reluctantly agrees, as we stand in silence awaiting the elevator's return.

Sliding the keycard into the blinking green slot in the door lock, he turns around, offering me a kiss and a half-hearted hug. Begrudgingly, I accept his gifts. His sour mood has transferred to me and by now, we are equally perturbed.

Leaving his bag by the door Foster asks, "What is so important it couldn't wait?"

"Foster, we need to talk. Several issues have emerged that I hadn't considered when accepting your proposal and this beautiful ring. I didn't want to bother you with them when you were out of town because I know you had so much on your mind. You know, life for me does not stop when you leave. Since you have been away, I have been dealing with an emotional and anxious roommate."

"And this couldn't wait, because?" he remarks.

My anger gauge is now at the maximum. I can no longer keep a civil tongue.

"Damn it Foster. You know how much family means to me and I consider Patricia my sister. Right now, she is very insecure about her future once we marry. I am so very sorry for interrupting your precious alone time, but now and always Foster, family must come first, or this marriage has no chance of ever working out. I know how exhausted you must be, but this cannot wait. I wish it could. Honey, please accept my apology, but I am at my wit's end with worry. These past few days have been stressful and most unnerving. I feel so selfish not considering Patricia before accepting your proposal."

He anxiously shifts positions on the foot of the bed. His eyes fill with concern as he listens.

Taking a cleansing breath, I continue, "Patricia is frightened, and rightfully so. Because of this emotional turmoil, she handed in a subpar essay and almost received a failing grade because she could not concentrate on schoolwork due to worrying about her future and where she was going to live once you and I move to Cincinnati. Her fears are valid, and I cannot allow her to worry any longer. This past week has been hell for Patricia and me both. We must come up with a solution to this issue tonight."

With his eyes fixed on the carpeted floor, Foster sits, stoically. He speaks no words, merely nodding in response to my statements. In full protective mother mode, I have never spoken to him in this manner. Looking up, in a childlike voice he says "sorry," as his eyes ask for forgiveness and acceptance of his apology.

Joining him on the foot of the bed, I place my hand on his thigh and apologize for not considering his need to relax before being hit with such a serious problem.

"I understand and should have held my tongue. Knowing how much family means to you, I expect nothing less. I deserve this verbal dressing down and am truly sorry for my thoughtlessness. I am just exhausted from the trip.

200

Before tackling this huge issue, is there any way we can lie here and nap for an hour or two?" He asks.

Nodding, I accept his suggestion. I too am tired. I have not slept well for several nights with all that has been preying on my mind.

Foster grabs me playfully and throws me to the left side of the bed and joins me. He kisses me passionately and whispers, "I love you Sylvia Rose Turner." I lay my head on his chest as his heartbeat lulls me to sleep. Unaware of how much time has passed, I feel Foster gently shake me, saying, "Wake up, Sleeping Beauty, it's time for that talk you spoke of earlier. Let's go to our favorite bench in the park, you know, the one by the pond. We can talk there."

He reaches over and gives me a kiss, accompanied by the smile which always melts my heart.

Sitting on one of the many wooden benches the park offers, we spend hours discussing every aspect of the future unfolding before us. I assure him we will adjust to the new city, his job and the life we are to build together. We talk about Hope's nanny. Foster says he knows how much Patricia means to me and cannot imagine how difficult things will be for us when it comes time to say goodbye.

"All we can do is make sure she is taken care of Sylvia, and we will do just that."

Foster's positive attitude does nothing to ease my heartbreak. Knowing we will make certain Patricia will live comfortably after we leave does not negate the fact, I am leaving a large part of me behind. She has helped mold my child into the loving, curious, and rambunctious little girl she has become. Our lives will never be the same. These changes, which I know are all for the best, remain difficult.

Together, Foster and I agree to renew my lease for two years. Unaware of the turn my life was taking, I signed a new lease a month ago and have eleven months until it expires. Foster agrees to leave the utilities in my name and pay them through this new thing called auto-draft from his bank. We will leave all furnishings, kitchen appliances and linens behind.

Foster suggests Patricia's financial obligations will not change. She can take in a roommate to help with groceries, which should allow her to save money for a car.

Satisfied with our decision on how to proceed regarding Patricia's living arrangements and financial future, we drive to the apartment to allow her to weigh in on the plan.

With a sound proposal in mind, we approach my nanny, hoping for acceptance of our recommendations. Refusing our proposition at first, as I anticipated, Patricia states emphatically she refuses to be viewed as a charity case.

Upset Patricia would say such a thing, I walk to my room and retrieve the newly signed lease. Handing it to her, I explain it was time to renew just last month, reminding her I had no way of knowing any of this was going to happen and pointing out that if I break the lease now, management will charge a hefty sum. To avoid steep fines and to keep a broken lease off my record, we must offer her the apartment or sublet it. Laughingly I say there is no way I can deal with subletters. I plead with her to consider the huge favor she would be doing for me if she were to stay in the apartment.

Through sobs, I tell her how hard this is for me.

"We offer you the apartment rent free for almost two years; at which time you will have graduated. You will pay no utilities for those years either. Patricia, if you need anything else, you will have our number. All you have to do is call. You are my family and always will be."

As we fall into each other's arms and cry together, Foster sits uncomfortably silent. Releasing our hug, Patricia rises to embrace Foster, thanking him for the generous offer.

"Hey, this isn't all me," says my wonderful man,

"Sylvia is putting as much money into this as I. You are family Patricia and as such, like Sylvia said, call if you need anything. We will always be here for you when you need us."

Chapter 38

Saying Goodbye is Never Easy

With the apartment situation settled and as everyone's stress levels return to normal, the next few weeks fly by. Foster is back in Cincinnati, familiarizing himself with his new job as I continue to work in Tupelo. Having given two weeks' notice, as expected, Ruby does not approve of my decision to move to Cincinnati. My daughter's God Mother and more like a mother to me than boss, she does not hesitate to voice her opinion.

"I believe you are making a big mistake, but you have to learn your lessons the hard way. Be careful not to lose yourself in the marriage, Sylvia. It is easy to become complacent and forget how hard you have worked to become the independent woman you are today."

Her statement, hurtful to hear, has a ring of truth. I have worried about the same thing. With no nanny or job, my world will revolve around Hope and Foster. It will be a harsh change, as I have never allowed myself to be reliant on anyone for financial support since I was fifteen. Although I believe it's the right choice for my little girl, the thought of us becoming reliant on one man's income is a daunting and unfamiliar prospect.

My last two weeks at The Tupelo Western are hectic. Ruby has put me in charge of training Richard, our newest hire. He has been a night auditor for several other hotel chains. In his late forties, he proves to be set in his ways. Unlike when they hired me, Richard knows what he is doing and believes he does not need my constant supervision. Our personalities clash several times as he insists on doing things his way, not ours. I finally decide to let him do as he pleases, knowing in time, he will regret his stubbornness. When Ruby asks how training is going with Richard, I explain he understands what we expect of him, but remains resistant to our company's methods.

Once Richard is comfortable with how we do things, I become a floater, allowing me to cover other shifts should someone call off. My last day finds me covering the morning shift. The hotel is awash with activity, leaving no time for employees to exchange pleasantries. The hotel is in for a busy weekend, as the Southeast Softball League's convention is being held here. To complicate matters, there has been a major mix-up with room assignments. I spend most of the morning rearranging rooms and floors for several guests. Some want a smoking room; others want the first floor instead of third, etcetera. As check in is not until 2 pm, I assure our agitated and impatient guests, their issues and concerns are being addressed.

Completely exhausted from trying to please our unhappy guests, I can finally sit back and draw a deep breath. I only have an hour left on my final shift. My serene state will not last. Candace runs from conference room three and yells to me,

"We have a problem. The maintenance crew did not set up conference room three to the league's specifications, and the coordinator is having a hissy fit. Can you please come down here and see if you can calm her?"

Pulling myself up from the comfortable office chair, I think to myself, *Just what I need in my last hour here, more problems.*

Candace walks at a hurried pace towards the meeting room in question. Ten paces ahead of me, I ask her to slow down as my feet are sore from not being able to sit for a second all morning.

"Can't," she answers.

"Things are pretty ugly in there."

205

Finally catching up with her, Candace grabs the door handle, and before opening, adds,

"I hope you're ready to see this mess."

As she pulls open the door, I gasp. Everyone I work with, apart from Joan, who is manning the front desk, is standing around a table in the center of the room. As they step aside, allowing me to get close, I see a large, colorfully decorated cake in the center. Helium-filled balloons fastened to the backs of chairs and crape paper streamers twisted and taped along the ceiling draw my eyes to a printed banner across the back wall of the room which reads,

"GOOD LUCK SYLVIA, WE WILL MISS YOU!"

Failing to suppress the emotions bubbling to the surface, I cannot control my outburst and cry uncontrollably.

Gazing at the smiling faces as I dry my tears, I thank everyone, letting them know how wonderful it has been working with them all. I cut into the beautiful cake Candace baked and decorated. Red roses made of icing cover the top with the words "We will miss you," piped in red in the center of the cake. I plate and hand each of my co-workers a slice as they ask various questions regarding my move, engagement, and Foster. I answer each question with an obligatory smile, all the while hurting inside, knowing I may never see them again. Ruby leaves the room to allow Joan to partake in the festivities, but not before asking me to meet her in the office before I leave the building.

With the room booked for the evening softball league's meet and greet, the farewell party gradually winds down. I thank everyone again, telling them how much I will miss each one, as I leave to meet with Ruby as requested.

My boss, the woman who is more like a mother to me than my own, sits, stone faced with fingers interlaced atop her desk. I reluctantly take a seat, apprehensive to hear what she is about to say. She pushes a manila folder towards me, asking me to review the contents. I remove from the envelope my employment record showing each day I missed and the one write up I received two years ago. Ruby asks me if everything looks in order and I agree it does. She hands me three pages stapled together, asking me to read, sign and date where shown. Never have I known Ruby to be so businesslike. A consummate professional, she normally conducts business with a certain informality when it is just the two of us. My hands tremble as I signed the documents, while uncontrollable tears fill my eyes. I am losing someone dear to me and am uncertain how to react to her cold, emotionless, and strict business attitude.

"You didn't read the documents, Sylvia. You signed the papers without reading them. Have I not taught you better than that?"

Her scolding tone cuts me to the core. "Yes, you have," I answer through tears.

She pushes the papers I signed back toward me, "Read," she demands.

I read every word. The document is a final review of the work I performed these past five years and as I flip to the last page, I read,

NOTICE OF TEMPORY LAYOFF

The letter states The Tupelo Western Hotel and Convention Center are temporarily laying me off. It further lists certain benefits the company is allotting me upon dismissal. The last page records the date of my termination as being today. I look up at Ruby, confused. I do not understand why she has chosen this course of action instead of just accepting the two-week notice I submitted.

Unable to hold in my emotions any longer, tears again well up in my eyes. I know she's angry with me but cannot understand why she would lay me off.

Ruby rises from her desk and closes her office door, touching me on my shoulder as she makes her way back to her chair. She asks me to take a deep breath and listen for a moment.

"Sylvia, I cannot allow you to quit. Please understand, I do not do this out of malice. I have laid you off for your own good. First, should you decide to work for this chain of hotels again, your employee file will show your dedication to the company. Second, you get a severance package, money I know you will need. Also, you can draw unemployment in Ohio. If I accept your resignation, you forfeit any chance of receiving unemployment. Can you understand now why I am doing this?"

I nod yes, but cannot speak. I do not feel deserving of such an act of kindness.

"Chin up, Sylvia, I know you are doing what is right for you and Hope, and I truly wish you the very best. I have not dealt with your decision to leave very well, and I apologize. Your severance package, along with a check, will be mailed to you today. You will need to be home to sign for it. Other than that, I can only say goodbye and thank you for all you have done."

We hug one last time before I leave her office. I cannot turn back to wave goodbye to Ruby and my coworkers, for if I do, the emotions bubbling deep inside will cause me to make a scene, which is not how I want anyone to remember me.

Exiting the lobby doors, a plume of cigarette smoke follows me out, escaping into the world, and dissipating within seconds. I turn around one last time, remembering the anticipation I had when I initially walked in that fateful afternoon in search of a job as a maid. My heart is heavy as my gaze shifts to my car. Tears blur my vision as I realize this will be my last time leaving this parking lot. The drive home is somber as I watch familiar landmarks pass by my car's window.

While making the preparations necessary for our relocation, Patricia and I talk of the life we shared within these apartment walls. We reminisce about good and bad times as we laugh and cry together. I tell Patricia how important she is to me and without her, my daughter would not be the happy, well-adjusted child she is today.

Packing our remaining belongings does not take long. I look upon the cardboard boxes containing what is essentially my existence, labeled, taped, and arranged in a tidy stack by the door of the apartment, a tangible representation of my unaccomplished goals. I stare at my belongings, aghast at how few personal possessions I have amassed over the course of five years. Ninety percent of these boxes contain Hope's toys and clothes. There are but two boxes labeled Sylvia. Feelings of fear and excitement cause me to weep silently.

Morning comes too soon. Having no witty or carefully chosen final words, it is with a heavy heart I announce it is time I drive to Cincinnati. My daughter has a death grip on Patricia's leg, crying and asking her to come with. Patricia bends down, strokes my little girl's face and in her most soothing and loving voice speaks to Hope as if she were saying goodbye to her own child.

"Hope, you know I love you. There are things I have to do here and can't come with you and Mommy. I promise to come visit as many times as I can. You are going to have to watch over Mommy and take care of her." Her nanny leans in and whispers loud enough for me to hear, "You know how much Mommy needs help around the house. I love you, Hope."

We embrace once again and tears flow like the mighty Mississippi.

"I knew this was not going to be easy," I say, "but had no idea how heartbreaking it would truly be."

Wiping my eyes, I hug Patricia, kissing her on the cheek and in between sobs mutter,

"I love you. Please remember that."

"I have always known that and always will." The

look on her face lets me know she means every word. "I love you, sis, and will miss you both. I hate goodbyes and if you both don't leave now, I will never let you."

I appreciate her attempt at humor; however, it is not enough to raise my spirits. Today is heartbreakingly difficult.

My baby girl and I leave the apartment, and Hope turns to wave goodbye one last time. My daughter and I somberly walk down the three flights of stairs for our last time. Securing Hope in her child seat, we prepare for our journey.

My foot presses heavily on the brake pedal as I deal with overwhelming memories and emotions. Weeping, I look up at the third-floor apartment I never dreamed of leaving. Farewells are never easy when leaving a place, and someone you love behind. My heartstrings are being pulled so taut the slightest tug may cause a catastrophic break. I cannot help but ask myself,

"Why do they call it goodbye when there is nothing good about it?"

Drowning in a pool of overpowering depression, I stick my head above the emotional deluge long enough to put my car in gear. Pulling away from our first home, we exit the parking lot as I say to my daughter,

"We are going to get through this baby girl, I promise!" After speaking these words, I am uncertain which one of us I am trying to convince.

Chapter 39

A New Family Moves into Hyde Park

𝕱oster is mentally and physically drained, working over sixteen hours a day. Seeing him so exhausted every evening, I cannot ask him for help in the search for a permanent place for our family to call home. He says he trusts my judgement and will be happy with whatever I decide. I'm searching for a comfortable place which exudes warmth and am not interested in just another average cookie cutter apartment. After weeks of looking, I have found two apartments which ooze cozy charm. The first has roomy closets and a lavish jacuzzi tub while the second offers a spacious living room with hardwood floors throughout. Hyde Park is a highly sought-after area with convenient access to local services. I chose this neighborhood for its boutiques, shops, and restaurants. Hope is over the moon with getting her own room while I force a smile to hide my lack of enthusiasm.

Foster works late into the night, constantly assuring me a set schedule is in the future. While I trust his intentions, I still doubt the process. Getting the new office up and running smoothly is my fiancé's focus. Right now, family comes second to career, leaving us alone and neglected. I give him the time and space he needs for now. If this pattern persists, a conversation will be necessary. I cannot marry a man who puts a job before family.

Spending a great deal of time in the tiny rental Foster secured for himself several months ago does not help ease my mood. The cramped living conditions cause tensions to rise. Mornings find Foster darting out the front door after finishing a cup of coffee. We never know when he will be returning home in the evenings. I spend my days taking care of Hope and shopping for furnishings for our new apartment. My little girl and I eat dinner without Foster and are in bed hours before he finally gets home. After quietly kissing Hope goodnight and joining me in our bed, he quietly slips under the covers. Most nights, I am too upset to speak, and pretend to be asleep. Without fail, he kisses me on the cheek, whispering, "I love you," before drifting off to sleep.

This morning is a carbon copy of every day. Foster pours a cup of coffee, kissing Hope on the forehead and me on the cheek as he rushes out the door.

"Gotta run, love you both," has become his standard goodbye.

The smell of pine and disinfectant lingers in the air of the new apartment I have chosen. This morning, we anxiously prepare for our new furniture to be delivered. Hope tells me she is excited to have her own room and how she cannot wait to see the pink canopy bed with matching vanity and chest of drawers she picked out. Loaded on the truck for Foster and me is a king-sized sleigh bed with matching nightstands, vanity, and a chifforobe all in dark walnut. For the living room, they will deliver a sectional sofa which reclines at each end. The tables and lamps, which were displayed along with the sofa on the showroom floor, were perfect, so I bought them as well. As the townhouse has a gigantic living room, this monstrosity will fill it nicely. As I show the men where to set the entertainment center, Hope is busy bouncing on her new bed. We spend the rest of the afternoon removing film from the glass of the entertainment center and arranging the bedroom furnishings. It has gotten late, and I do not want to cook dinner. Hope wants pizza, so we walk half a block to the Saucy Tomato Pizzeria. After enjoying our meal, I drive back to Cheviot, thankful this will be the last night my family spends in the cracker box home I have grown to despise. Once again, my little girl and I find ourselves in bed for the evening, unable to wish Foster goodnight.

We wake in the small house one last time, the scent of coffee inviting us to greet the morning.

"Gotta run, love you both," Foster says as he reaches for the doorknob.

"Hold it right there!" I shout. "You came in so late, we couldn't talk. Our new apartment is ready for us to move into tonight. You will find the two of us there this evening. Here is the key."

He takes the key as I give him a big hug and kiss, telling him I love him. As he leaves, I wonder where he will decide to spend this evening.

After packing most of our clothes, sheets, towels, and sundries, Hope and I are eager to settle into our new home. We spend the day putting everything in its place, and again, I am happily surprised by my daughter's propensity for order and tidiness. The thoughtful placement of her toys and belongings showcases the pride she has in her new bedroom. Once certain Hope and I have done all we can to make this apartment our home, I order Chinese takeout.

The hour grows late, and it is almost Hope's bedtime. Tonight, I do not have to remind her. Hope has already donned her pajamas in anticipation of me tucking her in for the night. When I ask if she is ready for bed, Hope immediately jumps from the sofa to the floor, sprinting to her new room without uttering a word. I can hear her excitement as the sound of the pitter patter of her feet fades down the hallway. Already under the covers by the time I make it into her room, she smiles as I tuck the top sheet securely under the mattress and reach for the book she has laid out on her nightstand.

"This is what you want me to read to you tonight?" I ask. "Yes, Mommy, please," she answers.

I read the Snow Queen to her as she falls asleep

within minutes.

Turning off the lamp, I exit her room, shutting the door slowly so as not to wake my little girl, who worked so hard today. Settling in for my next few lonely hours before bed, I curl up on the sofa alone and depressed. I miss Foster.

Expecting Foster to stay the night in the tiny hovel he has called home for these past months, I allow myself to doze off on the new sofa. A noise at the front door startles me as the rattling of the knob causes me to sit upright. There is nothing near me to grab for protection. Still groggy and not thinking straight, I racing to the nearest room and reach for the first thing I see—my cast-iron skillet. I remain silent with the lights off, shaking uncontrollably. At 9 pm, it is far too early for Foster to be home. I hear the door creak shut as cautious footsteps get closer, stopping just outside the kitchen. The sound of latches springing open on a briefcase causes me to draw a heavy sigh of relief. Foster is home, and I'm surprised he hasn't bumped into anything, considering this is his first time navigating the house in the dark. Reaching for the switch, I turn on the dining room light. Foster lets out a yell as he sees me standing in the kitchen doorway holding the skillet.

"Jesus Christ, Sylvia," he shouts. "You scared the hell out of me! What's with that?"

He points at the skillet and laughs as he walks over, gently removing the skillet from my hand and laying the most romantic and deep kiss on me, as if he has not seen me for years.

"I am home, baby," he says. "I am home, and this is my last late night."

Speechless, I kiss my fiancé passionately, desperately clinging to him and feeling scared that if I let go, this would all be a dream. We enjoy a quiet, relaxing evening at home cuddled next to each other on the sofa. I lay my head on Foster's chest, relaxing to his strong, rhythmic heartbeat.

Chapter 40

My Anti-social Daughter

$\mathfrak{T}$rue to his word, Foster no longer works late, allowing our family to settle into a comfortable routine. He always makes time for Hope in the evenings by cuddling together on the sectional and watching television while I prepare dinner.

After living in Cincinnati for several months, I notice something about Hope. She is content with spending time alone in her bedroom, entertaining herself in solitude with her dolls and toys. She never seems to have the urge to go outside and play.

Never has my daughter's antisocial behavior been on display more than today. As a reward for working so hard around the house, and for good behavior, I promise to take her to a local toy store where she can pick out a new toy. After making the short drive to the store, I park, and before entering, my little girl smooths out the wrinkles in her princess dress. The double doors slide open, and Hope rushes in excitedly, running down the aisles with no apparent plan. Sprinting to catch up, I grab her hand and explain we are here to buy one item. I scold her and remind her if she does not slow down and choose one new toy, we will leave with none. Releasing my hand as we enter the doll section, Hope runs down the aisle, stopping midway. I watch in horror as she pulls at a box containing a doll, which is already in the tiny hands of a little girl. The mother of the child stands shocked, as Hope grabs the package and turns her back to them, yelling, "Mine!"

Wearing the wrong shoes for this shopping endeavor, I run down the aisle, heels clicking loudly on the white tile floor. Trying desperately to keep my feet steady beneath me, I catch up to the crying girl and stunned mother. Looking sternly at my daughter, I exclaim, "You give that back now, Missy."

"Mine!" we hear again as Hope turns away from the little girl who attempts in vain to retrieve her doll from my daughter's deathlike grip.

Loosening the doll from Hope's arms, I give the box back to the shocked little girl and apologize profusely to her horrified mother.

"I am so sorry," I say, kneeling beside my daughter, adding, "she has never done anything like this before."

I search the young mother's eyes for a sign of forgiveness but find none. Pulling her daughter near, the mother snidely remarks, "They are called manners; you should teach them to your daughter." She grabs her little girl's hand and walks away, nose in the air, adding, "Come on, Abby, the nerve of some people!"

It is at this moment, in a fit of rage, Hope further embarrasses me by lying on the cold tile floor, kicking and screaming, "My doll, my doll!"

I could not be more ashamed and am taken aback by her unusual behavior, having never seen her act this way. Lifting her from the floor, I ask her to calm down, remarking, "do you see how upset you made the little girl when you took her baby? We don't do that Hope. This is unacceptable behavior."

The look of confusion on Hope's face speaks volumes. I have failed my little girl by not teaching her simple manners.

With most everything in my world settled, I must teach Hope social graces and proper manners. I have failed to notice she exhibits other signs of anti-social behaviors, some subtle, others not so much. Today's incident proves there are things we must address if we wish for our little girl to grow into a well-adjusted adult. Hope is ready to experience the world around her. She needs to learn the subtleties of socialization, which she can only gain through interacting with her peers. These are things Foster and I cannot provide. Hope must face the reality that the world no longer revolves around her.

Foster has mentioned daycare for Hope many times. Until today, I have rejected the premise, believing it to be in Hope's best interest to spend time with me, allowing our bond to grow. I must now acknowledge my fiancé was right.

Although far from perfect, Foster is everything I ever wanted in a caring and supportive boyfriend and father figure for my daughter. While I prepare dinner, Hope plays in her room, as Foster decompresses after a stressful workday. Refreshing my fiancé's tea, I ask if we can talk after dinner. Befuddled, Foster asks if it is anything serious. I hint that the discussion is important but not serious. With dinner complete and dishes clean, I join my family as we watch a few programs on the television. When the time comes, we put our little girl to bed, tucking her in and kissing her goodnight. Foster makes a beeline for the sofa, but I remind him we need to talk. Turning on the dining room light, I sit down at the table, waiting for him to join. A look of concern comes over his face, and, trying to ease his worry, I tell him everything is okay.

"We just need to talk about Hope," I reassuringly say. "Something happened today. Something I was not ready for."

Vividly, I describe Hope's behavior in the toy store. Foster interjects that he, too, has noticed our child enjoys being alone and is uncomfortable in social situations. To help Hope learn to socialize, we agree enrolling her in preschool is the best solution.

Now that I have his attention, I address another issue. "There is only so much cleaning I can do around here, and with Hope in preschool, I will have even less to do. I would like to find a job."

Apprehensive to bring this subject up, as Foster seems to truly enjoy being the sole provider for our family, I am pleasantly taken aback by his response.

"I was wondering how long it would be before you wanted to go back to work. I see no reason you shouldn't work if you like. You know I only want you and Hope to be happy. There is one other thing," he says with a mischievous smile.

Rising from the table, Foster retrieves his briefcase, pulling from it a manila folder. "I have taken the liberty of having adoption papers drawn up. I would like your permission to make Hope my daughter legally. Honey, when referring to Hope, you always say "my daughter." I know you do not mean to hurt me, but it does. I would love nothing more than to be her father legally and for her to be *our* daughter."

Unable to contain my excitement, bouncing up and down in my chair and clapping my hands, I repeat "Yes," several times.

"Oh, Foster," I cry, "of course, I will sign these papers." "Well, speaking of legalities, what about us?" Foster asks.

It has been over a year since Foster proposed. Since then, as a family, we have been so busy I have given little thought to a wedding, much less setting a date. "Foster, I don't need a piece of paper to know you're the man I love or to prove to the world we are a family. Besides, when am I going to find time to plan a wedding? I could never coordinate a time and date which would agree with your family and friends, or mine. No, a wedding will be a complete nightmare, and we don't need that right now."

With a look of great disappointment, my fiancé looks into my eyes so deeply, his stare touches the very depths of my soul. In a voice thoughtful and caring, he expresses his views on marriage. "Honey, this is not about doing what is right or moral. I am talking about being married, not just legally, but in the eyes of the Lord as well. Sylvia Rose Turner, I want… no, I need you to be my wife and ask that you reconsider. I want us to be a family once and for all."

He slides from his chair onto the floor. Now on his knees, he looks up at me, and I see pure love and devotion. Despite not being an overly emotional man, Foster's tears flow without shame. He lays his head on my lap, and as his chest heaves, whispers, "I need you."

Taken by surprise by his words and behavior, I can only react in shock, unable to speak. I stroke his hair, reaching deep inside my heart for the proper words to reassure this loving man.

Needing to clarify my remarks from before, I try to explain my reasoning. "I love you Foster, and I always will. I do not mean we will never get married, but a ceremony—do we need one?"

Offering him my arm for balance, I help him up from the floor. He reclaims his seat on the dining room chair, and we sit in momentary silence, holding each other's hands.

"Foster, I do want to be your wife. All I am trying to say is, who needs all the pomp and circumstance to be married? We can get a license and appear in front of a Justice of the Peace after we file these adoption papers."

His face lights up and eyes sparkle as he asks, "You mean it? We are finally getting married?"

"Yes," I confirm. "The moment we can get a date with the Justice of the Peace, we will become the Broussard family."

Rising from the table, we fall into each other's arms. Foster's heart pounds as he holds me tight. Gazing deeply into each other's eyes, we share a kiss. Lost in the moment, I bury my head deep into his chest as my lover places his arm gently around my waist, guiding me down the darkened corridor. He opens the door, and the soft ambient lighting flows from our bedroom, bathing Foster's silhouette in an angelic glow. My body quivers in anticipation as our uncontrollable passion ignites.

Gently guiding me onto our bed, Foster slides in beside me. We embrace, whispering words of love and devotion as night gives way to the morning light. Tonight, his touch is ever so gentle, yet his kiss is forcefully passionate, with an intensity which takes me to a fevered pitch of unrivaled desire. Entangled in a love so pure and deep, our souls become intertwined, traveling on a fragile ribbon of ecstasy and leaving the mortal realm behind. The very essence of who we are dances gracefully through the boundless expanse of the cosmos, a celestial waltz which whispers of timeless love and the enchanting connection between us. Spiritually, emotionally, and physically satisfied, we usher in a new day.

Chapter 41

Breakfast in Bed and a Birthday Surprise

𝕀 anticipate little to no fanfare this morning, having asked everyone to let the day slip by without mentioning my birthday or turning twenty-five.

Our bouncing ball of energy bursts through our bedroom door, holding a tray and surprising me.

"Happy birthday, Mommy," she proudly shouts. "I made you breakfast in bed!"

"I see that," I say with the biggest smile I can muster. "And such a pretty card you made, too!"

On the tray, beside the plate holding scrambled eggs, toast smeared with jelly, and slightly undercooked bacon, is a piece of red construction paper with the words "Happy birthday Mommy" written in white crayon. Crying, I give Hope a hug and kiss as I thank her for the thoughtful card and breakfast. "Breakfast smells really good," I say.

"Please don't cry, Mommy, it's your birthday. This is supposed to be a happy day."

"It is a happy day, sweetheart. Mommy loves your card so much; it made her cry happy tears." Truly not hungry, I allow Hope to watch me eat a few bites of the breakfast she prepared. Rubbing my stomach, I say, "Yum, that's some good stuff." I kiss her on the forehead and tell her it is time she has breakfast with her daddy.

Merrily, she skips towards the dining room as my husband asks me to join them soon, adding he too has a birthday surprise for me.

Reiterating my wish for this to be a low-key day, I ask for privacy, informing Foster I wish to shower and prepare for a quiet day at home. As I leave our bedroom, I hear him mutter something but cannot make out what he said.

After an unusually long, hot shower, I enter my kitchen. It looks as if every pot, pan, and dish we own is in the sink. Rolling my sleeves up, I sigh deeply and prepare to clean this disaster. Bolting from his seat at the dining room table, Foster grabs me around the waist. "Today is your day, and I will take care of everything here. Please sit down, relax. Hope and I have this under control."

Gently taking the sponge from my hand, Foster leads me to the dining room table, assuring me everything will be okay. He asks me to sit down with our daughter and to just enjoy my morning. His actions reveal he has a set agenda for today, and I sense that enjoying a quiet day at home is now a dream of mine which has long since faded.

I sit and listen as Foster and Hope work diligently to clean the kitchen. I jump slightly as the damp hands of my daughter reach around my neck for a hug.

"Daddy says I have to get dressed. Will you help me pick out something, Mommy?"

I cannot say no to her pleading eyes. Rummaging through Hope's closet, we find her favorite pair of bib overalls with colorful patches on each knee. I leave her to dress after she decides on a red T-shirt to complete her ensemble.

In the master bedroom, standing and staring blankly into my open closet, I cannot decide what to wear. An unexpected knock on the front door breaks my concentration. Groaning, I glance down at my watch and see it is only eight in the morning. The knock repeats and I wonder why my husband is not answering the door. Begrudgingly I walk down the hallway to find out who is interrupting my morning. Halfheartedly, I open the door. On our stoop stands

Tiffany Ambrose, twirling bubble gum on her index finger.

"Yeah, Mr. Broussard asked me to watch Hope for a few hours today," she says.

"Foster!" I yell. "Foster!" I yell louder, growing increasingly upset. "You get here this instant!"

Darting from the shadows of the hallway and nearly tripping over one of Hope's toys, Foster arrives quickly by my side.

A bit out of breath, he tries to explain Tiffany's presence while scolding her for being thirty minutes early. Turning to me with his sad puppy dog eyes, his face half covered in shaving cream, he apologizes. "She was not supposed to be here for another thirty minutes. I was going to tell you after I finished my morning rituals."

I angrily tug on my husband's arm, signaling to him I wish to talk, leaving the sitter standing by the front door. I pull Foster to the furthest corner of the dining room and sternly ask, "What the hell is she doing here?"

My husband tries his best to explain. "Well, I have somewhere I need to take you. I believe it is best we leave our little ball of energy here just for today. This birthday surprise is for Mommy. At the last minute, I had to call Tiffany and see if she could sit with Hope today." His expression begs for understanding, but this morning he will find none in my eyes.

"Foster, you know I prefer our weekends to be spent together as a family. I don't want to leave Hope with that girl today." I pray my anger and frustration are apparent.

Looking defeated, he asks, "Honey, please, allow me this one favor? It is important we do not have our little girl with us just this once. I know it's important for you, but believe me, honey, she will be happier staying home with Tiffany."

"Obviously, you have an agenda and chose not to

consult me." Unwilling to argue anymore, I turn away and walk to the bedroom, hoping to find an appropriate outfit for the day.

Roughly twice a year, sometimes three, Foster suggests a leisurely Saturday drive. He's using this as an excuse to get me to abandon the warmth and serenity I seek from our townhouse this morning. Knowing this to be an argument I cannot win; I dress and meet my husband as he gives Tiffany a few last-minute instructions before we leave.

As we take in the sights of some of Cincinnati's awe-inspiring neighborhoods, Foster navigates to an area known as Indian Hill, one of the city's most affluent neighborhoods. I grow increasingly uneasy and shift uncomfortably in my seat as my husband continues our drive down Shawnee Run Road. I do not care for this neighborhood and have made my disdain of Indian Hill abundantly clear. It is not so much the township of Indian Hill itself which makes me uncomfortable, but the pretentious attitudes of its residents. My unsettled energy does not go unnoticed, causing Foster to explain why we are in the neighborhood.

"I know you don't care for Indian Hill, but I thought it would be nice to drive around and see how the other half lives." There is a slight chuckle in my husband's voice as he attempts to lighten the mood.

Frustrated, I comment, "All I know is, I could never live amongst or belong to a social class who looks down their noses at others."

My statement seems to rock my husband to the core. Looking over, I see alarm and trepidation on Foster's face. He pulls the car quickly to the shoulder of the road. After putting on the hazard signal, Foster stares at me.

"Why are we stopped?" I ask.

Turning to face me, words stumble from his lips as he reveals the true reason for today's outing. Taking a deep breath, my husband begins, "I may have totally screwed up. I do not mean to upset you, especially on your birthday, and

224

an argument is the last thing I want. My God, I hope you can forgive me for what I have done. There is no turning back."

I have never seen Foster so upset and worried. This is important to him, so I relent, telling him with a giggle in my voice, "I promise to be a good girl from here on out and enjoy the scenery."

As the car slows, I notice an odd sight. Before us is a front yard, which seems slightly out of place. The juxtaposition between the weathered and worn ranch style wooden fence surrounding an immaculately manicured lawn is in stark contrast to the other expensive estates in the area. The intentionally rustic curb appeal hints that the owners may enjoy simpler things and perhaps come from humble lineage. To my surprise, Foster exits the car to open the wooden gate.

Uncertain why he is pulling onto this road, I ask, "What are we doing here? Won't we get in trouble for trespassing?"

He does not answer as he continues up the terra-cotta cobbled stone drive. Parking the car, he exits, rushing to the passenger's side. With his hand outstretched, he exclaims, "Welcome home, my precious wife." Stunned and in shock, I do not move, unable to speak.

There is a slight breeze this morning, bringing with it the smell of honeysuckle bushes and freshly cut grass. Accepting my husband's help, I exit the car. It is an unseasonably warm November morning with the temperature a pleasant forty-nine degrees. A fountain erected in the middle of the circular drive stops me from stepping back any farther as I look up at the huge blonde brick house with black and light gray trim. My husband stands close, holding my hand while I remain motionless. Emotions war within me. I feel honored to have such a thoughtful and generous husband, yet I am confused why he thinks we need such a large home. And even stronger than those emotions, I am

225

incensed he bought a house without even consulting me. I knew we would not live in our apartment forever, but I never dreamed this is where my husband wanted to live. Looking up at Foster, I smile and hug him tightly, realizing all he has gone through to make certain my twenty-fifth birthday is one I will always remember.

Foster interrupts our peaceful moment by asking if I am ready to see the inside of my new home. Taking me by the arm, he guides me to the large double entry doors. As he fumbles with the key, unable to place it in the lock, he looks at me pleadingly for help. Steading his hand, we insert the key together and enter the home. Gazing up at the *Gone with the Wind* staircase replica, I hear the echoes of my breath. The enormity of the moment is almost too much to bear. Awestruck, I watch as a rainbow of colorful fractals cascade downward, gently touching each spindle in the railing of the grand staircase. The vibrant colors draw my eyes upward where they fall on the source of the beautiful spectrum. Atop the staircase stands a stained-glass window depicting an angel watching over two children as they cross an old rickety bridge. On our second date, I mentioned the picture to Foster many years ago, describing how my mother always hung it above her bedroom door in each home we lived. I told him of my admiration for the painting and the emotional and spiritual security it brought to me as a child. The image allowed me to believe a guardian angel was watching over my younger brother and sister as I tried desperately to ease the struggles we faced as children.

This enormous piece of art, and the tremendous gesture from my husband, takes my breath away. Excitedly, I whisper, "This will be like looking through a kaleidoscope every day." With tears in my eyes, I stand on tiptoes while wrapping both arms around Foster's neck uttering, "Thank you for loving me."

Resting my head on his shoulder, I feel his heart pounding nearly as fast as mine. Kissing me on top of my

226

head, Foster reaches into his coat pocket, pulling out a light blue envelope that, as a loan officer in a bank, I am all too familiar with.

"Open the envelope," he says with a smile.

"It's a deed, Foster. I have drawn up several of these at work." "Read the first page, hon. It's important."

Opening the envelope, I read something which almost makes me hit the floor. The deed is in my name only. My bewilderment does not go unnoticed by this dear man, and he explains that because of certain issues within his family, he wants me to be the sole owner of this magnificent home. Deciding not to press the issue or bring up possible unpleasant memories, I change the subject, asking for a tour of this spectacular house.

It takes half an hour to tour upstairs as my husband points out the bedrooms, explaining each has its own full bath. He proudly escorts me to the last room upstairs. Opening the door, he remarks, "This is your house, honey, and always will be. However, I ask for this room to be mine as an office and a quiet space for me to relax."

The room is large with walnut wainscotting and Ducks Unlimited wallpaper. From the oversized couch to the deer antler lighting fixture, the room has a distinct masculine feel with the musky aroma of leather and wood. I assure my precious husband that no self-respecting woman would allow herself to be seen in this room.

The afternoon slips away sooner than expected as we tour the house and grounds. Growing exhausted, as the day has taken an emotional and physical toll on us, we agree it is time to go. The drive home is uneventful as Foster, and I exchange loving glances. Once back home, the rest of the day and evening becomes the peaceful one I had hoped for earlier.

Chapter 42

Adjusting Can Be Difficult

𝕴 have experienced the disorientation of uprooting my family and having to adjust to a new home multiple times throughout my life. I promise myself this will be my last move. The enormity of the task ahead of me to make this house a home fills me with dread. Foster has hired an interior decorator to help me with furnishing our new home in the most current style. With my unpredictable work schedule, I don't have the energy to organize this move. Busy with his own problems at work, my supportive husband has promised to take care of packing up our apartment and any other surprises that might pop up.

Many concerns dominate my thoughts. We are moving to a part of town known to house and entertain the extremely wealthy. I'm a girl who values simplicity and shies away from any unnecessary frills. The enormous house Foster has given me for my birthday is not who I am. Never having been a debutant, nor having been born with a silver spoon in my mouth, I will never pass as a Cincinnati socialite. I am a middle-class country girl who enjoys her anonymity. I will never understand why certain people feel the need to flaunt their affluence and status. The thought that I am expected to behave in the same manner just because I live in a certain neighborhood makes me physically ill.

The whispers I hear at the grocery store in Hyde Park are nothing compared to those I hear in the Village of Indian Hill. The instant I step foot into one of the many specialty shops or boutiques the area offers, I am met with an overwhelmingly judgmental atmosphere. Hushed conversations between women who view themselves as superior to me do not go unnoticed. They make certain to whisper loud enough for me to hear, yet just low enough to keep the harsh comments from drifting into neighboring aisles.

"Will you look at what she is wearing?" they whisper in their huddled cliques. "And that purse? Could it be more tragic?" Their judgment is more pronounced with each syllable they utter. "The poor dear. She doesn't know any better. I hear she is from Mississippi. Her husband is doing the best he can."

The only rebuttal I can muster is an occasional nasty glare in their direction. I dare not make enemies of the wives of the men my husband holds in such high esteem. The thought of having to mingle with these women who focus on what designer you are wearing or where you purchased your shoes makes my skin crawl. Now a permanent resident of Indian Hills, a new set of struggles and issues tears at me as I adjust to our new life.

Foster has never requested I dress or act in a certain way. However, I feel a certain sense of responsibility to my husband and obligation to maintain the image he wishes to portray to his cigar smoking, golf playing business moguls who frequent the country club. I am self-conscious when in social settings and always have been. It's off-putting to me to be amongst a group of high-class, uptight women who judge me before they get to know me.

I spend our first year in Indian Hill keeping myself busy as I fill the house with a mix of antique and modern furnishings. My decorator teaches me the new term "Objet D'art," saying I will impress the socialites with these overpriced items so carefully and prominently displayed throughout my home. A better description of these objects is the term I grew up using, nick-knacks.

The decorator adorns our home with all the newest fabrics, most trendy of furnishings and light fixtures. She explains that our old bedroom suites, sectional, and tables are not right for the new house and tries to convince Foster to donate them all to a local charity. Finally, having suffered enough from her backhanded snarky comments, I put my foot down. I will not lose all connection to my past. Some items I have had since childhood, such as the old oil lamp, several old books, and the first teddy bear I remember being given as a child. After a long argument, Foster agrees to allow me to keep any items I wish. We decide all furnishings from the apartment are to be placed in the mother-in-law-suite, sans Hope's bedroom set. My daughter's insistence on keeping the old furniture in her room fills me with great pride. The decorator tried to convince Hope to fill her room with antique dolls and toys, and a much more mature four poster bed, but Hope refuses those suggestions.

"I like my stuff!" she shouts.

My heart swells, knowing, like her mother, my child is happiest with her old belongings.

The decorator, finally satisfied she has made my home a worthy addition to the Indian Hill neighborhood, says my home is ready to host and entertain the highest members of society, and accepts payment, leaving with one bit of advice. "Now, dear, I suggest updating these furnishings every ten years. Here is my card. Try to keep up to date on all the latest decorating trends and must-haves for the modern home. It will serve you well. Call me." With a snobbish, "Tootles," she exits my home, and not a second too soon.

With the tedious chore of making my house feel more like a museum than home, I find it is time to concentrate on my appearance. The fashions worn by the younger women of today do not flatter me. I want to look good for my husband but cannot bring myself to ask a stranger for fashion advice. To solve this dilemma, I know of only one person I trust enough to help me with this problem; it is time for a call home.

Tonight, out of desperation, I reach out to my best friend and adopted little sister. Placing the call after dinner while Hope and Foster watch television in the living room, I ask Patricia if she will consider giving up her spring break to help me build a wardrobe suitable for a socialite. I share with her all the hateful remarks and shuns I receive from the other wives and mothers in this high society community in which I am forced to live. It is all I can do to hold back tears when telling her of the time my little girl came home with her dress torn, crying and hurt by the cruel things the children were saying about me while bullying her on the school's playground.

With no hesitation, Patricia states, "Let me check my schedule and get back to you with the dates I am available."

Patricia calls with her availability in a week's time. I make all the arrangements necessary and have airline tickets waiting for her at the check-in desk. Hope and I grow excited at the prospect of spending time with her again. My daughter and I spend countless hours getting the mother-in-law-suite ready. Today, we place fresh flowers throughout the apartment. Everything must be perfect. I want Patricia to be at ease and consider this her home. Beyond having her help me with a stylish wardrobe, there is a selfish ulterior motive for having Patricia come for a visit.

While waiting patiently in the terminal and feeling on edge, Hope yanks anxiously on my arm. Her forceful tugging makes continuing to hold her hand impossible, and I must release it. I watch joyfully as she rushes to the only other woman she has bonded with.

Patricia picks up Hope, rocking her from side to side. Through happy tears, she tells Hope how very much she loves and misses her. I watch the touching moment unfold before me as tears flow down my cheeks. Unable to wait another second, I rush over to hug my ex- roommate and best friend. While claiming her baggage, I attempt to describe to her the house and mother-in-law-suite. She waves her hand, saying, "I don't care about that; I want to enjoy our visit and, of course, help you with your wardrobe."

I watch as Hope skips alongside Patricia, happier than she has been in years, and I think to myself, *our family is together again.*

Lined with homes which make mine look like a pauper's cabin, Shawnee Run Road is a beautiful area. Patricia comments how she cannot understand why any family would need such large and extravagant homes. I sheepishly blush as we pull onto the cobbled stone road leading to the fountain proudly displayed in the center of our circular driveway.

"Wow!" Patricia exclaims, "this is your house? Dang, girl, you did good!"

Exiting my car with bags in hand, we approach the house. I am surprised when the door opens. Unbeknownst to me, my husband has taken the afternoon off to greet Patricia and help her settle into her new "digs." Dropping her bag, Patricia runs towards Foster, exclaiming how good it is to see him again. Then Patricia stands motionless, looking up at the stained-glass window.

"Oh, my freaking God Sylvia, that window. It's just stunning. Look at all the colors. So beautiful."

Unable to hide the pride in my voice, I exclaim, "Thank you. Foster had it specially made for me and had it placed right there to evoke just those emotions. He did good, right?"

Patricia nods as Foster excuses himself, mentioning he only took off a few hours and needs to get back to work. Hope and I show our guest to the mother-in-law-suite, which boasts a hand-carved oak door with a brass lion's head knocker and two gas lanterns hanging on either side.

"An exterior door inside? Odd, but nice," Patricia comments. I turn to her and laughingly say, "Foster wanted to give it the illusion of a separate home and not merely an

232

extension or wing of the house.

You are the first to use it." Opening the door, I add, "Come on in and see your new place."

"Wow," Patricia says again. "It's amazing, Sis." With a quick parting hug, Hope and I retreat to the parlor, allowing Patricia the space and time she needs to settle in properly.

Chapter 43

Dinner, Dishes, Decisions

𝕴 phoned Patricia in the mother-in-law suite to let her know dinner will be ready in one hour. Hope is quietly watching television in the living room until the sound of the front door opening draws her attention.

"Daddy, Daddy!" she yells.

I watch as our daughter, with outstretched arms and socked feet, slide into her father's open embrace. I meet my family at the front door, offering a kiss to my husband as I take his keys and announce dinner will be ready shortly.

"Smells good," Foster comments. "How's our guest doing?" "She is settling in. She's said little to any of us since you left to go back to the office."

I ask Hope to put her shoes back on before coming to the dinner table as Foster heads upstairs to change out of his work clothes. Freshly showered, Patricia joins me in the kitchen to offer a helping hand, which I immediately decline. I ask her to join Hope in the living room, explaining that we will eat soon.

Dinner is uneventful, and the conversation is minimal. With so much to discuss between us all, no one knows where to begin. Foster attempts to spark conversation by asking Patricia how things are going in Tupelo, but she responds with a simple, "Things rarely change there, all is okay."

I ask about school and her quick answer is, "it's going okay." Hope also only receives an "Okay" from Patricia when she asks about our old apartment and the neighbor's dog.

After everyone has finished dinner and in typical head of household fashion, Foster excuses the family from the dinner table. Patricia and I gather the dirty dishes as my husband rises from his chair, announcing he and Hope will be in the living room vegging out in front of the television. He gives me a slight peck on the cheek, adding, "I am sure you ladies have tons of catching up to do."

Uncertain if Patricia will be any more communicative now than she was at dinner, I remain silent as we tidy the kitchen, not wanting to upset the applecart. Taking a towel from the handle of the stove, Patricia dries the first rinsed plate and begins, "I am sorry about dinner. It's not that I didn't want to answer all ya'll's questions. I needed to talk to you first."

She takes the next rinsed dish from my hand and continues, "Sylvia, I would like to talk to you later about a serious matter regarding my future and which school I am going to attend next year."

After we finish cleaning the kitchen, Patricia goes to the living room to tell Hope and Foster goodnight. I finish wiping down the kitchen island, when our guest and I pass each other in the hallway as she return to the suite. We stop for a minute to hug and say goodnight.

The evening draws to a close and I find myself in an especially cheerful mood. Foster grabs my tush as we go upstairs to tuck our daughter in and say goodnight. Feeling frisky, my husband and I engage in a little naughty marital behavior before drifting off to sleep.

I wake up uncharacteristically energetic, ready to face a new day.

While enjoying my first cup of coffee this morning, I hear, "Good morning!" The words echo off the empty hallway walls, alerting me to Patricia's impending arrival.

Looking up from my mug, I greet her with an effortless smile, so happy she is here. After she pours herself a mug of coffee, we hug. "I am running a little behind or I would have breakfast ready for you," I say as we release from our tight embrace.

"No worries. With such a well-stocked fridge and pantry in the suite, there is plenty for me to cook should I become hungry later. What's going on with you today?" she asks.

"I'm off today, but still have to go in to finalize a home loan I've been working on for a young couple buying their first home."

Patricia walks me to the front door as I tell her how excited I am that we will go clothes shopping later. After years apart, my family is back together again, helping to make my usually frustrating morning drive tolerable.

Having completed most of the preliminary paperwork regarding the loan for an estate called Haynsworth Manor, I eagerly await the newly married Mr. and Mrs. Worley. Nervously, I repeatedly click my black pen, which sports the bank's logo in white.

Walking by my desk, the bank president asks, "Bored?"

"Oh, no sir, just waiting on the Worleys to sign loan documents."

"Surprised to see you here on your day off," he comments.

"Today is the only day this week they are both able to meet with me. It is imperative we process the loan before Thursday."

Walking away, he comments, "Always dedicated. I like that Mrs. Broussard."

Growing increasingly impatient, I wait for the young couple who obviously do not respect a loan officer's time. Frustrated, I pass the time counting winged toasters floating on the computer's monitor. Arriving nearly an hour late, I get right down to business as I have the Worley family initial, sign, and dates the loan documents I have prepared. Closing the manilla folder, I save the data entered to the hard drive of my computer and gather my things, calling it a day.

While I drive home, I attempt to formulate a cogent argument to convince Patricia to come back to Cincinnati after finals this semester. My hours are increasing at the bank, as are my responsibilities at home. Although I'm able to keep things together for now, I am torn between home and work. Hope needs me to drive her to dance class after school and occasionally to a friend's house, and she also has karate class on Wednesdays. Having balked at Foster's suggestion to hire a housekeeper, I am tasked with keeping this vast house clean. I feel there is no one can clean my house as well as I. My control issues make even the thought of a housekeeper stressful to me.

Arriving later than expected but somehow still in an unusually good mood, I place my purse down on the kitchen island.

Hearing my entrance, Patricia joins me in the kitchen. "Hi."

"Hi," I reply.

"Can we talk," she pauses, "in the suite?"

"Funny, I was going to ask you the same thing," I laugh.

We walk to the wing of our house, which has not been used until a few short days ago. I can't help wishing she would never have to go. Opening the door, I follow her into the living room as she offers me a seat on the sofa.

"This is a nice place you have here, and huge. I don't know how you manage this house, your career, and family. I know you've always been like a superwoman, but dang, I gotta tell you, this seems a bit much, even for you."

"Well, yes, it's large, and some days I am overwhelmed. There are times there is a lot to maintain, and to be honest, lately I have considered hiring a housekeeper, but it hasn't come to that yet."

"I can imagine," she says, nodding her head.

Unable to contain myself, I say, "Okay, look, I am no good at beating around the bush, so I'll just come out and say it. I want you to consider living here after your finals." I take a deep breath and continue, "There, I've just gone ahead and said it."

Patricia sits, mouth gaped open, eyes wide and face draining of color.

I panic. Perhaps I have said too much. "Patricia," I say. "Patricia, are you alright?

Eyes glazed over, she responds, "Yeah, kinda." She places her hand on her chest, and after a deep breath, she responds, "This is serendipitous. I wanted to talk to you about a few things too. You remember me asking about the best teaching hospitals in and around Cincinnati?"

"Yes," I answer.

"Well, there was a reason. Sylvia. I have gone as far as I can with my education in Tupelo. To go any farther, I need a school specializing in nursing, especially a nurse practitioner's degree. Jackson is the only city offering the comprehensive courses I need, but to be honest, I hate it there. So, I am left with choices farther away from Tupelo. That being the case, if I have to move so far away to obtain my degree, I was thinking, why not Cincinnati, Ohio? You guys have several teaching hospitals to choose from."

I am shocked but extremely happy. "Patricia, I'll be more than happy to go with you to check out schools. After all, you have come all this way to help this fashionably challenged woman."

"If I decide to pursue my education here, I will stay on campus in a dorm. It will be far more convenient, and I will apply for any and all scholarships to help pay for school. You know there has to be plenty of jobs to be had on such large campuses. I have given this a lot of thought." Her smile shows she is confident in her decision.

"So, what's wrong with the suite?" I ask. "Is it not big enough for you? What else can we provide? I think it will be far easier to have an apartment of your own. It will give you a reason to leave the campus life behind after your long day there is done. The mother-in- law-suite sits vacant, and I would love for you to live closer to us. Heaven knows your being here has already made Hope so happy.

Won't you at least consider it?"

"I can mull it over, but there is one problem," she remarks. "What about your husband? We cannot possibly consider such things until Foster has his say. Please know, I will never let my presence in Cincinnati be a problem for you or your family. I cannot consider living in this home without both of your blessings." My ex- roommate, best friend and little sister's tone is serious.

Attempting to calm her and myself, I tell Patricia we will talk to Foster after dinner.

"Oh no, Sylvia, I cannot be there when you talk to him. Please, this is between the both of you, and I know he may not be perfectly honest with his reaction if I am present during the discussion. We need to be sure he is okay with me being here."

Relenting, I agree to speak with Foster alone. I ask if she is all set to go shopping and remind her, we must watch the clock as Hope needs to be picked up from school in two hours.

As we leave for my shopping spree, a sense of utter joy overtakes me. Should my husband agree to allow Patricia to live in the suite, my life will feel complete.

Chapter 44

Our Happy Family

℘atricia's knowledge of fashion is unmatched, and she always knows exactly what colors and styles look best on me. She has a knack for finding the perfect outfits which fit me well. Because of her decisiveness, we breeze through the stores, wasting little time. We fill my little sedan with clothes, shoes, and accessories. Once done shopping, we pick up a little girl from school who can't keep her sticky and dirty hands out of the bags surrounding her.

Once home, I release Hope from her seatbelt, asking if she could help bring in some bags. Grabbing a pink and white vertically striped bag, she says with a big smile, "Sure thing, Mommy,"

After several trips to and from the car, we unpack my new wardrobe, laying individual ensembles across the king-size bed. Patricia retrieves wooden hangers from my enormous walk-in closet, placing one beside each new outfit.

"Wow," she exclaims. "Sylvia, there's hardly anything in this closet. How is it possible for someone with all your money to not have a closet full of clothes and shoes in every color?"

Having no answer, I simply shrug my shoulders.

We arrange the new clothes by color and season while Hope stays busy playing with the empty boxes and tissue paper. While standing back and enjoying my full closet, I thank Patricia for all her help in selecting my new wardrobe.

We adjourn to the receiving parlor for some much-needed rest while waiting for my dear husband to come home. There is much he and I must discuss later this evening.

"Daddy!" Hope shouts as she jumps from the loveseat. "Daddy is home!" Meeting Foster at the front door, our daughter stands with her arms outstretched in anticipation of her father lifting her high in the air and bringing her down slowly for a hello kiss and hug. Without fail, this ritual always melts my heart when I see the love between a father and his little girl.

"How's my little munchkin?" he asks.

"I'm okay, Daddy," she announces, kissing her father on his stubbled cheek. Letting her slide gently to the floor, Foster·places his briefcase on the table by the door and enters the parlor. "How're the girls?"

Rising from my favorite chair, I meet him in the doorway, offering a quick kiss and answering, "We are ok, just waiting for you to get home."

Tipping his newsboy style hat to Patricia, he announces he needs to go upstairs and get out of "this monkey suit." Foster has never been fond of having to dress in business attire and complains regularly about the discomfort such clothing causes him.

As her daddy heads upstairs, Hope asks if she can go play in her room. I bend down and kiss her on top of her head, telling her to be mindful of the noise. Patricia rises and asks to be excused, explaining she has yet to decide about what she is cooking for dinner.

"Aren't you going to have dinner with us?" I ask.

"Nah, Foster and Hope need to spend some time with you, right? And isn't there something you need to discuss with him?" I hear apprehension and worry in her voice.

Trying to ease her mind, I answer, "Don't worry Patricia. I am sure everything will be alright. You know

Foster wants what's best for the family. I am certain he will see things my way after I tell him what you and I have talked about."

"I'm keeping my fingers crossed that you're right," she says while hugging me before leaving for the suite.

I hope I am right, too. I think to myself.

Later, as I stand in front of the open refrigerator, I hear the unmistakable footsteps of my husband. They grow closer, finally stopping behind me. Placing his arms around my waist, he kisses me on the neck and laughingly asks, "Nothing for dinner tonight?"

"Seems I forgot to put something out to defrost this morning." Reaching around me, he shuts the refrigerator door, announcing,

"Chinese food will be delivered in less than thirty minutes." Again, my wonderful, thoughtful husband has rescued me.

Over dinner, I mention our guest has been considering completing her education at one of Cincinnati's many institutions of higher learning. I drop subtle hints regarding the possibility of her living with us. Foster does not immediately respond. I continue to prattle on about the benefits of Patricia pursuing her education in a city as large as Cincinnati. Growing agitated, my husband drops his fork on the empty plate in front of him, looks up, and says in an uncharacteristically gruff voice, "Nuff said. We will talk about this after we tuck Hope in for the night."

He must be terribly upset, as his Cajun accent becomes more pronounced when frustrated.

We spend the rest of our evening surrounded by an uneasy silence until Hope's bedtime.

Once tucked in and read her bedtime story, our little girl falls fast asleep. As planned, Foster and I spend several hours talking. My husband, ever the perceptive one, has seen the light in my eyes these past two days. Foster lays out a plan he has developed. He calls it a blueprint regarding our family's future and how he sees it unfolding. Carefully, he details his ideas and recommendations. I listen silently in awe as I look at this man while he continues to surprise me with how accepting he is regarding my and Patricia's decision for her to move to Cincinnati.

Early the following morning, I slip a note under Patricia's door. While enjoying my second cup of coffee, I wait patiently while mentally going over the talking points I need to share with her. I hear the brass knocker rattle as the door to the mother-in-law-suite opens. I am surprised to see a cup of coffee already in Patricia's hand as she joins me. Topping mine off, I pull out a stool, inviting her to join me at the island.

Not wanting to waste any time, I initiate the discussion. "Foster thinks it is best if you stay here with us, not only all summer, but during your first two years of school. That way, you don't have to pay for a dorm room and other living expenses."

Stunned, Patricia replies, "No way I'm doing that. We both know how we are. Neither of us like having to depend on anyone else. I have a say in this, so I'm gonna live on campus 'cause it's what's best for me. There are all sorts of jobs for students, so I will be able to make enough money to live off of." Voice trembling, she holds her head low, hiding the tears forming in her eyes.

Her unexpected reaction makes my heart sink; if she didn't agree to my first suggestion, there was no way she will accept what I have to say next. Attempting to calm Patricia, I continue, "Foster is also in disagreement with you regarding student loans. He believes it is best that we pay your tuition. I told him how badly you want to be a nurse and how much you are willing to sacrifice to get what you want. Knowing full well how long it takes to pay those loans back, my husband does not want you in debt after you graduate. This is no charity we are offering. If you agree, we will hire

243

you to stay here and take care of Hope and perhaps help me keep this enormous house clean. I will pay you a stipend for the work you do around here. Not only that, but consider this, you have been here long enough to notice I have no friends; your company will be greatly appreciated. Please consider all we propose. I am not asking for an answer now. Take all the time you need. You are my best friend, and I know you have it in you to be the best nurse ever. All Foster and I want to do is give you the best opportunity to allow that to happen."

Visibly upset, and perhaps slightly angry, Patricia rises, and turns to go back to the mother-in-law-suite without further comment.

These past few days have been unbearably tense.

Patricia has not left the mother-in-law-suite for three days. Neither Foster nor I attempt to approach her, both of us knowing it is best to give her the time she needs to weigh all her options. This afternoon, she emerges from the suite and joins us on the veranda, asking Foster and me to meet with her tomorrow evening in the apartment for dinner for a frank discussion. She apologizes for her anti-social behavior as she looks at me and states, "I pulled a Sylvia and made a list. I look forward to talking things over tomorrow evening."

"I understand. You had a lot on your mind. No apology needed," I reply.

As she closes the French doors behind her, Foster says with a laugh, "Sure took her long enough."

"Well, it's an important decision, and I can only hope she accepts our offer." Hiding the worry in my voice, I smile, admiring my understanding husband.

Anticipation, worry, and trepidation fill the air this evening. Foster and I are hoping for a certain outcome. However, I am nervous Patricia may have taken offense to our offer.

Patricia leaves a note on the kitchen island reminding

us dinner will be ready at seven PM.

As she opens the door to let us in, I notice the suite is spotless, with everything in its place. The only telltale sign someone is living in the apartment is the unmistakable scent of meatloaf lingering in the air. Patricia gestures for us to follow her to the dining room table.

She carefully pulls out my chair from beneath the table, offering Foster the seat at the head of the table. After a delicious meal of comfort food, Patricia asks us to meet her in the living room of the mother-in-law-suite. Scented candles are lit with artistically arranged flowers on the mantle and coffee table. Patricia finally breaks the tension.

"I want to start off by thanking you for the generous offer you have made. You two mean the world to me, and you've given me a lot to contemplate. I'm so grateful to both of you and can't thank you enough for all you have done for me already. Your rent money gave me the peace of mind to stay in Tupelo and concentrate on my studies instead of stressing about money. I can't even begin to express how much everything you did means to me. So, I hope you can understand what I am going to say next."

Patricia explains why it took her several days to decide on the next step of her journey. Politely, she acknowledges the generosity of our offer, telling us it makes her uneasy because of all we have done for her in the past. She points out three days is not enough time to process such a life-changing decision, and she asks if we can keep the offer open longer.

"With such little time left, there's no way I can process all of this. Besides, to be honest, I'm scared of leaving the only place I've ever called home."

Her words tremble with fear and unease. I hear the same vulnerability, insecurity, and fragility I observed the day she interviewed to become Hope's nanny. It was her honest, vulnerable demeanor which made me choose her over the two other girls.

In my arrogance, I failed to think of how a change of this magnitude would affect Patricia. I often forget not everyone has started their lives over again as many times as I have. Leaving Tupelo would be quite the change for her. To help ease her mind, I share with Patricia the difficulties I faced with each move I made, telling her, however difficult or unsettling, each move led me to where I am today. I reassure her Foster and I will be here to help her adjust to the new town and school.

The next few days fly by, and before we know it, Patricia is packing to leave for Tupelo. I will miss my little sis and best friend but am comforted to know she has not rejected our offer outright.

My heart nearly bursts from my chest when she calls us a week later. Through joyful tears, I tell Foster Patricia will enroll at the University of Cincinnati Medical Center in the fall, deciding to take us up on our offer.

Chapter 45

Time Marches On

𝕿he summer of 1990 brings unexpected changes to our home. Patricia has accepted a part-time job caring for an elderly gentleman who lives at the Dupree House. Those who reside in this affluent retirement community exude an air of superiority, and Mr. Miller is no different. His care does not require someone with LPN certification, but he insists upon it, stating he will not allow a home health aide to touch him. The cantankerous old man makes it clear he finds certain people to be beneath him. Even with her new hectic schedule, she always makes time for Foster, me, and Hope, fondly referring to us as her "adopted family."

Lately, however, Patricia seems preoccupied. Yesterday, she left a note on the counter, and in bold ink, asked for a family meeting. After observing a shift in her behavior over the past few weeks, this request does not surprise me. As we sit in the parlor, Hope plays with her Barbie while Foster and I nervously shift in our seats, waiting for Patricia to find her words.

"I love it here," she starts. "I have a lot going on at school and the Dupree House, and I need to prioritize those obligations. An apartment of my own would mean I can come and go without bothering you two. I'll still help Hope out when needed and stay on top of my duties here. I feel terrible about bringing this up, as you have both been so supportive and I can't thank you enough for the amazing opportunity you have given me."

We assure Patricia there is no need for thanks. Her success will be our reward. The emotional toll of Patricia moving out is difficult on all involved, especially Hope. We spend several weeks consoling each other and explaining to Hope that, although her nanny is moving out of the home, she will see her every day.

All too soon, the day arrives to help Patricia move into her new apartment. Not wanting Hope to become overwhelmed with emotions, we must be careful to prepare her for this difficult time.

We schedule a playdate with her best friend, Latisha, as a distraction and to keep her busy this afternoon. Patricia has accumulated very few items while living with us, so helping her move will take very little time. Placing the final container in her car, my heart grows heavy. Wiping away tears, I sit beside my husband in our car as we follow Patricia down our cobbled stone drive as she heads towards her new future. Knowing this move to be best for Patricia, my heart feels great emptiness.

After all her items are unloaded, we all enjoy a glass of iced tea as we relax on her balcony.

"Do you hear that?" Patricia asks. "Hear what?" I ask in return. "Exactly," she says with a smile.

"Quiet as a church mouse around here. I checked it out last weekend and was happy to find it this peaceful."

We rise to leave, telling her how happy we are for her. Hugging my best friend, I whisper, "If you need anything, let us know. I miss you already."

With goodbyes out of the way, we leave Patricia to begin her new life as a single, free spirited college girl hell bent on making it on her own.

As Foster turns the key in the ignition, I remember there are items I need to pick up at Kroger in Hyde Park. I ask him if he minds stopping there before going home, and he responds, "No problem."

Glancing over at me with his heart-melting smile, Foster mouths the words, "I love you."

Looking at my handsome husband, I cannot help but fall in love all over again. Reaching over and squeezing his knee, I say to him, "I love you too."

The last thing I remember is looking at my husband's smiling face and hearing a screeching sound followed by the loud crunching of metal. Then, darkness.

Chapter 46

How Could This Happen?

Beeping, humming, and muffled voices fill the room. Out of focus silhouetted figures draped in white surround me. I struggle to hear a man's echoing voice through the dense fog clouding my mind. "She's lucky to be alive."

I try to sit up, but a blurry figure presses on my shoulder, asking me to remain still. Straining to focus, I soon realize where I am.

Someone bombards me with questions. Do I know what date it is? How many fingers are they holding up? Who is the president? What is the last thing I remember?

The room continues to spin as I cannot comprehend the questions rapidly being thrown at me. With my head hurting and body sore, I have questions of my own.

"Mrs. Broussard?" someone asks. "Mrs. Broussard, can you hear me?"

My vision slowly returns. A young man stands over me.

"Mrs. Broussard?" he asks again, more impatiently than before. "Yes?" I answer.

"Good, you're awake," he says, releasing my arm and allowing it to fall to my side. "Mrs. Broussard, you have been in a serious accident. We're going to take good care of you. Can you tell me the last thing you remember?"

Closing my eyes, I search my mind. "My husband smiling." "Were you the passenger?" he asks.

"Passenger?"

"In the car, Mrs. Broussard. Were you the passenger?" "Oh, yes," I answer.

Then, it occurs to me, my husband is not in the room with me. Bolting upright, and through a painful grunt I demand, "Foster! Where is my husband?" I feel a sharp pain in my shoulder as my heart races.

"Calm down, Mrs. Broussard, please calm down. We need you to remain still. You'll pull out your I.V."

In his voice I hear concern as he orders the nurse to administer some cc's of something STAT.

A woman rushes to his side, placing a needle into the I.V. in my arm. Once again, I am rendered unconscious.

When I wake, Patricia is at my bedside, holding my hand. Looking at me with tear-filled eyes, she whispers, "Look who's finally awake. How are you feeling, Sylvia?"

"Sore, woozy, dizzy, and confused," I answer.

"I can imagine. They tell me you put up quite a fight earlier. You need to do your best to keep calm. You can't move around so much." She says this as she loosens the restraints.

"You have to promise not to move from this bed, okay? If you do, I'll have to put these back on. Do you understand?" she asks sympathetically.

I nod as she raises the bed and fluffs the pillow beneath my head. "What is going on? Why am I in a hospital? Have you seen Foster?" I ask.

There is a sadness in Patricia's eyes as she speaks. "I'll tell you what all happened, but you must promise to stay put."

Taking a deep breath, she sits on the side of the bed and relays in graphic detail what happened. "You guys left my place. At some point, an elderly man driving a box truck T-boned your car at a high rate of speed. From what I hear, he was possibly having a heart attack. Your little Honda was no match for the big truck as it hit the driver's side of your car. You are truly lucky to be alive. The impact was severe enough that EMTs needed the jaws of life to remove you both."

Panic causes me to interrupt her. "Foster?" I grip her arm firmly. "Please, you have to tell me where Foster is."

"Calm down," Patricia whispers. "Do you want them to knock you out again? Foster is in I.C.U. I have been up to see him a few times. He's not doing well, Sylvia. They are keeping him comfortable, but he has not regained consciousness since they admitted him. Believe me, right now, being unconscious is best. They have him in a medically induced coma, and he does not know what is going on. He is not in pain, and they are keeping him as comfortable as they can. There is nothing you or I can do for him. You need to concentrate on getting better so you can go upstairs to visit him. For now, he is in expert hands, and they are doing everything they can."

I can't help but notice Patricia has repeated certain statements. Confused as to why, I decide not to press the issue. As a nurse, she is always truthful, yet her eyes betray her, dancing away from mine as her body language suggests she is leaving something unsaid.

Patricia quickly rises and intercepts a woman who has entered my room, her white shoes squeaking on the tiled floor. Exchanging whispers, they leave, closing the door behind themselves. Finding this behavior odd, I wonder what they are talking about beyond earshot.

Patricia reenters the room with a host of people following her. "We have been talking," she announces.

"Yes, I know," I respond curtly.

"Sylvia, please, there is much to discuss when you are ready." "I am still a little foggy but can talk," I answer.

The young doctor from earlier steps to the bedside. Once again, he takes my pulse as he shoves a thermometer into my mouth. "Mrs. Broussard, we have some general questions we must ask you. Are you up to answering them?"

I nod yes, unable to speak because of this obtrusive device under my tongue.

"Do you know what day of the week it is?" he asks, removing the thermometer while checking the reading. "ninety-seven point six," he reports.

A nurse enters the numbers into a chart.

"The date, Mrs. Broussard. Do you know what day of the week it is?"

"Monday?"

"Correct," he confirms. "What is the date and month?"

"July twelfth, do you want to know the year too?" I clap back.

They must think I am an idiot and cannot see the whiteboard behind him, providing me with the answers to his questions.

"And the President of the United States?"

Now, there's a question not listed on the board, I think to myself before answering, "Bush?" I honestly could not recall at first.

"Good, good," he remarks. "It appears the bump on your noggin caused no serious damage. You may be tender and achy, but I have faith you are on the path to a full recovery. If you need anything, the nurse's call button is right there. I'll let you two visit for a bit. We'll be back in two hours to check in on you. Try to rest, Mrs. Broussard.

It's been a traumatizing day for you."

Patricia follows the doctor and his entourage out the door.

Now alone, I search for the remote device for the television, noticing severe bruising on my right arm. It is deep purple and painful, and it is now I realize the seriousness of the accident. The entire right side of my body hurts.

Patricia joins me in the room, and before she can sit down, I ask when they will allow me to see my husband. She guesses perhaps as soon as tomorrow. "Provided you are a good girl and don't give them any trouble."

I recognize her attempt at humor, but I cannot bring myself to laugh just now. Placating her, I promise to rest and be as quiet as I can. "Where is Hope?" I ask.

"We have turned the playdate into a sleepover. I have not told her about the accident yet. It's too soon. I will bring her to visit you tomorrow." With a nod towards the whiteboard, she indicates visiting hours are almost over, stating she needs to return home, as there are still things she needs to put away.

She kisses me on my forehead and leaves. I thank her for visiting and tell her I love her. Now, alone, there is a gnawing feeling in the pit of my stomach. I can't help but sense there is something everyone is avoiding telling me, and I do not like it one bit.

It is a restless night with the machines beeping. Someone in a room a few doors away is making terribly odd noises and yelling loudly. At 3 am, I cannot take any more of the constant crying out. I ring for a nurse in hopes of either another dose of pain meds or a sleep aid. Nearly thirty minutes later, the nurse finally shows up, explaining it was too early to give me more medication when I asked.

There is a lot of whispering outside my hospital room door this morning. Today, my pain has eased, and my mind is clearer. However, memories of the accident remain sparse. The whiteboard reveals my nurse for today is Navi and my doctor, Hirschbaum. I eagerly await my first visit with him because I have questions only he can answer.

To my dismay, Navi enters, followed by an orderly carrying a tray. "How are we doing this morning?" she asks in a chipper tone which immediately grates my nerves.

My answer is curt. "Well, I can't speak for you, but I am ready to go home."

"Now, now, Mrs. Broussard, you were in a serious accident and should concentrate on getting better instead of worrying yourself with things like that."

Her unbearably cheery tone makes me want to throw up. Deciding not to engage in continued conversation, I give short, concise answers to her questions regarding my pain level, comfort level, and state of mind. Pushing the tray of food from my bedside, I ask when the doctor will be visiting.

"He will be making his rounds this afternoon. He is in surgery right now." She appears annoyed by my attitude and lets me know, as her tone is no longer melodic and happy.

After taking my vitals, she exits the room without so much as a goodbye.

Flipping through channels on the television mounted above the scheduling board, I grow anxious. There has been no mention of Foster or his condition. Patricia is the only one to report on his status, and yesterday, all she could say was that they are keeping him comfortable, whatever that means.

Two hours later, the orderly picks up the tray from earlier, commenting that I did not eat. A different nurse comes and checks my I.V.s, announcing they will all be removed shortly. It is 2pm when Patricia finally comes for a visit. She brings Hope, however, I wish she had not. I do not want my daughter to see me battered and bruised. We engage in idle chitchat as we wait for the doctor's arrival. Hope is bored and climbs into bed with me to watch TV. My best friend and adopted sister scolds her for climbing over me, but I tell her it is okay. Patricia mentions it is a good sign to see all the equipment being taken from the room.

"Looks like you may be discharged soon," she comments. "Hope so," I respond.

Reaching over me, Patricia takes the remote from Hope's tiny hand and turns off the television.

"Hey, I was watching that," my little girl shouts.

"I know, I am sorry hon, but I need to talk to your mommy." Her sweet, caring tone calms Hope, and I see a serious look overtake Patricia's face. "We need to talk about the man upstairs," she cryptically announces.

"Now is not the time for a religious discussion," I answer.

"No, you don't understand." With an impatient look, she touches her eye, and makes the shape of a "c" with her hand and then points towards me, signing I.C.U.

"Oh," I acknowledge. "And how are we going to do that with...?" I point towards Hope.

"Not sure," Patricia laments.

A knock on the door alerts us to Doctor Hirschbaum's arrival. "Good afternoon, ladies. How's our patient today?"

"Okay," I answer.

He continues, "Mrs. Broussard, we have much to go over. You are a very lucky woman. Other than a broken collarbone, your injuries are minor. Some visible bruising, a few cuts and a couple of bruised ribs. We have you on pain meds and will prescribe some for you when you leave. There is no cast we can put on a broken collarbone. It will have to heal on its own. We will immobilize it, but you will still hurt for several days to come. We will set an appointment for you to meet with me in my office next week for a follow-up. Do you have access to childcare?"

"I'll be there with her," Patricia pipes in. She and the doctor make eye contact and nod at one another. Something is going on and I am not quite certain what. It becomes clear once Patricia removes Hope from the bed and announces, "We need to get this little one some lunch in her belly." Looking at me, she says, "We'll be back."

Patricia and my daughter leave as Doctor Hirschbaum lowers the bed rail and sits on the foot of my bed. "We need to talk about your husband, Mrs. Broussard. I assume your friend has informed you of his condition?"

"She says they are keeping him comfortable, and he has been unconscious this entire time, unaware of what is happening."

"Yes, but it's far more serious than that. Mrs. Broussard, there is no easy way to say these things." He reaches for my hand, and I instinctively pull away, anticipating words I'm not ready to hear. "Mrs. Broussard, your husband has suffered massive brain trauma, compounded by many serious injuries. Your friend authorized a feeding tube and ventilator to help him breathe. The staff has done all they can. This is difficult to say, but Mr. Broussard is not exhibiting signs of brain activity. The machines are the only thing keeping him alive."

"Please, stop," I cry. "When can I see my husband?"

Explaining the hospital has staff to watch over hope, he suggests I take Patrica with me when we visit Foster. He tries to comfort me by saying my husband is unaware of what has happened, and they have seen to his comfort. I know he is trying his best to be kind, but I grow angry. Angry at him, angry at the man who hit us, and angry at God for not protecting my husband. As he leaves, Dr. Hirschbaum hands me a box of tissues, reminding me the staff is just a button push away.

A nurse's aide helps me out of bed and into a wheelchair as I wait for Patricia to return. Unlike me, she has seen Foster and knows what to expect once we arrive at the I.C.U. unit. She has not, however, divulged the full extent of Foster's injuries. On the elevator ride up, she does, and I cry harder as she goes into vivid detail regarding the extent of my husband's condition. As the elevator doors open, she pushes me into the hallway. Taking my hand, she crouches beside the chair, whispering, "He needs us to be strong for him right now."

As we enter the double doors of the I.C.U. unit, a tall, bearded man introducing himself as Foster's nurse meets us. He reports my husband remains unresponsive but comfortable. We follow the nurse to a room full of machines emitting every kind of beep, hum and click imaginable.

My husband lies there, head bandaged, left leg and arm in casts, a tube in his throat and one inserted into his stomach. Patricia tells me to take deep breaths and hugs me as I bury my face in the comforting shoulder she provides.

"Oh God, it's worse than I could have ever imagined," I cry.

"It was a horrific crash, Sylvia. We are lucky he did not pass away at the scene."

I sob uncontrollably as my best friend holds me tight, saying not a word. A heavy sense of sorrow permeates the room.

As I face reality, I am numb. Unbearable silence overtakes my mind. This physical and emotional pain is greater than any I have experienced in my life. Crying uncontrollably, I watch as my husband lies there, motionless. I want to run and hide. I want to wake from this horrible nightmare.

Slowly releasing me, Patricia places her hand on my shoulder. In a calm yet eerily soft voice, she says, "They want us to talk about letting him go, Sylvia."

Angry at the universe and God, I respond, "I know that's why they brought me up here. I am not an idiot."

Knowing better than to say anymore, Patricia leaves the room, allowing me time with Foster alone.

I hold Foster's hand tightly and talk to him for over

an hour. My guilt for asking him to drive me to Kroger is almost unbearable. I blame myself for the accident, asking for his forgiveness. Had I not insisted on shopping, the accident would not have occurred. I thank Foster for his love and all he has given Hope and me, recounting precious memories and even times when he completely ticked me off. I recall my twenty-fifth birthday and seeing the enormous window above the staircase he had custom made for our home—the piece of art which, from now on, will represent his love and thoughtfulness.

"From this day on, I will see you in the beautiful colors which fill our hallway each afternoon." I stand up from the wheelchair and kiss my husband on the lips as I stroke his face, brushing hair from his closed eyes.

I feel pressured as the staff awaits a decision regarding Foster. How can I possibly leave behind the man who fills my heart with such joy and happiness? How will I ever be able to return home, knowing he will not be there to protect our family? How do I explain to our daughter that Daddy is not coming home?

After the doctor examines Foster, his lack of any response to forced stimuli confirms the bleakness of the situation. Writing something in a chart, the doctor sadly shakes his head as he leaves the room. The priest offers last rites and mentions how Foster's soul cannot escape to its final reward as long as it remains trapped within the shell we see before us. Anger towards God intensifies within me as I ponder how a supposedly all loving and knowing entity could inflict such pain and suffering on my family. Furious, I raise my eyes to the ceiling and ask how it is I am expected to choose my husband's fate.

Announcing her entrance with a "Knock, knock," Patricia asks me to step out of the room while the orderly performs his duties and the nurse administers more pain medications. Right now, I do not want to leave my husband's side, nor do I want to hear what is coming next. I've seen enough movies to know this is when the doctors decide to approach the patient's family with the "bad news," presenting them with a decision no family member wants to be forced to make.

Three doctors, a brain specialist, neurosurgeon, and my doctor, usher Patricia and me into a small office. After presenting us with the facts, they ask if we understand the seriousness of Foster's condition and his bleak prognosis. "I need time," I reply.

"Understood," Dr. Hirschbaum says as the three doctors leave the small office.

"I can't let him go," I cry.

"I know," Patricia says, "but think about what's best for him. What would he want? If you were in there instead, what would you want him to do? Do you want to see him this way for god knows how long? This is a choice no one ever wants to face Sylvia, and it is yours to make. I stand by whatever you decide. All I know is that as a nurse, I can tell you, for Foster, this is no way to live. Who and what he was, his very essence, has not been with us since the accident."

Accepting her words, I bow my head and answer, "I know you're right." Exchanging knowing tear-filled glances, Patricia holds my hand as we sit in silence.

My heart, my soul, my very being cannot let the man I love go. My mind, intellect, and sense of duty to this man, however, convince me his needs are greater than my own. It is selfish of me to keep him in this state just to spare myself from having to confront the overwhelming grief his loss will bring.

I see Patricia sitting quietly, wiping her tears away as mine continue to stream uncontrollably from my eyes. Barely able to speak the words, I reach for my best friend's hand. "I love him so much."

"I know you do, and so do I."

"It's time," is all I have the energy left to say.

With a nod Patricia wheels me towards the doctors, who have been impatiently waiting outside.

With documents signed, I hold my husband's hand, kiss him on the cheek, and say for the last time how much Hope and I love him. My heart breaks with each breath the machine forces him to take.

After they turn all machines off, within minutes, the last machine displays a solid green flat line, emitting a long beep. I cry uncontrollably as I reluctantly release the hand of the man who had so freely given me his heart.

Slipping the wedding ring from his finger, I clutch it tightly in my hand. Holding it close to my breast, I vow to keep him in my heart forever. To this day, I wear Foster's wedding ring on a chain around my neck, always keeping a part of him close to me.

Chapter 47

My Squatters

Never underestimate the greed of human beings. Despite obtaining an abundance of wealth, some people still feel a longing for more. Some are opportunistic, others outright ruthless, so it is with Foster's mother and sister.

The hospital insists I stay an extra day for observation and assigns a psychiatrist to help me deal with the repercussions of the accident and loss of my husband. On the day of my discharge, I am handed documents with aftercare instructions, along with a list of prescriptions. On a separate sheet, I find advice on how best to handle the pain of bruised ribs, and a broken collarbone. What I cannot find are instructions on how to heal my shattered world and broken heart.

Yesterday, Patricia brought my favorite jeans, T-shirt, and sweater along with my house slippers in anticipation of my discharge.

With keys jingling in one hand and Hope holding the other, Patricia enters my hospital room out of breath and obviously upset. Between haggard breaths she informs me, "We have an issue, Sylvia—one I have no idea how you are going to rectify all because I messed up bad."

She places Hope in my lap, causing pain to emanate from my shoulder. I shake it off, glad to have my daughter with me.

"Wait till you hear what's happened," with looks of concern and worry filling her eyes she continues,

"Well?" I ask.

"Sylvia, the funeral home, gave Foster's mother my number, and she called yesterday. She and some other woman have taken ownership of your house. It's my fault all this has happened. They flew in overnight, catching me off guard. You know how small my apartment is, so I offered to put them up in a hotel. They were having none of that. They insisted on staying in your house. I did not know what to do, Sylvia. His mother is so forceful and demanding. I took her to your house, offering them the suite. They refused, saying they were not going to be treated like hired help. I didn't have time to argue, as I had to work yesterday, and I left them there." Taking a deep breath, my distraught friend continues, "I went over to your house this morning to gather more clothes for Hope, and that woman would not let me in, saying it was her son's house, and Hope and I were not welcome. I have no right to refute anything they say, so I was forced to leave."

In the midst of healing physically and emotionally, I cannot deal with a demanding woman who thinks the world belongs to her. All I want is to enjoy the warmth of my home. From Patricia's description, it seems I don't have a home to return to. Angry and unable to believe what I am hearing; I mull over my options.

I could steer clear of the argument with Foster's mother and rent a hotel room.

I could go home, confront her, explaining they have no right to keep me or my daughter from entering our home.

I could call the cops and have them explain to this deranged woman she cannot lay claim to a property which does not belong to her.

Or I could call my lawyer and ask for his advice before doing something I may regret.

Option four seems best. I fear things between Foster's mother, and I are about to become unpleasant and ugly.

263

My lawyer advises me that the third option is most viable. Having the police escort me onto my property would be the best way to handle trespassers and might help to avoid any unpleasantness when I ask them to leave. He explains with law enforcement present, I will have witnesses.

"Take the higher ground," he advises. "She has no legal right to the home, so do not argue. Go get the deed to the house from your safe deposit box, hand it to the cops, and they will do their job."

I do not relish the idea of having to engage in legal battles. However, if Foster's mother wishes to make things difficult, I am more than prepared for a fight. For many reasons, my emotional state has reached a level ten out of ten, and this woman is giving me just the outlet I need to release my pent-up anger and pain.

Foster made certain our lawyers were meticulous in their work, leaving no room for legal loopholes or interpretation. My husband, being the great provider and planner he was, made certain Hope nor I would have any financial concerns should something happen to him. Never believing this day would come, I viewed the many visits to our lawyers as inconvenient and mere formalities.

I can hardly believe his relatives are behaving this way before we've even had a memorial service for Foster.

Patricia, my daughter, and I sit in my driveway awaiting the police. The front door to my home opens several times as a gray- haired, impeccably dressed woman peeks her head out, wondering what I am up to. She is about to learn, and a rude awakening is coming her way.

A police SUV pulls up behind Patricia's car as I exit, using a cane to steady myself. Although I am still extremely stiff and hurt, I will not allow my current discomfort to stand in the way of handling these unforeseen circumstances.

The officer yells at me to remain where I am and not to approach his vehicle. A second officer exits, rushing to the driver's side of Patricia's car.

"We were called here because of a domestic disturbance?" It is more of a question than a statement.

"Not exactly," I say, handing the officer the light blue folder with great effort and in incredible pain. "Here is the deed to my home. The women currently inside are trying to lay claim to my house. Officer, my husband died only yesterday. I am suffering injuries from the accident which claimed his life and truly do not have the strength or energy to deal with this right now."

After examining the deed, the first officer walks back to the parked SUV, his baritone voice echoing through the air as he speaks with someone over his radio. The second officer offers condolences for our loss as she shakes her head in disbelief regarding our current situation.

Finally rejoined by the first officer, he asks a few questions. "Have these individuals paid rent of any kind? Have they performed work for you in any way? Do they have your permission to be in the home?"

I answer no to the questions posed, and the officer informs me that my squatters are trespassing, and they have the authority to remove them by force, if necessary. A relieved sigh rushes past my lips as I watch the officers approach my front door. To make things more difficult, Foster's mother ignores the officer's attempts to speak with them.

The officers turn back and approach us, and my stomach tightens. Their furrowed brows tell me the news is not good. "We cannot force the occupants to open the door, ma'am. With your permission, we can ram the door and remove the trespassers by force. The call is yours."

Do I destroy my front door or allow these women control over me and my home? I wonder what my Foster is thinking as he watches these events unfold. As if he is speaking directly to me, I hear Foster's voice in my mind. "Honey, try the back door to the suite. I may have accidentally left it unlocked the other day after running the dishwasher in there."

I immediately ask the officers to try the back door to the suite. My squatters may not have thought to check it. If it needs to be forced open, the damage will be far less expensive to repair. They find the door unlocked, and I immediately feel a twinge of irritation toward my husband for not making sure our home was secure, but still grateful for his absentmindedness.

The officers enter the suite, entering through the laundry room of the guest quarters, catching my squatters off guard. Patricia and I follow close behind. Making it known they have no legal right to be in my home, the officers give the shocked women two options. Either exit my home of their own volition or be arrested for trespassing.

Flashing me a most hateful stare, Mrs. Broussard yells at me, "You wouldn't dare have us arrested."

Still angry and in immense pain, I cannot hide the disgust in my voice as I reply, "Try me."

Stepping between Mrs. Broussard and me, the second officer tells the women they have fifteen minutes to gather their things and leave my property.

They take ten.

Leaving through the front doors, Foster's mother looks back in my direction. "This isn't over missy; you haven't heard the last of me. This is my son's house, and I will see you on the street before I allow you to steal it. My lawyers will be in touch." She stops, and just before opening the rental car door, Mrs. Broussard turns to issue one last insult. "You are nothing more than white trash, and I will be the one to put you to the curb where you belong."

"Hateful bitch," Patricia remarks.

"Language," I chide, covering Hope's ears.

We watch as the rental car leaves my driveway, and I

apologize to my daughter. "I wish you didn't have to see or hear any of that, honey, but money and greed make people do and say horrible things."

Looking up at me with a confused look, my precious little girl asks, "Who is that Mommy?"

Looking into her eyes, and with great sadness, I answer, "I am sorry to say that, my dear, is your grandmother."

Unfortunately, this will not be our last encounter with this determined woman.

Chapter 48

Legal Battles Ensue

Dressed in the finest silks from China, Foster's mother strikes a statuesque figure. Her silver hair, deep inset eyes, and alabaster skin add to an already elegant woman. It is obvious she wishes to make a favorable impact on the judge, as this will be her only chance to leave a lasting impression. A savvy businesswoman, and no stranger to legal procedure, she wastes no time having her lawyers contest Foster's will. Before leaving to go back to Louisiana, Mrs. Broussard files her first affidavit against her son's estate. In doing so, her lawyers freeze all Foster's bank accounts, including Hope's trust fund.

As Foster's mother stands behind the hand carved wooden podium, facing the judge, confidence and smugness are not in short supply. However, I cannot boast the same. I feel my emotions rage and am glad the court has placed a bailiff between us as a buffer; as it is all I can do to resist the urge to wrap my hands around her pearl adorned, high- class neck.

In the case before the judge, I find my mother-in-law contacted my husband's life insurance company. As the gavel drops, she is dismayed to find I am listed as the sole beneficiary of his policy. Her plan to destroy me financially meets its first roadblock.

At least once a year, the Louisiana-based Broussard's legal team files frivolous lawsuits against Foster's estate to keep his assets frozen. Each time I appear in court, and provide all required documentation, the presiding judge summarily dismisses the current case before him. For the past five years, Foster's mother has been relentless. Mrs. Broussard, having money to burn, spares no expense in complicating my existence. I have offered her Foster's trust fund account. It is old Broussard money given to him by his grandfather and should go back to the family, but my mother-in-law's greed and pride will not allow her to settle. She wants nothing less than all my deceased husband's assets, including my house.

Dealing with the legal issues Foster's mother forces upon us over the years have been cumbersome and tedious and I pray this experience has been a great life lesson for Hope.

After the untimely death of her father, and years of legal battles, my daughter's outlook towards the outside world has changed. Hope, always a spirited child, becomes moody and withdrawn. I try but cannot console her. Being relentlessly sued, I could not lavish my daughter with expensive items and could no longer afford the designer clothes and shoes she wanted. An impressionable youth, she finds our lack of funds inconvenient. She blames me for her inability to keep up with the latest trends and fashions worn by her friends at school.

After exhausting all legal avenues for revenge, Mrs. Broussard ceases communication, for which I am grateful. With access to all bank accounts returned to our family, I can once again provide my child with everything she needs in the way of the latest trends and must-haves for a young girl growing up among Cincinnati's most prominent and wealthy children.

Hope counters any attempt I make to introduce my out-of-date values into her materialistic world with rebellion and arguments. She chastises me for my inability to understand the pressures she faces as a teenager. She accuses me of putting her popularity in jeopardy when I do not provide her with the latest $1000 tennis shoes. I understand my daughter's desire and need for popularity as I too must reluctantly purchase designer labels to blend in and gain acceptance from the local socialites. I try to instill a little wisdom in her, explaining she should not base her worth on materialistic items. I remind her of her father's legacy and his insistence that the Broussard family contribute to every charitable cause. I make certain his wishes are carried out. With all our family has done for the community and donations we make to each cause; the privileged residents of Indian Hill keep me at arm's length. Unlike my daughter, no matter how hard I try, I remain an outsider to the more affluent members of the Indian Hill community.

My husband, having come from "old money" and comfortable around those who flaunt their financial status, had no issues blending into the fabric of high society. His philanthropy and boisterous personality left a reputation to uphold. Hope takes great joy in living up to her father's legacy. I, however, still find it off-putting.

Today, Hope informs me she wishes for her twenty-first birthday celebration to be hosted in the Taft room at the country club as all debutantes before her. I reluctantly make the arrangements and hire a party planner, explaining to my materialistic daughter, this is to be her birthday gift from me.

Patricia regretfully declines the invitation to Hope's party via phone call, citing she has been offered employment in California. She gleefully reports she has secured her dream job as head nurse at Scipps Hospital La Jolla, one of San Diego's most prestigious medical institutions. Amidst the hustle of relocating for her new role and settling into a new city, she sends Hope a generous gift of a thousand dollars accompanied by a heartfelt letter expressing her sincere apologies for missing Hope's special occasion.

Hope's twenty-first birthday was both lavish and costly. The party organizer spared no expense in making the event one so successful, even the newspaper wrote about it. While I typically find country club functions tedious, I make an effort to smile and appear festive. Deep down, however, I recognize this lone event signals a new chapter in my life.

It has been a month since Patricia moved away, leaving me heartbroken. I understand the need to pursue her dream and am happy for her. However, now that my baby bird is twenty-one, she has decided it is time to leave the nest and test her new wings. Now an adult, and in control of the funds left to her by her father, I watch as she moves her belongings from her childhood room carrying with her not only her most treasured possessions but also what is left of my heart.

Asserting her independence, she rents a condominium in Hyde Park instead of moving into the dormitories on campus. I have voiced my concerns regarding such financial decisions but realize there are things she must figure out herself. My daughter's hard head refuses to allow parental wisdom to enter. Hope now lives for the moment, popularity, acceptance, and the instant gratification a life of privileged allows.

My daughter has grown up and is now living her life to the fullest, as I find my heart and home to be as empty as her childhood room. No one needs or depends on me any longer. Feeling my purpose in life has been full-filled, depression overtakes me.

Today, I stand as a middle-aged woman, recognized by locals as the solitary widow residing on Shawnee Road. My once vibrant strawberry blonde hair has turned listless and gray, losing its former thickness. The once supple texture of my skin has succumbed to age, now sagging in unexpected places. My weary eyes, once bright with hope and anticipation, now reflect fatigue, devoid of their former sparkle. Every line etched on my face, every crease, tells the tale of my life's journey. These wrinkles form a map, detailing an identity that once found validation and purpose through the love reciprocated by my family.

Navigating through the expansive and desolate

corridors of my home, the absence of life within its walls stands in stark contrast to the vibrant memories we once shared. Days blend into one another seamlessly, no more special events or plans to differentiate one day from the next. I find solace in the receiving parlor, surrounded by the comforting presence of framed photographs capturing happier moments from the past. Each image serves as a portal into the narrative of my life. This solitary room has transformed into my sanctuary, shielding me from the harshness of the outside world.

Chapter 49

The Surprise

𝔐y daughter has been a pain in my rump lately. Too often, she asks about her biological father. I am puzzled by her newfound interest in Chance, as she refuses to explain what sparked it. Three decades have passed since last I saw Chance, and now, with Mom gone, I can share with Hope her father's name. But I have no other information to give her. We talk about other things when she visits, but every time the topic of her father comes up, I sense a tangible discomfort in the air when I cannot provide more information.

Hope stops by to check in on me once a month, stating she is concerned because of my recent bouts of depression and loneliness. I reassure her my symptoms have lessened with the new medication regimen my doctor has prescribed, and I no longer dread the start of each day. Hope repeatedly suggests I rent out the mother-in-law- suite if not for the extra money, then just to give me someone to talk to, which may help battle the loneliness.

"I like my privacy," I rebut. "As your dad used to say, "Nuff said."

My routine remains unchanged. Each morning—weather permitting—I have my first cup of coffee on the veranda. Sitting on one of the two Adirondack chairs beneath the large outdoor umbrella, I admire the gazebo Foster built almost twenty years ago. The spacious back yard provides a spectacular view. This morning, a cool breeze carries upon it the strong, sweet scent of Jasmine while wild ducks and Canadian geese enjoy the pond. This beautiful and calming sight cause memory-filled teardrops to flow gently down my cheeks, reminding me of the times Foster and I relaxed out here and a stark reminder that I will face another day alone.

Refusing to allow sadness to take control, today I have made plans to join the bridge club. A new neighbor has become influential in ridding me of the overwhelming discomfort and unease I feel regarding leaving the house. Like me, she hails from the great state of Mississippi, and the first day we met, she shared with me her views about moving to Indian Hill. In her predominant southern accent, one like I had lost many years ago, she laments, "For the life of me, I can't understand why my husband insists I go to these stupid charity events and pretend to be one of these hoity-toity, holier-than-thou snobs."

From the moment those off-colored words flowed from her lips, I realized this was someone I wished to be my new best friend.

Jackie is a tall, young, voluptuous woman, and embraces her rugged side. Having been raised with four brothers, she mentions often going fishing and hunting with their father. Though I never engaged in such sports, I remember how important those activities were to Leif, and how they helped him fit in and find friends in Mathison. Jackie has become the yin to my yang, breathing life back into my once deflated world. She does not seem to see me as old— merely "seasoned," she explains. She intends to take advantage of my knowledge regarding the local customs and expectations, and I will depend on her to keep me up with the latest styles. I have long since lost touch with what is on trend.

After an enjoyable afternoon out with Jackie, I call it an early night. Our afternoon teas have morphed into what we colorfully refer to as wine tastings. However, unlike actual wine tastings, not a drop of ours goes to waste.

At 9 am, the phone rings, echoing throughout the foyer. Panicked, I cannot remember where I last placed my phone. I find it on the island in the kitchen, arriving too late to answer. Hope has left a voicemail. The message is confusing, and I cannot discern what she is asking of me. Per her request, I return the call. She asks me to stay home today, as she has something she wishes to discuss, and it seemingly cannot wait. I tell her of my plans with Jackie, and she begs me to cancel. Greatly disappointed, I oblige my daughter. Jackie, always the trooper and letting no last-minute changes upset her, reminds me family comes first. I apologize profusely, and we reschedule.

Plans halted, I await my daughter's arrival in my favorite chair. The rhythmic ticking of the grandfather clock lulls me into a twilight state. My mind, body, and soul are at peace, enjoying the trancelike state allowing me to escape the bonds of this earth. I retreat to precious memories of Foster and happier days, back when these now hauntingly silent rooms rang with love and laughter.

The front door opens as the sound of jingling keys interrupt my moment of Zen. Wearing a pink taffeta dress and patent leather shoes, my beautiful blonde granddaughter races towards me and jumps into my lap. Following closely behind is her mother.

"Grandma, Grandma! We have a surprise!" Artesia shouts before her mother can shush her.

"Artesia, not yet," my daughter cryptically says.

Unsure of what her visit is all about, I allow things to unfold as Hope sees fit. Squirming and unable to find a comfortable spot, Artesia climbs from my lap.

Tugging down on my sleeve, she asks, "Can I, Grandma?"

"Yes dear, go play," I answer, giving her a kiss on the top of her head.

Not wasting a second, she runs to the playroom opposite the library as Hope settles on the loveseat facing me, seemingly nervous and uncomfortable.

"What's going on?" I ask.

She does not respond. Nervous, her lips move, but no words come forth.

"You had me cancel my visit with Jackie. What is this all about, Hope?"

"Mom," a long pause. "Mom, I thought this would be easier." Completely dumbfounded, I sit and watch my little girl fidget with her purse straps. As awkward silence between us grows, my patience wears thin. I can no longer hold my tongue. "For the love of God, Hope, what in the world is going on?"

Taking in a deep breath, my daughter's angst-filled face finally allows her words to break through. "Mom, I am not sure how you are going to accept the surprise I have for you today."

"Hope, you know I don't care for games or surprises. Whatever it is, I am sure it's nothing I cannot handle. So out with it, young lady."

Flashing an impatient and rather perturbed look in my direction, she suggests I refresh my tea and we adjourn to the veranda. Hope says she feels being out in nature may help her relax and get through this. We say nothing more to each other as she walks me outside and asks me to get comfortable, saying she will be right back. Seething, I linger in the gazebo, awaiting my daughter's return. More than anyone else, Hope knows I do not have patience for this kind of behavior.

The honking of the geese and comforting breeze are not enough to calm me as I wait for a daughter who does not seem to value her mother's time. Facing the pond, I finally hear the opening of a door. Curious, I turn around and rise from the bench. Through the lace curtains on the French doors, I see the figure of a man. Too thin to be Hope's husband, for a moment I think I see a shadow from my past, someone I have not seen in decades.

"Surprise!" my daughter shouts as my knees buckle and the world turns black.

As I come to, I hear my daughter repeating, "mom? mom? are you okay?" I do not respond as she helps me up and into my Adirondack chair relieved it is only the two of us. For a second, I thought I had seen a ghost. Taking a drink of my tea, I look at my daughter with great confusion.

"Mom?" my daughter questions. "Yes?"

"Mom, are you alright?"

"Yes, a bit dizzy still, but I am alright. Why do you ask?" "Your reaction, Mom, it was, well, unexpected?"

"Sorry Hope, I just thought I saw—"

The French door opens, and from behind us I hear, "Here, I brought a damp cloth." Gruff and raspy, it is a voice I have never forgotten. As I turn around to get a look at the man behind the voice, I sit in shock. His golden locks, now white, his skin, aged and wrinkled and his once muscular frame now thin and frail, tell of a life ladened with hardship and strife. Beyond his time-ravaged outward appearance, his eyes still shine and his smile still as bright as the morning sun. It wasn't a ghost I saw. It is Hope's father, and if this is her surprise for me, I'm not amused. He approaches quickly, kneeling beside my chair. As he tries to place the cold dishtowel on my forehead, reflexes cause my arm to block his incoming hand and I watch as the damp rag he was holding falls to the ground.

"Whoa, hold on now, nobody's trying to hurt you," he says in a defensive tone.

Immediately remorseful, I apologize while reassuring him my anger is not directed towards him, but rather, a daughter who has a lot of explaining to do. I turn to Hope and ask,

"What have you done?"

Taking a deep breath she answers, "I have been

asking about my father, and all you provided me with was a name. Well, Mom, Google is a great tool, and it helped me find him."

She pauses for a response. I have none.

"Well, Mom, this—"

I cut her off mid-sentence as I stand to greet the man I have not seen in thirty years. "Chance Marlow." I say, still slightly in shock.

"Sylvia Rose Turner," he replies.

"It's just Sylvia now. I stopped using Rose shortly before Hope was born."

"Yes, she told me."

As the moment becomes more awkward, Hope excuses herself, reporting it was time she checks on her little girl. Once we are alone, I realize there are so many questions I have for him, yet I cannot seem to ask even one.

Sensing my uneasiness, the man I once loved more than anything begins, "You are as beautiful as the first day I saw you. All grown up and living in a mansion, of all things. I'd say you have done pretty well for yourself, Sylvia. And Hope, my goodness, she is so pretty and such a caring mother and wife. We have spoken a lot about her past. She speaks so highly of her dad and how she loved him." As the conversation lags, he adds, "So, how have you been?"

The last time Chance and I saw each other, I was living in a one- bedroom apartment in Mathiston Mississippi, a departure from the home in which I live now. Uneasy, and perhaps feeling guilty, I explain this house was a twenty-fifth birthday present from my husband, Foster. As we continue to talk, I tell him how Foster was there for me during Hope's birth. I don't go into detail how our relationship blossomed from that point on, there is no need. As we talk, he tells me of his bad fortune. I find out that shortly after moving to Tupelo, his wife's father opened another furniture store in Columbus, Mississippi. A year later he would find himself divorced, leaving him homeless and practically broke. Chance says after taking several construction jobs to make ends meet, a devastating injury left him unable to work.

"No one can live on the small amount the government pays for disabled people," he explains.

Chance reveals the many hardships he had to endure, and my heart breaks. He laughs and says, "I knew I would survive all the trials and tribulations. I just did not know how. Falling silent, he looks at me, his tone now serious. "Sylvia Rose, it was thoughts of you which kept me going. No matter how bad things got for me, I would remember all you went through as a child and the strength you showed when we first met. A fourteen-year-old girl who, despite having less than an ideal upbringing, never let life get her down. I never forgot that." He then tells me how he ended up in California. Fate would bring him in contact with a veteran who told him of California's social service programs, which provide extra government benefits, to help disabled people to live a better life. He tells of moving to San Diego and, through the kindness of a generous welfare program, was able to live a comfortable yet lower middle- class life. Then he says an illness sent him to the hospital for several months, leaving him unable to pay his bills and when he arrived home, he found himself homeless. The shame in his voice cuts me to the core. I try to hold back my tears to no avail when I think of all he did to ensure my family didn't struggle. Chance asks me not to cry, telling me everything he went through, and all he experienced humbled him and strengthened him. He says when Hope surprised him in California, it pleased him to learn our daughter grew up not having to experience the hardships he and I endured.

As if on cue, Hope appears from the French doors and states she and Artesia need to leave. "Well, I am riding with her," Chance says. "Been living with her and Gerry for almost six months now."

I look at Hope and yell, "He has been here six months and I am just now finding out?"

"We'll talk about it later, Mom. Artesia is tired, and I need to get dinner started for my family. Sorry, Mom, but we really need to get going. I'll bring dad back again, and you both can spend the entire day catching up. Is that okay?"

"Do I have a choice?" I ask.

"No, not really, unless you let him use the suite."

Not prepared for a houseguest, I suggest my daughter bring Chance back when it is convenient for him, and we can pick up where we left off today.

We all gather by the front door, and I kiss Artesia goodbye while her grandfather holds her, and Hope gives me a hug. Chance and I exchange nods, unsure how to end our visit without awkwardness.

Waving goodbye, I watch as the taillights of Hope's car disappear into the night, as visions of yesteryear stream from my eyes while I close the door and wipe the precious memories from my cheek.

Chapter 50

An Offer He Cannot Refuse

With the cat out of the bag, so to speak, the next few months pass quickly as Chance and I become reacquainted. I was not thrilled when Hope appeared out of the blue with her father. I often imagined how my life would be if he hadn't stepped in to ensure our mom and her children would have a secure and bright future. His generosity saved our family, and I have never forgotten my debt to him.

Hope calls before bringing Artesia over today, explaining the daycare has closed without giving the parents' notice or a reason why. It appears I will have my granddaughter during the day for the rest of the week. The thought of laughter filling this empty house brings me great joy. I eagerly greet my girls at the door, giving Hope a hug before sending Artesia off to her playroom.

Happily, the little girl turns around and skips toward her favorite room in the house as golden locks bounce on her shoulders.

Taking my hand, Hope guides me to the parlor as she shares with me the news of the day.

My daughter fills me in on what is going on at her home. She tells me Gerry longs to regain use of his man-cave. Hope also says she enjoys getting to know her father, but he is now getting underfoot. She complains that Chance is always wanting to help around the house, or worse, starting projects and never finishing them. She says he gets sidetracked easily, leaving a mess. Therefore, for the sake of family harmony, they need to find a place close by for

Chance to call his own.

Stunned and offended, I sit in silence for a moment. My dismay must be obvious, as my daughter immediately asks me what is wrong.

"What's wrong?" I respond. "What's wrong? I am hurt, Hope. Look at this place. I am alone in this house with more rooms than any one person needs. Why would you not suggest Chance move in here? Did you not suggest a few years ago that I rent out the suite? Can you sit there and honestly say it would not be the perfect place for your father to live? It sits there unused, collecting dust and cobwebs."

"We talked it over, Mom. Dad says it doesn't feel right for you two to live together. He wants to support himself and believes he will be happier living on his own. It's nothing against you, mom. Frankly, I agree with you; it would be perfect if he lived here, but he has made up his mind."

"You send him here, Hope, and after we talk, if he stills feels that way, I will drop the subject and we will never speak of this again. But you must convince him to meet with me and be open to what I have to say."

"I'll try, mom but can't promise anything." "That's all I ask, sweetheart."

Hope's phone chimes, "oh shoot," she says looking at her watch, "I completely forgot, I need to take Artesia to get a new dress for a birthday party she has been invited to this weekend."

"I'll go get her," I offer. Disappointed I will not have Artesia as planned, I make my way to her playroom.

I stand silently in the doorway as I watch my granddaughter play. She looks up while brushing her doll's hair and asks if I want to play.

"I would like to, honey, but your mommy is ready to go and asked me to come get you."

We walk to the front door where her mother waits

crouched down, arms wide open. I release Artesia's hand and watch as she runs into her mother's arms. I smile, reflecting on the days Hope would run into Foster's open arms the same way.

Still a bit perturbed regarding the insensitivity of Chance not even considering living in the mother-in-law suite, I have a restless night. This morning I wake, still upset with yesterday's conversation on my mind. In search of a distraction, I call Jackie to see if she wants to spend the day shopping.

"You don't have to ask me twice," she says in her usual, perky Southern accent.

We spend the day in the Kenwood mall. I enjoy and prefer the mall over specialized boutiques. I am a people watcher and enjoy seeing mothers try to reel in their overly excited children, young women pulling at their boyfriends who are so easily distracted by the scantily clad girls flitting about the mall, and the seniors who spend their time in jogging suits walking up and down the mall's isles. For my entertainment dollar, there is no better show to watch.

Jackie and I enjoy browsing the stores and soaking up the atmosphere the mall provides. She put off leaving as long as she could, but finally, Jackie announces she must get home as she and her husband have plans for the evening. As we search for her car in the parking lot, I share with her how disheartening it is to walk into a once lively home that is now devoid of life and laughter. Setting our shopping bags in her backseat, Jackie says she can understand the loneliness I must feel, and she insists I pick up the phone and call her anytime I need her. I thank her as we spend the rest of the drive home listening to the radio. As she pulls up to my front door, I remember vividly my first trip up the cobbled stone drive. Sighing, I exit her car and thank Jackie for a wonderful afternoon. Lazily, I unlock my door, throwing my keys on the table and climbing the stairs to my bedroom to deposit my purchases. Unusually exhausted, I stretch out on my bed, waking several hours later.

In a foggy state, I make my way to the kitchen to pour a glass of iced tea. Halfway down the stairs, I hear, "Ahem!"

Turning toward the sound too quickly, I scream and nearly lose my balance. Catching the railing, I see it is Chance, rushing up to steady me.

"Are you okay? I didn't mean to scare you. Hope dropped me off hours ago and let me in. She said you wanted to talk to me if I promise to shut up and listen."

"Yeah, well, a little notice would have been nice." I cannot hide the sarcasm in my voice, nor do I wish to.

Never one to mince words or waste time, Chance asks, "So, what's this all about? Why the demand to see me?"

"Let's take a walk," I suggest as we head towards the suite. Opening the wooden door with the tacky lion head doorknocker, I show Chance in, giving him a tour of the suite and ending up in the laundry room. Pointing to the door, I explain it is a private entrance. Chance is an intelligent man and knows exactly why he is receiving this tour. I tell him of the conversation Hope and I had regarding his current living situation and understand he wants to move out on his own. He gazes into my eyes as he exits the suite, and I can feel the warmth of his gratitude in his voice as he expresses his thanks but notes that if he were to consider the offer, it would make things too awkward.

"The very idea of living in the same house as my ex-girlfriend is quite unsettling, Sylvia. To be in such close quarters? Do you honestly think that to be a good idea?"

I grow irate, remembering how he gave us no option when it came to accepting his help so many years ago. His double standards are a bit too much, and I lose my ability to hold my tongue. "How dare you, Chance Marlow!" I shout.

"I promised you almost forty years ago I was going to pay you back for all you did for us. If you deny me this—" I stop mid-sentence to catch my breath to make sure my next words make an impact. "If you deny me this opportunity to provide for you as you did for us, I will never forgive you."

"You don't mean that."

"I do Chance. I am sorry, but I mean it with all my heart. You must let me do this. I need to be here for you like you were for me so many years ago. This is a no strings offer. I will not accept money from you or expect anything from you. You know damn well none of what you see around you now would have happened had you not sacrificed the way you did. You made certain a fourteen-year-old girl would have a better life. Now it's your turn to let go of your pride and allow fate to complete its mission. You are the father of my child, but even more importantly, you are family. You can come and go as you please with no expectations or demands. This mother- in-law suite will be your private home. I will never intrude. Take this for how it is meant, payment for all you have done for me and my family over the years. Take all the time you need to decide when you will move in. Don't feel rushed, just be aware, I am not accepting no for an answer."

It takes only a week for Chance to call and accept my offer. I try to dampen my excitement over the phone as the thought of him living here brings a sense of newfound excitement. My house might once again become a home.

A few months pass, and we both slowly grow accustomed to our new living arrangements. I ask Chance to have breakfast about twice a week. He returns my gesture with tasty and elaborately garnished dinners I had forgotten he enjoyed cooking. He keeps his place spotlessly clean, and I never overstay my welcome. We occasionally enjoy an after-dinner coffee and sometimes relax out on the veranda as we listen to the Canadian geese honk tirelessly around the pond. I feel my emotional walls slowly fall and wonder if he is feeling the same.

We take time to catch up on our pasts. I tell him of the accident which took Foster from me, and he shares the details of his divorce, which he considers the catalyst of his rapid decline emotionally, mentally, and physically. Not allowing things to become too comfortable between us, Chance excuses himself just before our conversations can reach a more intimate level. Kissing me on the cheek he thanks me for a wonderful evening before retiring to the apartment he now calls home. Nightly, I hear the door to the suite shut and contemplate the danger of allowing my feelings for Chance to resurface. Having lost him so many years ago, I feel the need to tread lightly, not acting too quickly out of fear of losing him again.

A year passes, and we continue to deny our attraction to one another. I am certain we both fear we may jeopardize the fragile balance of comfort and respect we share with one another. Neither of us can seem to admit the truth we desperately seek to hide in our eyes. We carefully dance around certain subjects to avoid mentioning or acknowledging any feelings we may be experiencing. I do not know about him, but I am insecure regarding my physical needs and longings. Chance has mentioned "hypotheticals," but never acts upon them. I try to drop not-so-subtle hints indicating my desire for him and then recant them nearly in the very same breath. I have called Hope many times asking for advice and suggestions. She is always kind enough to lend an ear, offering comforting words but refusing any advice.

Last night, it happened. Perhaps it was the full moon, perhaps it was the wine or new puppy we got a few weeks ago. Whatever it was, we finally stopped beating around the bush. As Chance hands me Harley, our new fur baby to take up to bed with me, sparks fly from our fingertips, igniting a dormant passion we have been so desperately trying to conceal. It seems old embers never die no matter how deeply we try to suppress them.

Together Chance and I decide to create a personal refuge from the outside world, and for a week it has been a dreamlike escape, allowing us to rediscover each other and reestablish our connection. Chance has not lost his gentle, loving touch, and I had forgotten how much of an unselfish and giving lover he is. We will spend today cleaning his apartment as we have agreed to share the house together. We opt for a peaceful cup of coffee on the veranda in order to unwind before tackling the monumental task. The apartment is usually kept spotless, but Harley, the newest addition to the family, had a few accidents indoors before becoming completely housebroken. We clean the carpets and other areas Harley has soiled by accident. We do not want those odors lingering once we seal the suite.

Over coffee this morning, I asked Chance if he has spoken to Gerry. He answers no and I must also admit to not having spoken to or even texted Hope all week.

"You think we may be causing them to worry?" he asks. "Maybe," I say. "I have a way to let them know we are ok."

With my phone, I take a picture of my freshly painted toenails resting comfortably on the wooden footstool as we lounge on the veranda with a slightly out of focus, tranquil pond in the background. I share the serene scene on my social media page with the words, *a peaceful start to our day,* in hopes the hidden meaning of those words will be deciphered.

"Hopefully she will see this and not worry," I say with a mischievous smile.

Chapter 51

Everything Comes Full Circle

𝔐y parents' unanswered calls and texts are confusing. It is uncharacteristic of Mom or Dad to ignore us. This morning, on her social media page, I saw a picture Mom posted of her sitting in her backyard with the caption, "A peaceful start to the day."

How can she post on social media but not answer her daughters calls or texts? How rude is that? Ticked off and angry, I decide to drive to Mom's house and confront her.

The plan is simple. Get her and Dad out on the veranda, and then I will explain that we can no longer be their mediators, and they must confront the feelings they are so desperately attempting to ignore.

As I park my car, nothing seems out of the ordinary. I ring the doorbell several times and receive no response, so I let myself in and am greeted by a cute, yapping, fluffy puppy whose little feet cannot gain footing as it excitedly slides helplessly on the rose marbled floor. Unable to contain my laughter, I kneel down and pick up the puppy, asking, "What's your name, you big 'ol ball of fur?"

I walk towards my dad's apartment. Using the brass lion's head knocker, I stand waiting with the squirming puppy in my arms. I give up after several failed attempts to get him to answer. I decide to check and see if Mom is still out on the veranda.

As I step outside, I immediately notice Mom and Dad, each enjoying a cup of coffee while relaxing beneath the unfurled umbrella. They seem blissfully unaware of how frustrated I am with them both. Fuming, I set the dog inside and shut the door behind me as I point to the puppy, now smudging the glass with his nose, and ask, "Who is this?"

"Oh, that's Harley, our Bernese mountain dog," Dad responds. "Whose puppy is it?"

"Hard to say," Mom chimes in with a slight chuckle in her voice. "He kinda seems to like us both."

Confused, I ask with whom the puppy resides.

"Funny you should ask," Mom answers with a smile. "Sooner or later we were going to have to tell you, anyway. Harley lives with us."

"You share him, then?" I ask.

"No, no, he lives with us, your father and I."

Attempting to make matters clear, Dad interrupts, "I no longer live in the apartment Hope."

Not what I expected to hear or how I expected this morning to unfold, I stand stunned and unresponsive as Mom rises from her chair to flash me a diamond engagement ring.

"We're getting married," she announces as her hand quivers uncontrollably.

Overcome by this news, I stumbled backwards. Luckily a nearby picnic table is there to catch me before I fall. "You're what?" I ask.

"Your mother is going to make an honest man of me," my father says with a laugh.

"I know you're caught off guard, honey. I am sorry. All this happened so quickly." Mom sits beside me on the picnic table and takes my hand,

"Our wedding is not going to be anything special. At our age, and this being a second wedding for both of us, we don't want anything fancy, only you, Gerry, Artesia, and a few friends. We are not going to make a big deal of this. Last Friday night, your father presented me with the ring. We have been as giddy as school kids and have spent days trying to come to terms with all of this ourselves. I am sorry for not answering your calls and emails. We couldn't deny our feelings any longer. Over the past year, we have grown to depend on each other. We are happy, and our lives have come full circle. You know very little of our history, but I owe your father my happiness."

"And I owe your mother mine," Dad adds.

Elated, I explain to my parents the reason for my visit was to confront them about being put in the middle of their insecure phone calls and emails. I tell them my intention was to rake them over the coals for not talking to one another. With the reason for my visit now moot, it is time I excuse myself and allow my parents to share this beautiful day together without outside interruption.

Dad begs me to stay and talk awhile. I tell a white lie and pretend we have a full weekend ahead, even though I'm yearning to stay and unravel the story of how this all happened. "I'll walk you out," my father offers.

Puppy energy on full display, Harley grows excited, getting underfoot as Dad and I enter through the French doors. With Harley in one arm and Dad on the other, we walk through the house, stopping just before reaching the front door. There, beneath the stairs, Dad looks at me with love and tears in his eyes. The sun shines brightly through the stained-glass window, and it bathes us in a rainbow of colors, accenting Dad's deep blue eyes and white hair.

"Never in a million years would I have dreamed this possible, Hope. Thank you for all you have done to make this a reality."

Dad slowly opens the door, taking Harley from my arms and I take this moment to gently wipe a tear from his eye. "It's been a long, hard road for you, Dad. You and mom deserve this happiness. Giving him one last long hug, I whisper into his ear, "I love you both so very much and am glad destiny stepped in to ensure my parents will enjoy their golden years together."

With a quick goodbye kiss on the cheek, I close the front door behind myself and just before entering my car, I turn around and look towards the house. I smile knowing that a couple, torn apart by the cruelest twist of fate, finally find themselves lovingly reunited so many years later. It is then a feeling of peace and great joy overtake me as I think, *what were the chances?*